Suddenly Annie felt like crying

Just what did she want anyway? Jeez, the more she changed, the more she stayed the same. Wanting the wrong guy and refusing to accept he was all wrong for her.

Nick had come to Bedford to get a divorce. He'd stayed to help her out. There was nothing more to it. And she was, once again, ready to play the fool for love—or lust or infatuation or whatever it was she was feeling right now.

She squeezed the bridge of her nose to hold back her tears. Time to get back to the original plan. Four days down, five to go.

How on earth would she make it through the next five days?

Dear Reader,

A couple of years ago during my nephew's wedding, a random thought popped into my head—what if a newly married woman left her husband?

Not that I wasn't paying attention, mind you—it was a beautiful, touching ceremony. And not that I wanted the bride to leave her new husband—they're perfect for one another. But when inspiration decides to strike, well, it doesn't necessarily wait for just the right moment.

Intrigued by the idea, I tucked it away and resurrected it later, mulling over a couple of key questions: What might cause a newly married woman to leave her husband? And what might bring the couple back together again?

I quickly realized that Annie is a woman longing to put down roots and Nick is a man searching for the place he belongs. To that beginning, I added a small town, some eccentric locals and a little humor—and this story was born.

I hope you enjoy Nick and Annie's story. Please visit my Web site at www.pamelaford.net or write me at P.O. Box 327, Grafton, WI 53024 and let me know what you think.

Pamela Ford

Oh Baby!
Pamela Ford

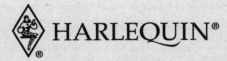

HARLEQUIN®

TORONTO • NEW YORK • LONDON
AMSTERDAM • PARIS • SYDNEY • HAMBURG
STOCKHOLM • ATHENS • TOKYO • MILAN • MADRID
PRAGUE • WARSAW • BUDAPEST • AUCKLAND

ISBN 0-373-71247-2

OH BABY!

This edition published by arrangement with Harlequin Books S.A.

® and TM are trademarks of the publisher. Trademarks indicated with
® are registered in the United States Patent and Trademark Office, the
Canadian Trade Marks Office and in other countries.

www.eHarlequin.com

Printed in U.S.A.

To my parents, Don and Rita, for raising me to dream; and my husband, Jay, and our children, Margaux, Ella and Laurel, for their support as I chased that dream. And to Aaron and Nancy, without whom, had they not had the good sense to fall in love and get married, this book might never have come to life.

CHAPTER ONE

NICK HADN'T SEEN ANNIE since the week after their wedding—six years ago last month.

She'd married him, just as they'd agreed. Had left him a week later, just as they'd agreed. And he'd filed for divorce, just as they'd agreed.

He cleared his throat and tapped his fingers on the steering wheel as he practiced aloud a new version of the speech he had been working on for days now. "Annie, our divorce was never finalized. I left the country and never followed up with the lawyer to make sure everything got done."

She was a practical sort, Annie was. She'd probably offer him a cold lemonade and they'd have a laugh over how irresponsible he once had been. Then she'd sign the new set of papers he'd brought with him and he'd kiss her on the cheek when he left. And they'd go back to life the way it had been for the past six years.

Unless, of course, she'd remarried.

He pulled his Range Rover to a stop in front of a big pale-yellow Victorian house and lifted his sunglasses to squint at the sign in front.

Unless of course, he'd made her a bigamist.

Bailey House Bed & Breakfast. He drew a breath. This was the place, exactly where the old woman at the gas station on the edge of town said he would find it. Small-town Wisconsin at its finest.

He shoved open the car door and stepped out into the late afternoon summer sun. A crumbled fast-food bag and a toothbrush dropped out onto the pavement. He scooped them up and tossed them onto the passenger seat.

Why was he nervous? Annie would still be Annie. Whether she'd married or not, all she had to do was sign the papers and they'd slip back into their lives—no one the wiser. Well, no one but her *other* husband…and the judge who would have to remarry them…and a couple of witnesses—

He buried those thoughts and headed across the walk and up the stairs to the wide front porch, noting the paint just beginning to peel on the old wood. There were layers of buildup underneath, layers that would make this place a nightmare to scrape and paint. Thank God he wasn't the owner.

He jabbed the doorbell and put a pleasant expression on his face. After a long minute without a response, he pushed the bell again. Maybe he should have called.

No, it was bad enough they were still married. It would have been far worse to tell her that over the phone.

Suddenly the door swung inward and Annie stood before him, in cutoffs and a T-shirt. Barefoot. Radiant. Deep blue eyes shining. Tawny blond hair pulled back into a ponytail, a grin on her face as though she were ready to take on the world.

Annie.

He couldn't remember the Annie he knew, the waitress in the all-night coffee shop, looking so gorgeous.

"Hey, Annie," he said.

Her eyes widened. Her grin disappeared.

An older woman's voice floated down the hallway from somewhere behind her. "Tell Vivian I'll be right out."

"Get out of here," Annie said in low voice. "Now."

What? He took a step toward her. "I know this is a surprise, but I need to talk to you."

The older woman spoke again, her voice closer, louder, with each word. "Annie, dear, I'll be back in time to help you flip the mattresses."

Panic stole over Annie's face—panic that was instantly replaced by an expression of fierce determination. In one nearly seamless movement, she launched herself out of the doorway and into his arms and began to kiss him like he was the long-lost love of her life.

She pressed herself against him as if willing him to put his arms around her, and, for a brief, stunned moment, he pulled her close and returned the kiss. Then his brain kicked into gear and he took her by the arms and pushed back a bit.

"What—" he choked out.

"Good heavens!" the older woman screeched as she came through the doorway and spotted Annie in his arms. "He's here!"

Behind her, a gold-and-black, watermelon-shaped mutt bounded out onto the porch and began to bounce around them, barking.

Nick tore his gaze from Annie and focused on the diminutive gray-haired old woman; every line in her soft face angled upward from her joyous smile. Almost dancing with excitement, she reached up to tug his head down and kiss his cheek.

And the dog kept barking as if he'd just dug up the bone of his dreams.

"Chester! Quiet! Chester!" Annie shouted.

"I'm Luella!" the old woman cried over the chaos.

"Be quiet!" Annie grabbed hold of the dog's collar and dragged him toward the door.

"So happy to finally meet you," Luella said in a voice still loud and high. "I've been the inn's housekeeper for twenty years. I keep your Annie from overworking herself, what with that little bun in the oven."

Bun? His heart seemed to slow. Pregnant? Husband?

He shifted his gaze to Annie just as she snatched up the squirming dog and spun around, the desperate expression on her face a mixture of horror and hope.

Bigamist?

Her eyes locked with his.

"I, ah—" he stammered.

Behind him a car horn blared and he jumped, startled. He turned as the driver slammed on the brakes of her silver Lincoln and skidded to a halt just inches behind his SUV.

"Oh! Vivian's here!" Annie almost screamed in panicked glee. "You don't want to be late for Women's

Club." She shoved the dog into the house and pulled the door shut before he could escape.

Luella shook her head. "That old lady. Always has to make a grand entrance."

The blue-haired woman at the wheel laid on the horn once more, and then a third time.

"Oh! She's in fine form today. I'll just have to hear everything later." Luella patted him on the arm. "Just wait until Vivian hears the news."

She headed down the steps. "I believe this calls for a glass of Chablis with our supper, don't you think?"

"Have two," Annie called. "Take your time."

Luella glanced back at Nick and grinned. "Oh, yes, dear. I see what you mean. We'll make it a long meal."

She had hardly gotten into the car and closed the door before it sped off, leaving the faint smell of burning rubber behind.

"Good God," Annie muttered. "This is going to be all over town in half an hour."

"What the heck is going on?"

Annie sighed and shook her head. "You might as well come in. Want a lemonade?"

At least he'd been right about one thing. "Sure."

Annie pushed open the front door and the dog leapt out again, whining excitedly, tail whipping from side to side. Thankfully the mutt wasn't barking.

"Just ignore him, he'll calm down," Annie said.

Nick followed her to the kitchen, a big, bright room filled with the delicious aroma of cookies baking.

"I always have homemade cookies for the guests." Annie took a pitcher of lemonade from the refrigerator. "Bake up a fresh batch every couple of days so the cookie jar is always full."

She poured him a glass of lemonade, a slice of lemon floating on the top, and he took a seat at the old oak table in the center of the room. He looked out the tall windows facing south, to the kind of view most people only dreamed of having. A long expanse of lawn sloped gently toward a sandy beach on a lake that looked to be surrounded by pristine forest.

A moment later, Annie set a plate of warm cookies on the table and took the chair opposite him. The dog collapsed on the floor beside her, apparently exhausted from all the energy he had expended barking.

"I guess I owe you an explanation," she said.

He waited.

Annie swallowed hard. "Two years ago I bought this B & B with the money you gave me. Well, first I went to college so I could learn how to run a business. Then I found this place."

Her voice quivered and she reached down to rub the dog's head. "It's a great little town…."

"Annie—are you pregnant?"

Her expression shifted as though the question caught her completely off guard. She looked about to say something and stopped herself, then drew a slow breath and exhaled. Avoiding his eyes, she stared at the ceiling for a long moment before finally bringing her gaze back to rest on him. She bit her lower lip and made a futile gesture with one hand, as though the motion might give him an answer.

He raised an eyebrow.

She nodded.

Shit. "Married?"

"No."

He let out a breath. At least he hadn't made her a bigamist. He picked up a cookie.

"So where's the father?"

She locked eyes with him and he waited.

"I'm looking at him."

He jerked his head around to look behind him; no one else was in the room. His mouth opened, but the only word he could manage was "What?"

"Everyone thinks I'm married to you...."

"Wait a minute, wait a minute, wait a minute—" He tried to force his brain to catch up with the conversation.

The words poured out of her. "I didn't plan for it to happen—it just did. I've been meaning to put an end to it, really I have, but— Ohh, now that you're here, they're going to know I'm a fraud. They're going to think I meant to lie. Well, I *did* mean to, but it's not what you think. I didn't intend it to go this far."

She heaved an agitated sigh and flopped back into her chair. "Everyone in town is going to think I'm just another fake from the city willing to take advantage of their trust—"

"Hold it! You're not making any sense. How did *I* get into this story? What about the real father? Isn't he interested at all?"

"Interested?" She shook her head. "He doesn't even know."

"That's your first mistake! With all due respect, don't you think it might help if you told him?"

"Sperm donor."

"Huh?"

"Artificial insemination."

"Oh." *Oh.* He found his brain empty again. How did one respond to such an announcement? *Gee, I see it worked. Gosh, I'm relieved that some guy wasn't sleeping with you and left you hanging like this? Why would you get yourself artificially inseminated, anyway?*

"So you did this on purpose." A bit inane, but at least he said something.

"No."

His eyes widened.

She snorted. "Well, of course I got pregnant on purpose. How else do you think one gets artificially inseminated?"

"No need to get testy. I'm not the one who lied about who the father was."

"I didn't lie about the father."

He frowned.

"I lied about being married. Everyone just assumed who the father was."

"Oh, well, then it's okay," he said irritably.

"I didn't mean for it to happen like this. I was researching B & Bs so I would know how to run one when I finally bought a place. I came here to visit because it was called Bailey House and it was in *Bedford.*"

She gave a sheepish grin. "You know, kind of like the movie *It's a Wonderful Life.* But there was this college kid who was doing yard work for the summer who kept asking me out. It was just easier to say I was married. Besides, I thought I'd be gone after a week."

The timer sounded and she jumped up to slide a tray of cookies from the oven. "But then I got to talking with the owner. She and her husband wanted to retire. *They wanted to sell.* They hadn't put up a For Sale sign because they were being really picky about who they'd sell to."

"You're losing me."

Annie turned to face him. "They'd raised their family here. They loved this place and wanted to pass it on to someone who would love it like they did. Someone who would raise their family here. Someone who was *married.*"

She turned her attention back to the cookies and began to lift them off the sheet with a spatula, her words coming faster now. "And there I was, *married*—or so everyone thought. Somehow, suddenly, I was buying the place from them and staying on. Eventually I was going to say we had gotten divorced, but I couldn't do it too soon or everyone would be suspicious."

She looked him straight in the eye. "You know what I mean?"

"Not really." He took a large swallow of lemonade and had the fleeting thought that by the end of this story he was going to wish he had something stronger to drink.

"Didn't anyone ever wonder where your husband was?" Nick couldn't keep the incredulity out of his voice. "And—how did you explain—the pregnancy?"

Annie shook her head. "You're a top-secret military guy. The only way we ever got to see each other was if I met you at military bases around the world. So every

now and then I took a trip. That's when I got pregnant."
She glanced away. "I didn't see any hope for love—or
marriage—in my life. So I decided to quit hanging my
hopes on some guy I had yet to meet and go for it
alone."

"Annie! This is no little white lie—you've created a
whole other world. Didn't your mother ever teach you
not to lie?"

"I don't need a lecture, thank you, Mr. Not-So-Pure-
Yourself."

She picked up what looked like a miniature ice-
cream scoop and began to attack the bowl of cookie
dough, scooping and dropping neatly rounded balls of
dough onto the baking sheet. In silence, she filled the
tray and slid it into the oven. Then she sat in the chair
opposite him and sighed.

"It was never supposed to go this far." She gave
him a pointed look. "And you were never supposed
to show up. What the heck are you doing here, anyway? Don't tell me you just decided to drop by so we
could rehash old times, 'cause if you do I might just
kill you."

"We're still married."

"In the eyes of everyone in town, yes."

"No, Annie, I mean we're still married. The attorney
never filed the papers.... I left California right after
you did—actually, I left the country—thinking it was
all settled."

She gaped at him, eyes wide. "Are you kidding me?
I knew it! I knew something wasn't right! I tried to call
you once to make sure everything had been finalized

but your line was disconnected. How could you have let this happen?"

"I assumed the lawyer would do his job."

She snorted. "Why wouldn't you call him to make sure?"

"*I was out of the country.* I didn't go back to California for more than five years."

"I should have known I couldn't count on you to follow through." She slapped a hand on the table. "I upheld my part of the bargain. I married you and left you. You got your trust fund seven years before you were supposed to. The only thing you had to do—the only thing—was make sure the divorce went through."

"And pay you $250,000. I did that, remember?"

"Fine." She shook her head. "If only Luella hadn't seen you. I've made a life in this little town. For the first time, I belong. I'm part of a community. Now, with you showing up, I'll lose it all."

Sympathy stirred within him. He remembered what she'd told him of her childhood. How she'd grown up an army brat and hated always being the new kid in school. That just before her father retired from the army, her parents had died in a car accident, and the kids were split up among the relatives. How she'd been on her own since the day she graduated high school.

He started to reach across the table toward her but stopped himself. "I'm sorry."

"Sorry? Sorry won't fix this." She gave a rueful laugh. "How am I supposed to support myself when I'm run out of town? Alimony?"

She leaned sideways in her chair to grab a short

stack of envelopes from the counter and wave them in the air. "As the husband in this family, you should know the bills are due. The lawn needs mowing, the storm windows need to be washed before fall comes, and, oh, in case you hadn't noticed, the exterior could use a coat of paint."

"I noticed. Look, Annie, I know this is a bit of a shock."

"The master of understatement strikes again."

"All we need to do is get divorced for real. That's why I'm here. I've got the papers in the car—you just have to sign them."

"I guess you don't know that you can't file for divorce if the woman is pregnant?"

His blood seemed to slow. "What?"

"Not in Wisconsin, anyway. Business law 101."

"You learned about divorce in business law?"

"We got off on a tangent." She gave a cynical laugh.

"Some tangent. Look, that just doesn't sound right to me—"

"It doesn't matter how it sounds. What matters is that it's true. I'm pregnant—you can't divorce me. The law is written to protect the unborn child. It's probably the same for every state."

Irritation flooded through him. Irritation and panic. He was supposed to marry Melissa Morgan in six months—the date was set. Everyone agreed Missy was the perfect woman for him—gorgeous, fun *and* she liked the outdoors. Plus, he loved her, he was sure of it. Not in a head-over-heels, gasping, stomach-flopping kind of way, but he did love her. Which was a lot better than many people ever got.

Everything had been great. But then, two weeks ago he learned his divorce had never gone through. His attorney had assured him a divorce could be finalized in time for the wedding, as long as he found Annie and got her to sign the papers right away. Who would have guessed she'd be pregnant?

He raked a hand through his hair. "Wait a minute. What about those quickie divorces people talk about. You know, in Mexico, or Las Vegas, or someplace like that?"

Annie just looked at him.

He plunged onward. "We could get one of those. We'll just fly out—like tomorrow—get the divorce, and then go our separate ways."

"That's rich. My husband arrives on a military leave to announce he's taking me on an exotic vacation—to divorce me while I'm carrying his firstborn child."

Nick tried to grin but the expression on Annie's face told him she didn't find his comment funny. "Okay, so it sounds bad," he said without missing a beat. "How about if you don't tell anyone we're getting a divorce right now—just say we're taking a trip. Once I've gone…back to the military…you can pretend you're married for the whole pregnancy if you want. No one has to know we're not. Then six months from now—or whenever—just say we've gotten divorced."

He paused, weighing whether or not he should tell her about Melissa. Well, why not? She was a female, she'd understand how upset Melissa might be about all this. Besides, it wasn't as if he and Annie were ever *really* married. "Look, Annie, the thing is, I need to be single…soon. So I can—" suddenly the words felt awkward "—get—married—again."

A sharp laugh burst out of her. "I can't believe this is happening. I'm living a bad daytime soap opera. Nick, the problem is, Luella and Vivian will already have spread it all over town that you're back. No one's going to believe we'd leave on vacation right away—especially when this is your first trip home." Her voice turned pleading. "Couldn't you just stay a while and pretend you're on leave?"

He was sure he could make her see reason. "Annie, I've got a fiancée. I can't just hang around here and playact. We need to get divorced. Now."

She fixed an unreadable look on him and he waited for her to give in. A minute passed and then another without a word spoken. Her expression grew thoughtful.

"You need a divorce. And I need a husband. Seems to me we can work this out."

He squinted at her and nodded. *This was totally unlike her. Just what was she up to?*

"I might be open to flying off to who-knows-where for a quickie divorce…" She smiled and he felt a noose drop around his neck.

"Yes?"

"If my *husband* were to stick around for a while."

He exhaled. "Annie—"

"Come on, Nick, if it wasn't for me, you wouldn't have gotten your trust fund early like you did."

"You were paid handsomely."

"I helped you out in your time of need. Now it's my time of need. All I ask—"

He crossed his arms over his chest. "Do you have any idea how much this will screw up my life?"

"About as much as it has mine?"

Touché. "What exactly do you want?"

"Nine days—"

"Nine days? Are you out of your—"

"A mere nine days pretending we're happily married and I promise I'll go wherever we have to go, do whatever you need me to do, to finalize our divorce."

"Three days at the most. *Three.*" What had happened to easy-to-influence Annie?

"Not long enough. Look, you were granted a leave to come home to see your pregnant wife. You wouldn't stay just three days."

She leaned toward him, eyes glistening with excitement. "Besides, it'll be easy. You won't have to answer any questions about what you do—it's top secret, remember?"

"I'm engaged to someone else."

"I didn't say you had to fulfill the connubial duties—"

"That hadn't even crossed my mind. How do I explain to Melissa that I'm staying out here another nine days? She doesn't even know I've come to see you. She thinks I've been divorced for years."

"Do you even work?"

What did that have to do with anything? He sat up straighter. "You bet I work. I'm a writer. One of those guys who travels all over the world, rafts down rapids, climbs mountains, eats fried bugs in exotic countries, and then writes articles about it—sometimes books."

He sat back in his chair. "In fact, right now I have a

proposal in with my agent for a television-book deal that just might make me a household name. I want to track down the Almasti in Mongolia. Ever hear of them? They're kind of like Big Foot—some people think they're Neanderthals who survived."

A slow appreciative grin filled Annie's eyes with warmth. "You did it. You actually did what you wanted to do with your trust fund money?"

He nodded.

"I have to admit, I thought you'd blow the whole fund on the L.A. party scene."

She knew him better than he would have guessed; he might have done just that had he stayed in L.A. "About two weeks after you left, I took off for Nepal. Sold my first story from there and didn't go back to L.A. for years."

No need to tell her that L.A. reminded him of a night-shift waitress he used to tell his dreams to in a dive restaurant at two in the morning, a waitress he'd once married—and had never really forgotten.

"Perfect." She jumped to her feet and paced the room, her voice all business now. "Then you don't have to ask anyone for time off from work. Just tell your fiancée you're doing another story. Right here in Wisconsin."

"Oh, she'll buy that. There's *lots* of adventure to write about in this little town."

"Snobbery is not attractive," she said. "Make it up. She's not going to know—after all, you're not actually writing an article. How can you? You're a top secret military kind of guy—not a writer."

He stared at her.

"You owe me," she said. "Think of it as repayment."

Repayment was not the word he would have chosen to apply to this situation. Perhaps *extortion* would be better. "One week. I'm pretty sure the military only gives its really important guys leave in very short increments."

The noose around his neck seemed to tighten.

"Nine days. I spent an entire childhood moving from base to base—the military gives leaves in any amount of time they darn well please."

He threw his hands up in frustration.

"Nine days?" Her face glowed with hope, and at that moment, he might have agreed to anything just so he wouldn't be the reason she'd lose that glow.

"This is bordering on the absurd," he said, stalling.

"We can do it."

"We hardly know each other."

"Nick, we faked it well enough to get married six years ago."

She was right about that—to this day no one had a clue the marriage had been a sham. The day after the wedding, Nick's parents had flown back to Chicago, and as far as they knew, Annie didn't walk out on their son until six months later. They'd accepted without question the reason for the divorce—that the two had married too quickly and soon learned they were completely incompatible.

"My parents never quite got over why you left me," he said. "I think they couldn't believe that *anyone* would leave a Fleming."

Annie laughed. "If we can fool your family, we can fool people who don't know you at all. Come on, Nick."

"A week. I'll give you a week. What difference does it make, seven days or nine, as long as I play my role right?"

She sighed. "It has to be nine. There's a ribbon-cutting at the new general store museum, and I chaired the fund-raising committee…." She grimaced. "We've, ah, made a donation—"

"We?" General store museum?

"Well, I couldn't very well ignore the fact that I was married when I made the donation, could I?"

"Is my name on your checking account, too?"

She bent to peer into the oven. "Looks like the cookies are done."

"Annie! You took this all the way, didn't you?"

"One thing just seemed to lead to another," she said slowly as she pulled the cookie sheet from the oven. "It was kind of like a snowball rolling downhill."

"I think the snowball just smashed into a tree."

"Not if you stay for nine days."

"I don't remember you being so…"

She spun to face him and grinned. "Stunningly beautiful?"

"Pushy," he said.

"I do remember you being irresponsible."

The truth of her words stung. "Not anymore."

"Prove it."

He met her gaze and held it, saw the challenge in her eyes, and knew he wanted to stay, wanted to help her. With her looking at him like that, strong, competent, vulnerable all at once, what he wanted to do right now was make things right.

He exhaled. "Nine days? Eight nights? And then we fly off to get a quickie divorce and everyone thinks I've gone back to the military?"

She nodded.

"Promise?" What was he thinking? Nine days? Melissa would never buy it. She thought he was writing an article about driving from California to Chicago—which he was. What she didn't know was that he had made a little detour into Wisconsin to find Annie.

"Promise."

"And today is day one?"

She nodded.

"Okay." *He had lost his mind.*

She beamed at him, her relief palpable. "Thank you."

What the heck—might as well roll with it. He raised a wicked eyebrow at her. "So tell me, what do we do now...*sweetheart?*"

CHAPTER TWO

ANNIE LOOKED AT HIM and frowned. "What am I thinking? This isn't going to work—you won't have enough clothes to last nine days. No way you'd come home for nine days and only have enough clothes for a weekend."

She tapped her lower lip with her finger. "I suppose we could say the airlines lost your luggage. That would be a good excuse for why you're buying new stuff. Yeah, that might work for—"

"I didn't fly—I drove."

"From L.A.?"

"I'm doing a story about driving cross country to Chicago. I've got a duffel in the trunk. With a job like mine, you have to be prepared."

A grin spread across her face. "You *have* changed! What are we waiting for? Let's get you moved in."

He held up a hand. "No, no. I'll get it."

He started across the kitchen, but Annie jumped to her feet and pushed through the old-fashioned screen door ahead of him. "I'll help you carry something," she said over her shoulder.

The door banged shut behind her.

He shrugged. She was about to see just how much he

hadn't changed. He followed her down the driveway to his dark green SUV and popped open the tailgate, stifling a laugh when he heard Annie gasp at the sight inside.

Okay, so it looked even worse than he remembered. Sure, his tent and sleeping bag were rolled up nice and neat. And there was a duffel just like he'd said there would be. Admittedly, it was nearly empty, but at least he had one. Everything that had once been in it was strewn across the back end in a sea of assorted newspapers, magazines, bottled water and empty snack bags.

He grabbed the dirty jeans that were draped over the back seat and shoved them into the duffel. Wrinkled T-shirts came next, and socks and—uh, those silky boxers Melissa had given him the night before he left.

"I see organization is not one of your strengths," Annie said, eyes riveted on the mess.

He scooped up the boxers in an armful of clothing. "Too much order stifles creativity."

Suddenly she smacked him hard on the shoulder. "Drop that stuff! Get out of the way!"

He dropped everything and jumped back just as she slammed the tailgate shut.

"What the...? You almost broke my fingers!" Was the woman nuts?

Smiling, she ignored him, looked right past him and waved at a heavyset, middle-aged man in a gray sweat suit power-walking down the sidewalk toward them. "Hello, Father."

Father? He glanced quickly at Annie.

"Priest," she whispered. "Father, I want you to meet

my husband, Nick. He's home on leave. Nick, this is Father Thespesius. I've mentioned him in some of my letters."

The priest pumped Nick's extended hand. "It's so good to finally meet you. Welcome to Bedford! How goes the secret service?" He waved a hand back and forth. "No, don't tell me. I don't want to jeopardize our national security."

He started to walk around them in a circle, arms swinging. "Have to keep moving. If I stop too long my heart rate drops and I don't get the full cardio benefit. You're a lucky man to have a gal like Annie. And a baby on the way. Twice blessed." He strode off down the sidewalk, glancing back at them to call "See you in church."

Nick looked at Annie and found himself nodding along as she did. *Church?* He hadn't been to church in years. "You go to church?"

"Everybody goes to church in a small town."

"Everybody? Annie, don't you think we should keep a low profile for the next week? Can't we pretend we just want to spend all our time alone together?"

"You'd rather the whole town be talking about *why* we're not in church and what we're doing instead on Sunday morning?"

"Oh, come on. No one will even miss us."

She laughed knowingly. "Not only will they miss us, but the next time they see us, half the town will probably comment on why we weren't there—and the other half will be snickering. Welcome to Bedford, population 7,500."

What had he gotten into? And what had happened to Annie? She was taking charge here like a general with a mission. He contemplated this change in her and realized he didn't find the difference unattractive. Quite the contrary; the Annie he used to know could have used a dose of self-confidence.

Annie motioned at the driveway that led to the big garage behind the house. "Why don't you pull your car up so you can repack your duffel in private. I'll get out the laundry soap— maybe you'd like to do some *wash.*"

She smiled sweetly and headed up the front steps into the house.

He slipped into the driver's seat, muttering under his breath, "Maybe you'd like to do some wash." Snapping up his cell phone, he called Melissa and was relieved when she didn't answer. He left a quick message—a lie—that he'd received a sudden assignment that would keep him in the Midwest and he would call her later.

He pulled his SUV up to the garage and dialed his attorney, this time disappointed that no one answered. He left a detailed message—the truth—about Annie, Wisconsin law and the situation in Bedford.

Ten minutes later, after throwing his dirty clothes in the washer, he joined Annie in the living room—parlor, he supposed they called it in an old house like this. He set his duffel on the floor and stopped to take in the picture before him.

Annie sat on the brocade sofa, one elbow on the armrest, chin cupped in her hand, her face a vision of apprehension.

"It just dawned on me—where are you going to sleep?" she asked.

"Don't you have an empty room?"

She nodded. "But it's not that simple. Luella would know—heck, my guests would know. Married people sleep in the same room. Especially married people who hardly ever get to see each other."

The thought of sharing a room, and a bed, with Annie slowed his brain. He walked over to the hearth and forced his thoughts to organize. "We can do that," he said finally.

"I suppose you could sleep on the floor."

Floor? "Hardwood?"

"Uh-huh."

"A couple of throw rugs, I bet."

She tilted her head. "Your point exactly?"

"I'm not sleeping on a wood floor for the next eight nights. Surely you've got enough room in your bed."

"Surely you jest."

"Surely not. I stay nine days—eight nights—I sleep in a bed. Those are *my* terms."

She just looked at him.

"Annie?" He rested a forearm against the mantel and waited for her to respond. A framed picture caught his eye, a wedding photo set next to an antique oil lamp. He leaned toward it for a better look and a rush of tangled emotions raced through him. It was them—him and Annie—on their wedding day six years ago, smiling at the camera with all the enthusiasm of young lovers.

A week later, Annie had left. At the memory, a long-forgotten ache touched his gut. Once he'd lost his late-night confidant, he'd found all he wanted to do was get out of L.A. The superficiality of the place became all the more obvious without Annie as a counterbalance. In retrospect, her leaving had jump-started him into his dream of becoming an adventure writer.

He shoved aside the memory and the feeling of loss. "Nice prop. I was wondering how Luella recognized me."

She shrugged sheepishly. "How could I be married and not have a picture of us out?"

He sat beside her on the sofa. "Annie, you were safe with me that week after our wedding. You don't have to start worrying that I'll take advantage of you now."

"I know, I know. I can't very well tell Luella to put another bed in the room." She sighed. "Okay, so we share a bed. That's the easy part, anyway. The hard part is making sure we don't make any mistakes in public. So tell me some things about you I should know, as your wife."

"Like what? I grew up outside Chicago. My dad's a retired banker from a long line of successful—and rich—bankers. I have a sister—"

"I know that stuff already."

"My mom died last year."

Annie's eyes softened and she reached out to cover his hand with her own. "Oh, Nick. I'm so sorry. How's your dad taking it?"

"It's hard for him to be alone—they were married forty years. I was going to stop by and surprise him after I left here—guess that'll have to wait nine days." He grinned.

"And your sister?"

"Still in Chicago, too. Working for the family bank, which is good for dad in a lot of ways. Not the least of which is that she's seriously dating some guy who's also in banking—"

"Ah, kind of like the number-cruncher son he never had."

"Something like that. He doesn't bug me to join the bank anymore. I think my mom's death made him realize life is too short to be disappointed that your kid isn't a financial wizard."

A long pause hung in the air between them. Finally Annie spoke. "So, do you still drink your coffee black?"

"I hate coffee."

"Really? Then why were you always stopping in the restaurant in the middle of the night for coffee?"

He cocked his head and stared at her a moment. "You were the only person who ever took my dreams seriously, who ever seemed to believe I might make them come true." *And you had this goodness about you, an honest realness, which was really hard to find in L.A.* He shrugged. "As for coffee, I still drink it—black— when I need a jolt. You?"

"Pregnancy's put an end to my coffee-drinking. Now it's decaf, with cream. What else?"

"I don't know. I eat red meat. Does that help?"

"Yeah…"

"I run. Seven or eight miles every day."

"What else?"

"You tell me. You're the one who's created a profile. What do I do exactly?"

She flashed him a grin. "Something for the military. It's so top secret even I don't know what it is."

"Well, that makes job questions easy. So, is it safe to assume we've been married for six years?"

"That would be correct."

"When's the baby due?"

"Six months."

"You're three months along? You don't even look pregnant."

"Oh, I do. You should see me without clothes on."

He raised an eyebrow.

She blushed. "Forget I said that."

"So where'd you get your degree?" he asked. "What's it in again?"

"Hotel and restaurant management. University of Wisconsin-Stout—"

"Hence the bed-and-breakfast." He gestured toward the doorway. "Why don't you show me around while we have this conversation so I can really get up to speed?"

"Good idea. This is the parlor. You've already seen the kitchen and basement." She smiled like a proud parent and led him across the hall into a second sitting room and the dining room. Both were decorated with antiques, in a style reminiscent of the late nineteenth century.

"On the second floor, I—*we*—have five guest rooms." She mounted the stairs and glanced at the dog bounding ahead of her. "Oh, something else you probably should know—everyone thinks Chester is yours."

He gave the mutt a long look. "I hate little dogs. And I don't like big ones much better."

She threw him a dirty look as they continued up the stairs. "He's twenty pounds. And how can you be a man and not like dogs?"

He shrugged. "Never had one, never saw the need to have one."

"Well, since everyone thinks this dog is yours, you'd better put on a good show."

"Would a man pick out a mutt that looks like that?"

Chester wagged his hairy tail as though aware he was the topic of conversation.

"You did."

Ahead on the landing, Chester waited for them, prancing excitedly, tongue hanging out of his happy grin.

"We're acquaintances," Nick said to the dog. "Not friends. Remember that."

He turned his attention back to Annie. "Is there anything else I should know about myself? Like, I sing opera or paint my toenails, or…?"

Annie rolled her eyes and led the way down the second-floor corridor. "Offhand, I can't think of anything, but who knows? I've been embellishing on you for quite a while."

"Somehow I'm not flattered."

She pushed open the doors to a couple of unoccupied guest rooms. Each had a similar flavor—lace curtains at the windows, antique furniture, patchwork quilts, faded Oriental rugs. The look was warm and welcoming. By the time they reached the third floor, Nick was beginning to think this might not be the worst situation he'd ever gotten himself into.

Annie opened the first door they reached. "This is my—our—room."

He stepped over the threshold. "A double bed? Couldn't you at least have a queen?"

"*Queen* isn't historically correct."

"Ha! But it *is* a lot more comfortable for two people."

"Two people hasn't been a concern of mine since I bought the place," she said with a sniff.

"Never?"

"I'm married, remember?"

How could he have forgotten? He dropped his duffel on the floor next to her dresser.

Annie looked at it for a long moment, as though only now realizing Nick was really going to share her room. Then she smiled. "I'll empty some drawers for—"

"Yoo-hoo, anybody here?" An elderly female voice came up the stairs from the front hall. "Annie!"

Panicked, Annie spun toward the door. She grabbed hold of his forearm. "Oh, my gosh! Luella's back already! She can be nosy, so when in doubt, keep your mouth shut."

Annie hurried into the hall. Chester ran ahead of her, tail beating the air in excitement.

Nick followed, pausing in the doorway for a last look at the cozy room. Old-fashioned and feminine, with its flowered wallpaper and white chenille bedspread, the room was a picture of an era gone by, of stolen romantic moments between a young man and young woman, while her father sat in the backyard smoking his pipe and talking politics. He grinned and wondered whether such thoughts ever crossed Annie's mind. Another picture popped into his head, of Annie lying across the bed in a general state of undress. The thought took him aback. This was his friend, Annie. And he was engaged to someone else. What was the matter with him?

He swallowed hard and hurried down the hall after her. *Maybe this bed-sharing thing wasn't such a good idea after all.* He almost ran her down in his haste to catch up, stopping behind her to stare over the balustrade at the gathering of women below them in the foyer—one, two, four, six, eight. *Holy cow.*

Eight faces crowned with silver hair smiled up at them—and said nothing. And then the sound of heels clipping briskly upon the hardwood floor of the corridor was followed by Luella's face, and her gasp. "Oh, my dears, I thought I gave you enough time. I had no idea you might still be upstairs."

Annie's face flamed. "Inquisition," she muttered. "There's going to be an inquisition. And I'm going to be hung."

Nick took her by the elbow and gently guided her down the stairs. "Not if I can help it," he murmured in her ear.

"Ladies, you'll have to excuse our surprise," he said when they reached the bottom step. "It's been some time since my wife and I have seen each other."

The small group let out a collective embarrassed laugh and suddenly the women were chattering around them, introductions flying as each shook Nick's hand.

Luella spoke over the clamor. "As soon as the ladies

heard he was here, why, they insisted we cut supper short and come right over. I tried to discourage them, said you two needed time alone, but it was to no avail as you can see."

"Oh, it's all right, isn't it, *sweetheart?*" Nick gave Annie a loving smile.

The endearment seemed to loosen her up. "No problem at all, *darling.*"

"I'm just glad to finally be able to put faces to the names Annie has mentioned in her letters. I've heard so much about all of you I feel like I know you already." He hoped he wasn't laying it on too thick.

Annie gave a slight nod of approval for his quick ad-lib. Okay, this wasn't so hard. All he had to do was charm, charm, charm. "Ladies, I think we'd all be a bit more comfortable in the parlor. Would anyone like a lemonade?"

"Oh, what a dear," someone said.

Annie smiled.

"You go on and sit down." Luella bustled toward the kitchen door. "I'll get the lemonade. Don't you talk about anything important until I'm back."

Nick and Annie settled onto the sofa, while everyone else took a nearby seat, some pulling in chairs from the dining room, to gather around the two as though Nick were a movie star come to visit from Hollywood. Nick draped a casual arm around Annie's shoulders and pulled her close, letting his fingers play with the soft strands of hair that had pulled loose from her ponytail. He was the perfect picture of the long-absent husband unable to keep his hands off his wife.

Annie tried to subtly shift away, but he held her firm.

"It really is wonderful to finally meet Annie's husband," someone said.

"No talking, no talking!" Luella's voice rang out from the hall. A minute later, she appeared around the corner with a wooden tray filled with glasses of lemonade. She passed out the drinks. "All right. Now you can talk."

The women tittered and said nothing, suddenly tongue-tied. Finally one spoke. "Are you back for good?"

Nick put a disappointed look on his face. "Just nine days, I'm afraid. Then it's back to business as usual."

The room filled with sighs of disappointment and clucks of the tongue.

"Poor Annie," one lady murmured.

"Annie says you work for the military. What exactly do you do?"

Nick pursed his lips in contemplation. The women straightened, hanging on his every word.

He smiled apologetically. "I—well… It's classified. Top secret. I could tell you what I do…" He leaned toward the woman who had asked the question, holding in a laugh as everyone leaned forward in expectation.

"But then I'd have to kill you," he said in a stage whisper.

With a collective gasp, the women sat back in their chairs. He grinned and let out a sharp laugh.

"Nick!" Annie slapped him on the arm.

He laughed again. "Just kidding. Truthfully, though, I'm really not at liberty to talk about it."

The women chuckled nervously.

"You must be thrilled about the baby," another woman finally said.

"You have no idea what an effect that baby is having on me," he said with a smile.

"Oh, Annie, he'll be such a good father."

One woman bent forward. "Some of us were beginning to wonder whether you weren't a figment of Annie's imagination."

Annie's smile faltered a bit. "Nick, this is Vivian. We sit together on the board of the new museum."

"The general store." Nick nodded as though he knew everything about it. "I'm so proud of Annie's involvement here." He pressed a kiss to the side of Annie's brow and ran his fingers over the skin at the back of her neck. Soft.

"We're actually quite pleased you're here, Nick, because we have another reason for stopping by," Vivian said. She focused her attention on Annie. "Who better than Nick to help judge the Women's Club flower-arrangement contest?"

Right. Who better than the man with the black thumb?

He felt Annie tense. She shook her head. "I thought you had the judges all lined up."

Vivian turned to Nick. "The Fletchers got a last-minute conflict and canceled out. The contest is in two days."

"Wouldn't it be better to get someone who has more experience with flowers?" Nick asked.

"Annie tells us you're a gardening whiz."

He slanted a look at Annie. *Gardening whiz?* Her eyes widened slightly and she nodded.

Maybe he was going to learn he painted his toenails, after all. He gave Annie's shoulder a gentle squeeze as he smiled humbly at Vivian.

"That Annie of mine. She loves me so much, she sometimes exaggerates my abilities just a bit." *He couldn't even keep a cactus alive.* "What else has she told you about me?"

The ladies laughed again.

"Oh, lots of things. How you love dogs…"

As if on cue, Chester came over and sat at his feet, tail whipping from side to side. Forced into the moment, Nick reached down to give the dog a pat and was rewarded with a series of fast, slobbering licks on the hand. *Nice touch.*

He wiped his hand on his pant leg. "That's me. Never met a dog I didn't like."

Luella smiled. "You can tell how much Chester loves you. A dog always remains devoted to its master no matter how long it's been since they were together."

"So, will you do the flower judging?" Vivian asked. "It's a worthy cause—part of our annual Flower Festival. All the arrangements are auctioned off and the money is used to fulfill our pledge to the new museum."

"Well, I…"

"Ple-e-ease."

Annie was going to pay for this. He looked to her for help and she gave an almost imperceptible shrug.

"All right." And then because he thought that sounded sort of lame, he added, "It'll be fun." *It'll be fun? If anything was lame, it was that comment.* What was he thinking? A flower-arrangement contest? He had to get out of here before he agreed to anything else.

Taking Annie's hand, he stood and pulled her to her feet. "Ladies, I really hate to be a party pooper, but my wife promised to show me the lake—and of course, some of the gardens."

Clasping Annie's hand tightly in his, he towed her toward the doorway. "It was very nice to meet all of you. I'm sure we'll be seeing one another around town."

"Only if Annie will let you out of her sight," Luella shouted with glee.

He waited until he and Annie were in the kitchen before he pulled her close enough so she could hear his whisper. "A gardening whiz?"

"I didn't think you'd ever actually be here."

"And a dog lover? You're so far from the truth, this gig will be over before it gets started." He glanced back toward the parlor and discovered several of the ladies craning their necks to see down the hall. The last thing these busybodies needed to talk about was a spat between Annie and her just-returned husband. He had no choice but to make it good—fast.

Without warning, he drew Annie against him and kissed her. She didn't exactly melt in his arms, but she didn't do too badly for the spur of the moment. More stiff than she'd been on the porch, but then she hadn't had much practice in the past few years.

He grinned as they gently pulled apart. He opened the door. "Show me the lake, love."

"That's enough!" she said under her breath. Her cheeks glowed pink.

He let go of the screen door and it slammed behind him. "The ladies were watching."

"That's no reason."

"Oh, but it was reason enough for you to kiss me when I arrived at the front door."

"That was different." She glanced away.

"Was it?"

"Yes, you're over the top. All that touchy, lovey-dovey stuff in the parlor. All those honeys and sweethearts. And then a kiss in the kitchen?"

"You're my wife. *I've missed you.* I'm just acting the way any red-blooded American man would act if he hadn't seen his wife in months."

He put an arm around her as they headed across the wide back lawn toward the water.

"Nick—" Her voice was full of warning.

"Don't look now, but the ladies are all at the kitchen windows."

She jerked her head around. "Oh! And you're egging their curiosity on with all this romantic stuff."

"I'm just doing what you told me—make 'em believe we're married. Now, put your arm around me. If you want them to believe we're in love, you're gonna have to act like it."

She rolled her eyes but complied. "Lots of married couples save these public displays of affection for private moments. We could be one of those types."

He let his arm slide down her back until his hand rested on her derriere. "Nope, I don't think so. Not after how the ladies saw me acting in there. I have to be consistent."

"Get your hand off my butt or I'll deck you."

He laughed and gave her rear end a pat before letting go of her. "Don't tell me we have trouble in paradise already?"

He sauntered onto the pier and sat on the bench across the end of the dock.

ANNIE STOPPED TO WATCH him for a moment, to drink in all that was Nick. His black hair was longer at the neck than current styles dictated, his T-shirt worn and faded as if he'd had it in his closet for years. His jeans, obviously old favorites, hugged his hips and fell straight to his ankles, creasing just a bit at the top of his running shoes. Lean and muscular, he still walked as if he owned the world.

It was amazing, after all these years he still had an effect on her—and he still had no clue about it. She knew she was overreacting to the affection he was showing as her long-absent husband, but every time he touched her she found herself fighting feelings she thought she'd gotten over a long time ago.

They'd never been anything more than friends, though she'd always thought that, given half a chance, she could have fallen head over heels for him. She, an army brat. He, the son of a wealthy banker. Nothing would ever have been less likely.

Well, it didn't matter now. The man was engaged and it was just as well. The last thing she needed was some casual fling with an irresponsible charmer who was about to marry someone else.

Although, she had to admit, it would sure fit her pattern. She'd always chosen the wrong kind of guys to get involved with—and it had taken months in therapy for her to finally realize it. She wasn't going down that path again. No way. Nick Fleming had "bad choice and broken heart" written all over him. Besides, she had a baby to think of now, and somehow, she didn't think Nick Fleming would ever be the fatherly type.

Problem was, the way Nick was acting, the way he was touching her, was bringing back every old feeling she'd ever had for him. She sighed inwardly and joined him on the bench.

"Thanks for being so nice to the ladies. And for agreeing to judge the flower arrangements."

"Just doing my job. If I'm going to be here for nine days, I might as well have something to do."

"Well thanks for being so gracious, anyway."

He shrugged. "This is beautiful." He gestured at the lake shimmering under the late afternoon sun.

A few houses down, almost out of earshot, a group of kids were doing cannonballs off a dock, trying to outdo one another with the size of their splashes. In the distance, a couple of sailboats slid slowly across the nearly flat water. "I almost feel like I'm on a movie set."

"This lake was half the reason I bought the place. Most of the land is state forest so it can't ever be developed. The view will stay like this forever."

"And you can live here happily ever after, as long as we pull off this charade."

"Maybe." She sat in silence for several minutes. "I've got about eighty acres over there."

She nodded toward a heavily wooded area that bordered her manicured lawn. "A stream runs through it. The thing is, if the B & B doesn't start making more money, I'm going to need to sell the land just to stay afloat. I've heard from a couple of developers. The question is, what will they put up? A resort? Condos? All I picture is lots of powerboats and Illinois license plates."

"Hey, watch it. I'm from Illinois—a long time ago, anyway."

She grinned. "Sorry. I'm feeling a little protective. Could be lots of Wisconsin license plates, too. Either way it changes everything around here."

"Annie, you're not thinking like a business person. More tourists would mean more business for you, too."

"Yeah, I know. It's just…the wrong kind of development would wreck the whole charm of this place."

She gestured across the bay. "Picture it. A big aluminum-sided complex of condos along here, just like every other development you see in every other community. A perfectly manicured lawn that no one ever walks on, let alone plays on. Or just as bad, maybe a massive four-story brick hotel with hundreds of rooms—and an outdoor swimming pool right next to the lake. Just not my idea of paradise."

She stood, suddenly wanting to get away from the pictures in her mind. "Let's walk. I'll show you all the flower beds I'm sure you'll be itching to dig your gardening fingers into. That is, of course, after you walk your dog!" She grinned wickedly.

Nick jumped off the bench and came after her and she took off running, laughing with glee.

He caught her by the arm and spun her around. "I should be really mad about all this."

Annie could see the twinkle in his eyes. "But you're not."

He brushed his lips across hers, a gentle, spontaneous kiss. Her heart leapt and her brain chastised her for allowing herself to respond to his touch.

"But I'm not," he said. "Now, show me the flowers."

CHAPTER THREE

NICK SLID INTO THE DRIVER'S seat of his SUV and picked up the cell phone. He'd just spent an hour looking at more flowers than he'd ever wanted to see in his life. Not that it would help him during the flower judging, but at least he now knew the difference between delphinium and phlox…or was it flax?

He wiped the back of his hand across his mouth and brushed away the crumbs from the chicken sandwiches Luella had brought out to them. She'd practically dragged him and Annie out of the flower beds and onto the porch to make sure they ate. Then she'd sat across from them the whole time, beaming. The woman was definitely happy Annie's husband was back.

With a sigh, he punched in the code to retrieve his messages.

"Hi, Nick." Melissa's sultry voice came on the line. "I can't believe you got an assignment out there. I'm leaving, too. Just got a photo shoot in Paris—an emergency. The girl they hired broke her leg—they need me there the day after tomorrow. I'm missing you already. And now we won't see each other for three weeks."

Her voice rose a notch. "Leonard called. There's a

party tonight at Marlene's. I wish you were here to go with me. Call my cell later and I'll pass it around so you can say hi to everyone. I miss you. I love you. Talk to you tonight. Ciao. Oh—I'll be at the Hôtel Grands Hommes in Paris."

If he wasn't so tired, he might be envious. L.A. was rocking and he was stuck here. The whole town of Bedford probably closed down at ten o'clock.

The second message was from his lawyer. "Nick, she's right—you can't divorce her in Wisconsin if she's pregnant. We could pull it off out here, but you don't meet California residency requirements anymore. Give me a few days do some checking. Call you back when I know something. Hey, bummer about the baby."

Bummer big time.

Well, the lawyer had nine days to figure it out, and the man better have an answer for him soon. He let his head drop forward until it rested against the steering wheel. What was that old saying? Marry in haste, repent at leisure? It was beginning to sound very profound.

He looked at his watch. Seven o'clock. The sun was only now beginning to drop on the horizon. He'd really pushed himself yesterday, driving almost all night, stopping once to sleep in the car for a couple of hours at a truck stop before putting in another seven hours to reach Annie's. He let his eyes close for a moment and felt himself immediately slide toward sleep. It would be early to bed for him tonight.

He stuck the phone in the case with his laptop, stepped out of the car and pushed the button on his key fob to lock the door. He stopped and looked at the keys in his hand. Did people lock their car doors in small towns? How about their house doors?

The sound of a car interrupted his musings, and he looked up to see a black Volkswagen bug pull into the driveway. The driver door flew open and a woman dressed entirely in black stepped out and strode toward him. Black thick-rimmed glasses framed her eyes and her fuchsia hair hung stick straight to her shoulders. She looked as though she belonged in L.A., not small-town Wisconsin.

"Nick Fleming? Francis Troutline." She reached out to vigorously shake his hand. "You can call me Minnow."

He raised an eyebrow. "Girl Scout camp?"

"What?"

"Your name."

"Oh, no. Never went to camp. Everyone calls my dad Trout. I was the baby of the family. Get it? Minnow. It just stuck."

He nodded.

"When I heard you were here I couldn't wait to meet you," Minnow said. "I cut Annie's hair—and other people's hair, too— so if you need a trim…" She cocked her head, inspecting him. "You're looking a little shaggy around the collar—"

Excuse me? "I like it this way. If you don't mind… Minnow…I was just going inside."

"Oh yeah, me, too." She strode past him up the stairs and let herself into the house. He watched her for a moment, gave his head a shake to clear his brain, then followed her up the stairs. He paused in the doorway.

Minnow had Annie in a big hug and was babbling something about how she couldn't believe Nick was here and Annie hadn't told her he was coming. *This woman wasn't really a friend of Annie's, was she?*

Minnow spotted him. "Hey! Shut that door! The mosquitoes around here are so big we fry 'em for dinner."

He stepped into the kitchen and the door smacked against the jamb with a bang. Someone really should fix that.

"Uh, sorry," he said.

"Just joshin' you. A little up-north humor."

The diameter of her neck looked as if it would fit nicely between his two hands. He suppressed a grin at the thought.

She looked at his computer case. "Is that briefcase full of secret military papers?"

He opened his mouth, then shut it, struggling with an answer. "Kind of. It's a computer."

"Have you had the house swept?"

"I'm sure Luella takes care of that," he said with effort.

Minnow snorted. "For bugs. You know, listening devices?"

Was the woman nuts? "I don't think we'll need to worry about that."

Minnow looked incredulous. "Considering your line of work, I'd think you could never be too careful."

He looked at Annie for help and she burst out laughing.

Fine. So Annie was nuts, too. "I'm going to put this stuff upstairs."

"She knows," Annie whispered.

"Knows what?"

"About us."

He looked from one woman to the other. Minnow was nodding at him. Careful, careful, he didn't want to blow anything here. "Knows…?"

"About our marriage, our divorce." Annie's voice rose a notch. "She knows—"

"Everything!" Minnow said.

Luella came through the doorway carrying a vase filled with wilting flowers. Petals dropped to the floor as she crossed the room. "Who knows everything?"

The three of them froze.

When it was clear the two women were incapable of getting a word out of their mouths, Nick finally said, "Minnow. She knows everything about…" He faltered. He didn't even know the woman. "Oh, just everything, I guess."

Annie nodded. "Right. You know how she's always reading—"

"Movie-star magazines and spy thrillers," Luella answered.

"She does know hairstyles," Annie said.

Looking at her hair, dyed as it was that odd shade of reddish fuchsia, Nick thought Annie was stretching it a bit. "She does seem to know a lot about…espionage," he offered. "You know, I think I'd better get this stuff upstairs."

"I'll help you." Annie grabbed the computer bag from his hand and raced from the room.

"Me, too." Minnow followed her out.

Nick looked at Luella and shrugged before heading upstairs himself. So there was someone in this town who knew all of Annie's secrets. This certainly put a new twist on things.

He walked into the bedroom just in time to hear the end of Annie's explanation of how Nick had come to be in Bedford. Minnow flopped back into the pillows on the bed. "Wow. Exciting. Nine days, huh? This is kind of like a book I read last year. The hero is in love with this woman, but the Russians are after him, so to protect her, he ends their relationship, but the Russians kill her anyway and make it look like his own guys did it, and—"

Nick held up a hand. "No Russians, no love story, no murder. How is that anything like this?"

"Well, *I* think it is," Minnow said. "What do you really do, anyway?"

"I'm a writer."

She sat up straight. "For the movies?"

"No. I do manuals on how to run machinery."

Annie laughed. "Just ignore him. He writes stories and books about adventures—you know, white-water rafting, mountain climbing…" She brought her hands together with a clap. "Well, the important thing, Nick, is if you're ever about town and get into some sort of trouble with the story—"

"Your *cover,*" Minnow said.

"Right, your *cover.* Then Minnow might be able to help."

"I'll bet," he muttered.

"Consider me one of your operatives," she said. "I own a hairdressing shop in town—Whoop de Do."

"As in *hairdo?*"

"That's right." Minnow pulled a business card from her back pocket and handed it to him. "Like I said… When you're ready to take care of that shaggy stuff on your neck, give me a call."

"And like I said, I like it that way."

"Never let it be said that I failed to warn you your haircut is woefully out of date." She pointed a finger at him. "All that aside, what this operation needs right now is a name and a plan."

Great, she was going to stay awhile. Nick dropped into an overstuffed chair in the corner, pulled off his shoes and stuck his feet up on the ottoman. "A plan for what?"

"Where you'll go each day, what you and Annie will do, code words for if there's been a breach in security—"

He fought to keep his voice level. "Minnow. This is a no-brainer. I've already got the garden club ladies convinced. The rest of the town will follow suit. Believe me, this *operation* doesn't need a plan."

"Let's think about this," Annie said. "On the one hand, we'll be spending most of our time here at the house, so how many people will Nick actually see? On the other hand, we can't keep him captive here for nine days or people will begin to talk." She stood and paced the room. "Still, will a plan help us or complicate things unnecessarily? Life is not the same as paint by numbers—"

"Annie! We don't need a plan. Don't overanalyze this." Nick couldn't keep the exasperation out of his voice.

"I think he's right, Minnow. Sorry."

Minnow looked from Annie to Nick and back again. "Get real. Don't tell me you're just going to wing it for nine days?"

They nodded and she heaved a long-suffering sigh. "At least we should have a code word in case there's a security breach."

Silence stretched out between them.

Annie caved first. She sat on the edge of the bed and cast a hopeful look at Nick. "I suppose a code word might be helpful in an emergency."

He snorted. "How about Deep Throat?"

"That's a code *name*—not a code word," Minnow said. "But now that you mention it maybe we should have code names, too. I could be…Barracuda."

Oh, brother. "I think a code word will be plenty."

"Really? All right." Minnow tapped a finger on the side of her head as she concentrated. "Question is, what should the code word be? How about, ah…" She sat up straight and threw her hands in the air. "Hold it! I've got it! We're worried about a breach in security. Babies can be in breech position. Annie is pregnant." She paused and looked into each of their faces as though the answer were obvious. "Our code word will be *baby!* It's perfect. If any of us says *baby* to one another, it means something's gone seriously wrong."

Nick mentally groaned. "And what happens if Annie mentions that the *baby* just kicked? Are we supposed to panic then?"

"Oh. Yeah. Okay, we need a modification. The code word will be…let's see…*Oh* Baby. Oh Baby! How often would you use those two words together?"

Nick could think of a few times he'd used that combination, but thought better of relating them in mixed
company. At this point, it seemed smarter to humor the
woman rather than keep this conversation going any
longer. "Fine."

Annie seemed relieved. "If it works for Nick, it
works for me."

"We should also have a rendezvous point," Minnow
said. "How about if anyone uses the code word, we
meet at the fountain?"

Nick restrained the urge to roll his eyes. "Sounds
great."

"Do you know where the fountain is?" Minnow
asked pointedly.

Caught. "No."

"It's in the city park. Do you know where the park
is?"

"I'll show him tomorrow." Annie rubbed her eyes.

Nick stifled a huge yawn. "Ladies, I hate to break
up this mission-planning session. I know it's not that
late. But I've been driving for days and I need to get
some sleep."

Minnow scooted off the bed. "We should all be well
rested so we're sharp tomorrow. Oh! Cell phone numbers—have you got one? We need to be able to get in
touch."

She grabbed a notepad and pen off the nightstand
and scribbled a number down, then handed the pad to
Nick. He let loose with what he knew was a melodramatic sigh, penned his number on the next sheet and
tossed the pad back to her.

Minnow grinned as she shoved the paper with his number on it in her pocket. "Super! See you guys later. Don't forget—*Oh Baby!*" She strolled out the door humming the theme song to *Goldfinger.*

Nick turned to Annie ready to make a smart-ass comment, but she beat him to the punch.

"Don't say a word. I know she's a little eccentric. But she's about as true a friend as anyone could find. And at this moment in my life, I can use every friend I've got."

"I wasn't going to say anything," he lied. "Except that I really need to get some sleep."

Annie stood. "I forgot to empty out a couple of drawers for you."

"Don't bother. I'll live out of my duffel. It's no different than how I live whenever I'm on assignment."

"You're sure? Then I'm going back downstairs. I've gotta get some things ready for breakfast tomorrow, lock the back door, put out the dog…"

"Post a guard, patrol the perimeter…"

She laughed. "Right. You just…do whatever you have to. Bathroom's through that door…towels are in the closet. If you need a toothbrush or anything, let me know. I keep a supply of new toiletries for guests who forget something." She took a step toward the doorway and stopped. "I—are you sure—"

"Go. It'll be fine. I'll probably be asleep before you get back."

"Right. Okay, good night." She slipped out of the room.

He clicked off the switch on the standing lamp beside the chair and cast the room into hazy gray stillness.

The only illumination came from the glow of the street-lamps filtering through the white lace curtains at the windows. A sense of peace washed over him, a remembered feeling from childhood, of sleeping overnight in the front bedroom at his grandparents' house.

He closed his eyes and let his mind drift. Minnow was making this more complicated than it needed to be. The poor woman, she must be so desperate for excitement she was turning this charade into her own version of a spy thriller. Still, she was Annie's friend. And she'd kept Annie's secret so far.

He forced open his eyes and pushed himself up out of the chair. What he wanted first, before climbing into bed, was a hot shower to wash away the dust of traveling. He reached up to pull the shades, then peeled off his clothes and let them drop to the floor in the darkness.

ANNIE LET CHESTER OUTSIDE and spotted Minnow's car idling in the driveway. Music blared out through the open car window, while Minnow, illuminated by the dome light, punched through the radio buttons looking, apparently, for the perfect song. Annie hurried down the steps and over to the driver's door.

"Can you believe this is happening to me?"

Minnow looked up with a start. "At least he's cute."

"Oh, yeah. He always was."

"You still like him?"

Annie shrugged. "No. Anyway, he's engaged."

"Liar. If I had a husband who looked like that, I'd be fighting him every step of the way to the lawyer. You ought to think about keeping him on."

Annie let out a burst of laughter. "Like I have anything to say about it. Get out of here."

Minnow's face took on a know-it-all smile. She put the car into Reverse. "I'll talk to you tomorrow."

Annie watched her drive away, then dropped her head back and stared up into the black never-ending sky, her mind a jumbled mess of conflicting thoughts about this grand deception she and Nick had put together. She hoped she wasn't making a big mistake.

Thank goodness, things were a bit slow—only two rooms rented tonight. She didn't think she could handle having a full house to deal with right now. As it was, with Luella around all the time, this would be a tough charade to pull off. They'd be on stage almost every minute of the day.

She climbed the back steps and waited on the porch until Chester ran out of the darkness to join her. She looked down at him disapprovingly. "Couldn't you have taken your time tonight? I'm not in a real hurry to go to bed."

The dog wagged his tail.

"Yeah, I know. Blah, blah, blah. Come on."

She held open the door for Chester, then followed him in, locking the door behind her.

The problem was, Nick was so much the same as he'd been six years ago—still handsome in a rugged sort of way, still charming, still used to getting what he wanted, *still able to make her heart pound*.

At least now she was smart enough not to go there. When she'd married him, there had been this part of her that had dreamed of a Cinderella story—that he would tell her he actually loved her, that he didn't want them to divorce. Sure, there was no denying she'd wanted the money he'd offered her to marry him.

But she would have married him even if there had been no money involved at all.

Because she'd been a dreamer then. A hopeless romantic. She shook her head, remembering. She'd followed a boyfriend out to the West Coast, certain he was *the one*. Within a month of her move, he'd dumped her for some beautiful aspiring actress. And there she'd been stuck. No money. No friends. And a crummy job as a waitress in an all-night diner.

Nick was a 2:00 a.m. regular at the diner, and somewhere along the way, he told her about the trust fund his grandmother had left him, how he couldn't get it until he turned thirty-five—or married. So she'd agreed to marry him—for $250,000. She'd rationalized it as a means of getting herself back on her feet. But once they'd actually wed, it had broken her heart to leave him. The thought of never seeing him again nearly did her in.

After leaving L.A., it had taken several years and a couple of other short-lived relationships before she finally realized that while she was spending her time romanticizing, the men she was dating were walking all over her. She'd finally learned her lesson—never again would she throw her own life to the wayside because of some guy.

As long as she remembered that, she'd be fine this next week. Absolutely fine.

Problem was, she had to share a bed with the man.

Minnow would say this was an opportunity, not a problem.

Maybe. Maybe if the guy weren't already engaged. Maybe if Nick Fleming was the kind of guy she wanted. Maybe if she were the kind of woman Nick Fleming found attractive. She gave her head a shake. This train of thought was a complete waste of brain waves.

She sighed. The muffins were mixed and ready for baking in the morning, the table set. Luella had long since gone to bed. Annie moved around the dining room table, straightening a knife here, a fork there. She filled the salt and pepper shakers and checked the sugar bowl. She swept the floor and washed the windows in the cabinet doors. She made a list of chores for the next day. And she yawned as she tried to think of more things to do. She yawned again and gave up stalling. Ever since she got pregnant, she couldn't stay up late anymore.

"Come on, Chester, either we gather our courage and go upstairs or I collapse here and now." She flipped off the last light switch.

Slowly, she made her way to the third floor, gave her bedroom door a little push and peered inside. Darkness stretched across the room. Good. He was asleep. She grabbed her nightgown from the hook behind the door and tiptoed to the bathroom to change. Maybe this room-sharing arrangement wouldn't be so hard after all.

She tugged open the bathroom door. Light flooded out at her and she blinked a couple of times to adjust to the sudden brightness.

Nick.

In a towel.

A little towel.

Various, disjointed thoughts flooded her brain—

what great shoulders…look at those arm muscles…he must lift weights…why isn't he in bed?…perfectly flat stomach…oh, my gosh, you're staring at him, say something quick—

He probably figured her to be insane.

"Thought I'd shower. Hope you don't mind."

"No—no absolutely not. I'll wait—" She took a couple of steps back and reached out to close the door, but Chester bounded past her into the small room, leaping with joy as though he'd just discovered someone new in the house who needed greeting. He jumped up at Nick and his paws dislodged the towel.

Good God! Annie reached out and slammed the door shut, heart pounding at the sudden sight of Nick in all his Roman statuesque glory. She drew a breath and tried to still the racing of her pulse.

The door opened six inches and the dog slid out of the bathroom on the end of Nick's foot. Chester barked at her and wagged his tail excitedly.

"Oh, be quiet. Sometimes you're more trouble than you're worth."

A minute later the door opened again and Nick stepped into the room wearing running shorts and a T-shirt. Annie sighed with relief. One part of her brain had been afraid he might sleep in the buff.

Avoiding his eyes, she slipped past him into the bathroom and took her time getting ready for bed. When she was certain he had to be asleep, she took several quick steps across the room, slid under the covers and tried to forget that a foot away from her a man was sleeping in her bed.

Not just any man—*Nick Fleming.*

Her heart thumped. At this rate it might be hours before she fell asleep. She could hear Nick's breathing, slow and deep. At least one of them would wake refreshed tomorrow.

Chester leapt onto the bed and climbed over her to find a spot for the night. Annie could feel him go through his nightly routine, digging at the bed with his front paws, then turning in a circle several times before finally settling down with a loud groan of pleasure. For Chester, all was certainly right with the world. If only her own life were so simple.

She closed her eyes and let the sound of Nick's rhythmic breathing lull her toward sleep. One day almost over. She turned onto her side and hugged the edge of the bed. Really, this wasn't so bad. Tomorrow morning they'd get up, rejuvenated, and work out a plan for the day. Before they even knew it, another day would pass, and another, and another, until finally it would be time for Nick to leave Bedford. And time for her to go back to life as she knew it.

This really wasn't so bad after all. One day down, only eight more to go.

THE SHRILL RINGING OF a telephone jarred her awake. Nick shot from the bed and fumbled in the dark for his computer bag until he found his cell phone and turned it on.

"Hello?" he murmured in a voice heavy with sleep. "Oh, hi sweetheart." He yawned and rubbed his eyes. "I went to bed early. What time is it?"

Annie glanced at the clock and without thinking said, "One o'clock."

Nick jerked around and slashed the air with his free hand, warning her to be quiet.

"Sorry," she muttered.

He climbed back into bed and shoved a couple of pillows behind his back so he could lean against the headboard.

"It's not a big deal, really," he said into the phone. "Just a story about all the things there are to do in Wisconsin. I figured as long as I was already out here—" He paused.

"I miss you, too, but I'll be home before you know it. When you're back from Paris, we'll go away for a couple of days— What? No. I'm really beat—it's two hours later here— No Missy, I don't want to talk to anybody else— Melissa, hey— Oh, hi, Chelsea. Yeah, good to talk with you, too. Having fun?"

There was a long pause, as though Chelsea were filling him in on every little detail. Annie grimaced.

"Give me back to Melissa, will you?" A moment later, he said, "Hey, Miss— Oh, Bill, thought you were Melissa. Give her the phone, will you?"

Annie grinned at the growing exasperation in his voice.

"Missy, I'll talk to you later, I'm really tired. I was already asleep— Of course not. No, I'm not mad at you. Talk to you tomorrow. I love you, too."

He shut off the phone and dropped back into the pillows. "Sorry. She's at a party."

"It's okay." Annie rolled onto her side and closed her eyes.

"She misses me."

"Umm." She had nearly fallen asleep again when his voice dragged her back to full consciousness.

"She's pretty young."

"Sounds pretty ditzy, too," Annie muttered under her breath.

"What?"

"Nothing." She turned onto her back and looked at him, a shadow in the dark room. "Is something bothering you?"

He didn't answer for a long time. "Remember when I'd come into the coffee shop and we'd talk about all the things we were going to do with our lives?"

"Uh-huh."

"I don't remember ever—did I ever—do you remember…"

"Spit it out."

"Was I going to get married?"

She laughed and her heart warmed. "Only to me. What's the matter? You getting cold feet?"

He shrugged. "Sometimes it doesn't feel exactly like I thought it would. This being engaged—getting married—thing."

"Can't help you out there. I only did it once and that was fake." *Even though she wished it hadn't been.* "Nick, as long as you love her, it's going to be okay."

"Yeah. And I do. Love her." He drew in a long breath and exhaled. "Well, good night."

"Good night." She wanted to reach out and run her hand over his hair, down his cheek. Wanted to somehow make him feel that it would be all right. This was the Nick she remembered. The one who was trying to find his place in the world, trying to figure out who he was. Despite all the places he'd been, all the adventures he'd had, he was still searching.

Her heart twisted and she mentally recoiled from the feeling. She couldn't care for him—not again. He was here for nine days and after that he would be gone, off to marry the woman he'd chosen.

It was a long time before she finally fell asleep.

"FOR CRYING OUT LOUD!"

Annie's eyes flew open and she heard a thud as Chester's feet hit the floor. She could see Nick sitting up in the darkness.

She tried to force her sleep-muddled mind to waken, her eyes to focus on the bedside clock. The red numbers glowed three-thirty. God help her if Nick was one of those light sleepers who woke all night long.

No, God help him.

"What's the matter?"

"Your dog was sleeping on my pillow."

"So?"

"Dog breath. Not exactly minty fresh. And he sure stretches out—we're like sardines in here with the three of us."

"He sleeps on that side every night. I bet he thinks you're stealing *his* pillow." She yawned.

"Get him a basket. He can sleep downstairs while I'm here."

Annie sat up. "He's supposed to be *your* dog. How

will it look if the day you come home you banish him from the bedroom?"

"Like I'm taking my rightful place?"

"He's been sleeping on the bed since I got him. He won't understand if suddenly he's banished to the floor."

"We're only talking eight nights here. All I want is a good night's sleep. Problem is, your dog wants the whole bed."

Annie sat up straighter, prepared to give Nick a lecture about compromise. Then reality broke through her sleep-befuddled mind. If Nick was miserable he might decide not to stay the whole nine days. And if that happened, the jig was up. She'd have to deal with all the questions about her marriage and why Nick was leaving after just twenty-four hours home. Her whole lie—her whole life—would fall apart.

Put that way, it seemed reasonable that Chester could sleep somewhere else for a few nights—it would be his sacrifice for the cause.

"I'll get him a basket tomorrow."

CHAPTER FOUR

NICK DROPPED DOWN ONTO the bottom stair and laced up his Nikes. A nice long run was just what he needed, a chance to clear his head and try to forget he'd agreed to pull the wool over the eyes of everyone in town. Not to mention he now was a father-to-be.

Annie left the house before he'd even gotten up. "She's off on errands," Luella had said. She'd frowned at him as she put a plate of strawberry-filled crepes in front of him at the table.

Then her frown had turned into a scowl and she'd sweetly but pointedly said, "Seems to me you two would want to be spending the morning together." He'd gulped down his food and escaped the kitchen before she could press the issue.

Shoes laced, he leaned against the wall and began to stretch his calves in anticipation of the miles to come. After so many days in the car, he couldn't wait to get some exercise.

"Here's the leash."

He turned to find Luella holding out the dog's leash and some plastic sandwich bags. Chester leapt around her legs excitedly, biting and tugging at the end of the leash.

"Annie said you wanted to take the dog running with you while you were home."

She did, did she? He forced the corners of his lips to curve upward. "Yeah. I do."

He took the leash, one of those fancy types with a molded plastic handle and retractable cord.

Luella shoved the bags at him. "For the poop."

"Thanks." He waited until she had returned to the kitchen, then snapped the leash onto Chester's collar. "Come on, mutt."

He stepped out into the sunny morning and headed down the narrow road that wrapped around the lake. A cool summer breeze slid over his skin and he inhaled deeply, savoring the freshness, reveling in the deep scent of pine in the air. He had to admit the smog in L.A. left something to be desired.

Chester ran alongside him, roaming out the full fifteen feet the leash allowed, stopping to investigate just about everything he spotted or smelled on the side of the road. A quick tug at the leash and the dog would race to catch up and bound past him.

Nick cast his gaze at the canopy of trees arching overhead and the thick woods that bordered the road. A sense of peace settled over him. The dog ran ahead, turning back every now and then, a wide canine grin on his face.

"Don't get too used to it, mutt. I'm out of here in eight days. Then Annie can walk you."

Nick's feet hit the blacktop in a steady rhythm and he broke a sweat. He glanced at his watch. Perfect— he was on track for a six-minute mile. Now, if only

Chester would mellow just a bit. The dog was outpacing him, straining against the fully extended leash as if the effort would allow him to get even farther ahead. Nick gave the leash a slight tug and moved to shift it to his other hand.

With a sudden explosion of barking, Chester tore into the tall grass at the side of the road, ripping the leash from Nick's fingers and disappearing into the woods.

Nick let out a sharp exhalation and drew to a halt. "Chester!" he shouted. "Chester! Come!"

He waited and shouted again. When the dog didn't appear, he slapped his hand on his thigh in disgust and set off into the woods. "You'd better keep hiding. Because, you dumb mutt, your days are numbered."

That stupid dog probably ran home. Actually, with his luck that mutt would be deep in the woods with the handle of the leash caught in a bush. Was there some reason why Annie couldn't have a normal leash? The kind with a loop at the end for your hand so a dog wouldn't be able to escape like this?

He shouted for Chester again and turned in a circle. The dog could be a mile away by now. He began to trudge deeper into the woods, shoving branches out of the way, swearing as brambles in the underbrush scratched his legs. Swatting at the mosquitoes that were feasting on his sweaty skin, he let loose with a string of curses.

After a few minutes, he reached the bottom of an esker. He started up the side, slipping once on the damp soil to land on his knees in mud. *And Annie wondered why he'd never wanted a dog?* If he couldn't spot the mutt once he reached the top, he was abandoning the search. Only a lunatic would expect to find a dog in the middle of a woods.

Reaching the top of the ridge, he looked down the other side, hoping to spot Chester. His breath caught.

A river wound through the ravine below him, racing on its path through pristine forest. The sight drove all anger from his mind.

"Wow," he said in awe. "Is this the *stream* you were talking about, Annie?" He let his gaze sweep the nearby area—pine trees, hardwoods, scrubby bushes, wildflowers. He inhaled slowly and started down to the river to get a better look.

From the bushes behind him came a frenzied rustling sound, and he scooped a thick stick off the ground and spun to face whatever was coming after him. With a staccato of barks, Chester burst out of the underbrush, tail wagging excitedly.

Nick swore and grabbed the leash. He threw one last look at the river before turning to retrace his steps. He couldn't believe Annie owned this property. She was so worried about finances, and here she was sitting on a gold mine. Cross-country skiing, hiking, rafting, tubing…all she had to do to fill her rooms was offer her guests a little adventure.

Once back at the road, he wrapped his fingers around the leash handle and gripped it as tight as he could. He looked at the dog. "Mutt. You're not getting away from me again."

He took some satisfaction in the fact that Chester finally had the decency to look chagrined.

ANNIE HEFTED THE WICKER dog bed into her arms, pushed the door of the hardware store open with her hip and headed down the sidewalk for home. She loved days like this—warm, sunny, dry. Made you appreciate being alive. Even if half your life *was* a big fat lie.

She shifted the basket in her arms as if to shift her thoughts and focused her mind on her dog. Chester, her loyal companion for the past four years, was about to be relegated to the corner. She sighed. Maybe he wouldn't mind.

Yeah, right.

She only hoped he didn't whine all night long. Then again, there might be some poetic justice to the situation if he did. Poor Nick still wouldn't be able to get a decent night's sleep.

Eyes downcast, she kept her stride brisk so she looked purposeful, on a mission, with no time to chat. Avoidance was her key word today: she didn't want anyone to stop her and ask questions about Nick.

The smell of fresh-cooked bacon wafted through the air and she hurried past Tommy's Diner without looking up. Maybe tomorrow she'd feel differently, but right now she needed a little time to work into this whole charade, a little time to—

"Annie!"

She jerked her head up. Busted.

Turning slowly, she watched as one of the middle-aged waitresses from the diner chased her down. "You stop right there!"

"Jeez, Carol. You almost gave me a heart attack."

"No way you're walking right past us and not stopping in."

Annie smiled apologetically and gave a shrug. "I'm in kind of a hurry."

Carol grabbed her by the arm and steered her through the open door of the diner. "Honey, that handsome hunk of a husband can wait a few minutes longer. We've been dying to talk to you since we heard the news."

She lifted the basket from Annie's arms and set it on a chair, then went to take her place behind the counter.

Annie sighed. It was probably better to get this over with right in the beginning. Maybe then everyone would leave them alone for the rest of Nick's stay.

She dropped onto a red vinyl padded stool at the counter and looked up into Carol's grinning face. Behind her, a balding head peered over the high pass-through into the kitchen.

Yep, even the owner didn't want to miss out on the latest news about town.

"Hey, Tommy," she said. "You'll be able to hear better if you come out here."

Carol set a brown ceramic mug on the counter and filled it with decaf. "On the house. In celebration of Nick's first visit home."

"Thanks." Annie peeled open a creamer and poured it into her cup, swallowing a smile as Tommy nonchalantly wandered out of the kitchen.

Carol leaned her elbows on the counter and rested her chin in her hands. "Well? Talk, girlfriend. Tell us everything."

NICK ROUNDED THE CORNER on the highway at a moderate jog and cursed. No town in sight. He'd left the country lane behind a while ago, and now all he could see was acres of farm fields and the two-lane road on which he was running. He usually had an incredible sense of direction—how could he have gotten lost?

He looked down at the dog loping alongside him—and the dog looked back, tongue lolling out, dripping saliva onto the hot blacktop. "I know just how you feel," Nick muttered.

He glanced at his watch; sweat dripped off his face onto his arm. His shirt, wringing wet, stuck to him. It had to be well in the eighties by now. He wouldn't be surprised if steam was rising off his back. He squinted at the sky, perfect clear blue with not even one cloud to provide some respite from the heat. The best he could tell, he'd probably gone eight or nine miles already, but it was hard to know since he'd had that pleasant little dog-chasing break in the middle. He should have driven the route beforehand so he'd known where he was going.

No, what he should have done was not head north at that intersection way back. The road had gradually veered due west, forcing him to go in the wrong direction. Then he'd had no choice but to follow it until he came to a crossroad so he could work his way back to where he thought Bedford was.

Bedford. Since the moment he'd arrived here, not one thing had gone according to plan.

Not that plans were that important to him; he'd always flown by the seat of his pants. But the events of the last day were just so unexpected—even for him.

Annie had always been the planner, insecure, wanting to force her life into a starry-eyed mold, searching for a permanence she'd never had. Obviously, she'd found it here. And he was glad for her. She'd changed. Had a confidence he'd never seen in her in L.A. *A confidence that allowed her to fly by the seat of her pants and come up with a harebrained idea about pretending to be married.* Who would have ever thought Annie McCarthy—

His arm jerked backward at abrupt resistance on the leash. He glanced behind him to see Chester stretched out on his belly, exhausted, on the gravel shoulder of the road.

"Oh, no. Come on, Chester." Nick tugged at the leash. "It can't be far now."

The dog didn't even lift his head from between his front paws, just looked up with big brown eyes and wagged his tail back and forth very, very slowly. Nick gave another, more assertive pull on the leash. "Move it, Chester! Come!"

The mutt refused to budge. Nick felt a stirring of sympathy and sat on the road next to the dog. "Had enough, boy?"

His only answer was the thumping of Chester's tail.

"Yeah, me, too." He sat there, forearms resting on his bent knees, waiting until he cooled down a little and his breathing evened out. Then he picked up the dog and began to walk with him in his arms.

"I'm just carrying you awhile," he said. "Because it's either that or sit here for an hour. We're still not friends."

Fifteen minutes later, the front of his shirt drenched with a new layer of sweat from carrying the dog, he reached the gas station where he'd asked directions yesterday.

He set the dog on the ground. "Let's go, Chester, we're in the home stretch."

They passed the Welcome to Bedford sign and he felt a grim satisfaction. Not too far to Annie's place now, just through the downtown and then another half mile up the road. He began to salivate at the thought of a tall, cold glass of water.

Ahead, a sprinkler rotated across a front lawn, spraying out a steady sheet of water that glistened in the sun before falling to the earth in silver droplets. Nick stopped. He looked at the dog. Chester perked up and his tail whipped back and forth.

"You thinking what I'm thinking?" Nick glanced in either direction to make sure no one was around, then ran into the yard, into the spray, pulling the dog with him. The shock of ice-cold water on his overheated skin made him laugh out loud. Invigorated by the spray, Chester began jumping and barking, and Nick laughed again as the water fell on them both, soothing away the heat.

Eyes shut, he stuck his face close to the sprinkler head and let the water gently pummel his face while he opened his mouth to drink from the icy stream. He cupped his hands together and held them under the sprinkler, then stepped away from the spray to let the dog lap up the water he had captured in his hands.

Chester shook himself; droplets of water flew out

in every direction. Nick pushed his wet hair back from his face and shook his head in much the same manner.

"My sentiments, exactly. Come on, dog. Let's go home."

Dripping, they headed down Main Street toward Annie's bed-and-breakfast. Nick glanced at each building they passed, checking out the town that would be his home for the next week and then some.

Tavern on the corner.

Bakery. He inhaled. Was there anything as mouthwatering as the scent of fresh-baked bread?

Insurance agency. Antiques store. Beauty parlor—must be Minnow's place. He made a point of not looking in the window, hoping she wouldn't notice him going by and rush out to tell him he needed a haircut.

Tavern. Laundromat. Screaming kids ran out the door and he dodged left and then right to avoid them.

Hardware store. Tavern. Flower shop. Tavern. Hmm, there was a definite pattern here.

Diner. An old-fashioned root beer sign in the window caught his attention and took him right back to childhood. He looked in the large storefront window and contemplated whether they'd let him run a tab for a frosty mug of Dad's root beer.

A SENSE OF RELIEF rolled through Annie and she smiled at the diner staff. She'd gotten through her whole story about Nick and no one questioned a thing.

"That's about it." She swiveled back and forth on her stool, suddenly confident beyond words. "Nick's got eight days to spend in Bedford before he has to report back to Secret Ops."

As she swiveled to the left, she caught sight of a strange man staring in the front window—surely an escapee from an asylum—his hair slicked back and sticking out in places, his clothing soaking wet and clinging. Beside him, a wet, scraggly dog had its paws up on the window, and his tongue, hanging out, was dripping saliva onto the glass. She stared back, all words lodged in her throat.

He smiled at her.

She closed her eyes, counted to five, and opened them again.

He waved.

She watched as he tied Chester to a sign pole, pulled open the door and sauntered over to her.

"Fancy meeting you here," Nick said.

"Fancy." Her heart went schizophrenic, alternately pounding in horror and leaping in ardor. "Carol, Tom, this is…Nick."

Nick reached out to shake hands all around. "I was out for a run and ended up cooling off in someone's sprinkler."

Annie gave a weak smile, completely at a loss for words. Her "husband" looked like a lunatic. At least he didn't stink.

Nick leaned over to kiss the top of her head. "Boy, am I glad you're here, honey. I was dying for a root beer. And *my dog*," he said as he hitched his thumb toward the outside, "could use a bowl of water."

"You came to the right place," Carol said, clearly unable to control her smile.

Please. The woman was almost giddy.

Tommy's head nodded up and down like a Bobble-head statue and Annie had the sudden urge to run screaming from the diner and put a For Sale sign in front of her house.

"Glad to meet you," Tommy said. "Root beer's on the house. Are you hungry?"

Annie shook her head. There was no way she was going to let Nick be in this diner any longer than she had to. God only knew what people might ask him, *what he might say.* Anyway, it wasn't even eleven-thirty yet. "No, thanks, we're having lunch at—"

Nick dropped onto the stool next to her. "Famished, actually. How about a burger and fries with the works? Fried onions—not raw. Onion rings."

"You got it." Tommy headed back to the kitchen. "Annie, anything for you?"

She forced her voice to remain light. "I guess I am a little hungry after all. Pregnancy does that to you. I'll have the same."

She turned to Nick and whispered between clenched teeth, "Stay quiet and let me handle any questions."

Carol set the glass of foam-topped root beer in front of Nick and plopped a fat red straw into its center. She handed Annie a bowl of water for the dog and turned her full attention to Nick.

"I swear there were times I started to wonder if Annie had made you up. The way this girl talked about you, I thought no way there's one package with all those ay-tributes—an exciting job, handsome, muscles, brains, and—

Annie's heart stilled. She waved a hand in the air in a desperate attempt to cut Carol off. "I'll take one of those root beers, too!"

"Hot-blooded to boot," Carol finished.

Annie could feel her face burning, could tell Nick had swiveled his stool so he could look directly at her.

"I'll give the dog his water." She jumped to her feet.

Carol just kept talking. "But now that I got a good look at you, she weren't exaggeratin' none. I could go for a little *hot-blooded*."

The woman leaned her elbows on the counter so she was eye-to-eye with Nick. "You got any older brothers?" she asked in a conspiratorial tone.

Nick laughed. "Nope."

"Shoot." Carol straightened. "If Annie ever throws you over, I get first dibs. Another root beer coming up." She sashayed down to the other end of the counter and tossed a grin over her shoulder at Nick.

Annie fled outside, set the bowl of water on the sidewalk by Chester, and waited while he drank his fill. What could Carol be thinking, saying this stuff to Nick? The man was going to think Annie spent all her time talking about him. Okay, so maybe she had when she first moved here, but it had been more than a year since she'd been so forthcoming with information about her mysterious husband.

Maybe she should just escape this madhouse and go home, not even go back into the diner.

Yeah, right. If she left Nick unattended, there was no telling what kind of troublesome conversations he could get into. He could blow their whole operation. She glanced into the window and watched him chatting with Carol. Jeez, what was she thinking? He could blow their whole operation while she was out here on the sidewalk.

Snatching up the bowl, she forced down the panic rising inside her, put a pleasant expression on her face and went inside. She slid onto the stool beside Nick, determined to regain control of the situation. He put his arm around her and pulled her close. Beneath his damp shirt she could feel the hard muscles of his chest— what were they called? Pectorals—yeah, pecs— His lips touched her ear and a jolt raced through her.

At this rate, she'd be lucky to control her drooling, let alone the situation.

"Hot-blooded?" he murmured. His warm breath tickled the side of her neck and her stomach flopped.

"So I got a little carried away." She could hear the defensiveness in her voice and forced herself to lighten up. "After all, you didn't really exist. If one must create a husband, he might as well be perfect."

"Are you implying I'm not already perfect?"

Hardly. She was relieved when Carol set the burgers in front of them.

"Eat up, folks." Carol lay the check beside Annie's plate and went off to wait on a group of teenagers who had settled at a nearby table.

As the clock drew close to noon, a steady stream of customers came into the diner. Time and again, Annie introduced Nick. And time and again, the response was the same—they'd heard he was in town, and how was the military, and would he be staying long, and, congratulations about the baby, and gosh, didn't he want to quit his job and settle down here for good?

Thank goodness all this preliminary-introduction stuff, plus the fact they were in the middle of eating, kept everyone from being too nosy. Only problem was, that meant the really hard questions would come in a day or two. Maybe she shouldn't have insisted he stay nine days.

She wondered what Minnow, the resident espionage expert, would have to say about how visible Nick had suddenly become. Clearly this couldn't be a good development for a covert operation.

As if on cue, the door opened again and Minnow breezed inside, dressed all in black and grinning from ear to ear. She slid onto the stool next to Annie.

"Hey, Annie. How's married life treatin' you? Hey, Nick. Saw you slink by the shop earlier. Thought you might be stopping in to get that stuff trimmed on your neck."

Nick gave her a wan smile, tossed his napkin on the counter and stood. "Sorry we can't stay to chat, Minnow, but we were just leaving." He motioned with his head to Annie and started for the door without waiting for a reply.

"Yessir." Annie restrained the urge to give a crisp salute. She pulled a few bills from her wallet and threw them on the counter as she stood up.

Minnow reached out to take hold of her arm. "Have you shown him the rendezvous spot? The fountain?" she whispered.

"No, but I will. Call you later." Annie grabbed the

dog basket off the chair and caught up with Nick outside, where he was untying Chester's leash from the parking meter.

"You didn't have to be so obvious."

He looked up, all innocence, his fingers working the knot in the leash.

"I can tell you don't like Minnow and she probably knows it, too."

At the flash of irritation on his face, she walked away quickly so he couldn't answer without shouting. He and Chester were beside her in seconds.

"Doesn't the woman have any boundaries?" he asked. "She's obsessed with my hair."

Annie looked at the dark, thick hair curling at the back of his neck, just begging for someone's fingers to play in it. No, not just someone's fingers—hers. *Yeah, well, Minnow wasn't the only one obsessed with his hair.*

"Annie?"

She jerked her eyes to his face and felt heat rise up her cheeks for the second time in half an hour. "Uh, Minnow is kind of a free spirit. She can't help the way she is. Her parents were into flower power, and telling it like it is, and all that laid-back stuff."

"It's all coming together for me now."

"So go easy on her. She means well."

Nick's noncommittal grunt made Annie a little apprehensive about mentioning the rendezvous spot. She wasn't in the mood to have Nick go off about Minnow's obsession with all things related to espionage. One part of her agreed with him that the idea of having a rendezvous spot seemed ridiculous, but another side of her figured, better safe than sorry. Finally, she took a breath and dove in.

"Hey, Nick, before we go home... I want to show you the fountain...remember? In the park."

He raised an eyebrow.

"I know it seems silly, but just in case, let's make sure our bases are covered. Humor me. Please?"

He handed her the leash. "Lead on. You take the mutt, I'll carry the basket."

"It's pretty easy to find." She led him down a side street and into a large park. "Sidewalks from each corner lead to the center. Find a sidewalk and you'll find the fountain."

A few minutes later they were standing in front of a hulking, circular sculpture from which water was shooting out of several openings and cascading down a multitude of uneven faces.

Nick stared, his expression one of incredulous disbelief. Speechless, he walked all the way around the fountain. "Chester, maybe *we* should get into the fountain-designing business. We couldn't do any worse than this."

The smile that had been tugging at Annie's lips burst into a full grin and she laughed. "I thought the same thing the first time I saw this...work of art."

"What is it? Don't tell me they paid someone to make this."

"Second question first. It was designed and donated by Minnow's parents—"

"Why doesn't that surprise me?"

"—after they moved here from New York, because they wanted to get back to nature. It's an abstract stone sculpture."

He looked at the fountain through narrowed eyes. "Abstract I get, but come on, this abstract stuff always symbolizes something—so what is it? You know, a mother and child…or the world at war, or…" His voice trailed off as he walked around to the other side, stopping every few steps to look at the monstrosity from a new angle.

"I really don't think it's anything but a bunch of shapes," Annie said. "You know, that sixties mod look."

Nick set the basket on the ground and squatted down to tie his shoe. He looked up at the fountain. "Maybe." He didn't sound like he believed it.

His eyes widened. "And maybe not."

He straightened slowly, never taking his eyes off the piece. "Oh, my gosh. Don't tell me you don't know what this sculpture is."

"What?" She moved to stand beside him.

"Come here." He threw an arm around her shoulders and pulled her right up against him.

Twice in one day, body to body with Nick. She prayed her knees didn't give out.

"Do you see it?"

"See what?" Her eyes refused to focus with him this close to her.

"Bend over a little. Now tilt your head—to the left." He put a hand on her head and gently forced her to bend farther. "It's not real obvious. Just let yourself feel it."

Oh, she could feel it, all right. From the tips of her toes to the top of her head. *Lust.* "Give me a hint."

"Okay, it's a couple."

"A couple of what?"

He exhaled in exasperation.

"Ohh. You mean, like a man and woman." She frowned in concentration. "I don't see it."

"They're, ah…kissing."

"Are you crazy? Show me again!"

He pulled her directly in front of him and reached over her shoulders to put a hand on each side of her face and turn her head. The touch of his fingers almost sent her stomach into spasms. And she thought it was hard to concentrate before.

He pointed. "See how he's bent over her—"

"No."

"How his hand is behind her head—"

"No."

"Come on. Look, she's got one hand around the back of his neck, her other hand is on his shoulder…."

Her forehead furrowed as she tried to concentrate on something other than Nick. She pointed. "Is that her leg?"

He snorted. "No, that's nothing—just an abstract shape." He moved her head down and to the left, then rested his hands on her shoulders.

Weak. She was getting weak with all this nearness. Nick was going to have to carry her home.

And then, suddenly, she saw them, the couple, *nude,* arms around each other, engaged in a kiss of unmistakable passion.

She gasped. "Oh, my gosh, I see them. You're right. They're…oh, my…they're…kissing, all right. I almost feel like a Peeping Tom." She twisted round to look Nick in the face.

His eyes met hers and something flared there. *Heat.* He was going to kiss her. Her heart began to hammer. And she was going to let him.

Her dream was about to come true.

"Hey Annie," he said softly. "I've got something to tell you."

He'd never forgotten her, either? "Yes?" She moistened her lips and raised her chin a bit in anticipation.

"When I was out running this morning…" He took a step back and picked up the wicker dog basket.

Huh? The thudding of her heart skidded to a stop.

"The dog ran off and I had to chase him into the woods. How much of that land is yours?"

"What?"

"The land in there is incredible. I wouldn't doubt if there are eagles nesting."

"Yeah—"

"There's a river—is that your property?"

She nodded. "I told you there was a river." *What the heck happened to the kiss?*

"You called it a stream. That's a river. Forget selling to the developer. Put in some landings and you can offer tubing, rafting, canoeing. Cut some trails through that forest for hiking and in the winter use them for cross-country skiing. That's how you can bring more bookings into the B & B."

She felt as if she'd just fallen into the river. Nick the

dreamer. She remembered this guy from six years ago. "Yeah. I'll do that in my spare time." *With a baby on my hip.*

"Annie, think of how this would help your business."

She let out a sharp breath. "Nick. Everything I'd make, I'd have to spend to keep the trails groomed and the rafting going. Close, but no cigar."

He hadn't changed a bit. Lots of big ideas, most of them not grounded in reality. "Let's go home. I've got to change for a museum-board meeting this afternoon."

She didn't want him to kiss her, anyway. *Yeah, right.*

"Okay, but I'm telling you. The answer to all your problems lies in the woods next door."

CHAPTER FIVE

ANNIE RESTED HER CHIN in her hand and looked at the spreadsheet detailing the amount of funding that was necessary to run the museum once they opened the doors. They had yet to hit their fund-raising goal, but then again, they had yet to hear from some of the foundations to which they had applied for grants.

At the head of the long oval conference table, Vivian was droning on about the need to set yearly fund-raising goals in order to ensure the museum stayed viable. The other members of the committee were bobbing their heads in agreement. Annie nodded along, her thoughts leaping from the museum's financial situation to her own.

Too bad she couldn't do some fund-raising of her own in order to keep the B & B viable. Nick may think her answer lay in the woods, but his ideas weren't exactly the kind of thing a single woman with no experience in outdoor adventures took on alone. Especially one with a baby on the way. The more she thought of it, the more she became convinced the only thing his ideas would bring her were more headaches.

She rubbed her forehead with the palm of her hand.

Her life had been going along just fine until Nick showed up. Well, okay, so she'd hit a little rough water here and there and financially she could use a few more bookings every week, but, by and large, she was doing pretty well.

Who did he think he was, anyway, coming up with ideas for her business when she hadn't even asked him for help? She didn't need Nick to save her. She'd been running her own life for so long now, she didn't need a man to validate what she was doing or to come up with more work for her as he was walking out the door and—

"Annie? Is that all right with you?"

She started and looked up to see the other eight members of the board staring at her.

"Ah...could you repeat that, please? I drifted off a moment there. Late night. Sorry."

Vivian smiled. "No need to apologize. We all understand your mind might be on other things now that Nick is home."

Annie replied with a weak smile.

Vivian continued, "We were thinking, since you helped write the original grant proposals, you might follow up with the foundations regarding their possible donations. It has been quite a long time since we filed the paperwork. Maybe they need a little reminder that we haven't heard *anything* from them yet."

Oh, no, she hated doing that kind of stuff. It felt too much like begging. "Sure, I'd be happy to."

"All right, then, with seven days until the grand opening we still have plenty to do. You all know your assignments. Let's get to it. We are adjourned." Vivian tapped her pencil on the conference table as if she were holding a gavel.

Annie pushed back her chair and looked up just as Nick stuck his head through the conference-room doorway. She mentally groaned. Couldn't the man stay home? The more he showed up around town, the more likely he would be caught in the middle of interrogations from nosy community members.

Vivian put on her "welcome to my parlor, said the spider to the fly" smile. "Nick. What a surprise. How nice to see you again."

Annie jumped to her feet, hoping to get him out of the building before Vivian had a chance to ask any questions. "Hi, honey, we're just breaking up."

Before she could hurry him out the door, others in the room stepped forward to introduce themselves, and engage him in that oh-so-familiar small talk about the military and his marriage, and his upcoming baby, and just how long would he be able to stay in town?

"I've heard so much about the new museum, thought I might be able to get a preview tour." Nick flashed her a smile and she had to force herself not to be affected by the warmth in his expression.

"Oh, I don't really have time right now," she said. "How about another—"

"I'll show him around." Bill Baken, one of the town old-timers, reached out to shake Nick's hand.

Annie had to consciously hold herself back from kicking Bill in the shin as he rambled on. "Once the museum opens, I'll be one of the volunteer guides—might as well get some practice."

The two set off down the hallway that led to the museum. Annie watched them for a long minute, then threw her hands up in frustration. With a sigh, she set off down the hall after them. Someone had to make sure Nick kept his story straight. And someone had to know when to interrupt long-winded Bill or this tour could take all afternoon.

She reached the two men just as they halted in front of a wall of photographs. Century-old black-and-white photos of Bedford hung next to modern-day color shots of the same locations. It was a stunning contrast between then and now.

Annie waved a hand. "Bill, I can take over—you don't have to stay. I've actually got a little more time than I thought."

"Oh, I don't mind. It's good practice." Bill launched into a story about the founding fathers and how Bedford began as a farming community. He sailed from that into a description of the stagecoach routes through the town. From there he rolled into a telling of how Bedford became a summer destination of Chicagoans who arrived by rail to vacation at resorts on the lake.

Hands shoved deep into the pockets of his shorts, Nick turned his head slightly to raise an eyebrow at Annie. She swallowed a grin. Time for a well-placed interruption—just as soon as Bill came up for air.

Bill pointed to the thick forests on an old aerial map and dove into a history of logging in the area.

Nick straightened and pulled a hand from his pocket to trace a logging road on the map. "These roads still there?"

"Yup. Some are pretty grown over by now. But—"

"Where's Annie's—our—house?"

Bill searched a moment, then pointed it out.

Nick nodded, a thoughtful expression on his face. "So here are the woods…and there's the river. Look at this." He grabbed Annie by the arm and pulled her closer to the map. "We've got a logging road on our property, honey."

"You planning to cut down some trees?"

He laughed, threw an arm around her shoulder and pulled her close enough to kiss her temple. She let herself sink against him and drew a shaky breath. This would be way too easy to get used to.

"No. But I am planning to do some canoeing and tubing. And I need to be able to get the boats in."

"Bet you could do some fine cross-country skiing in that woods," Bill said.

Annie turned to stare at him, mouth hanging open. She shifted her gaze to Nick and then back to Bill again. "Have you two met before?"

Bill pointed at a section of the map. "Look at the topography. The glaciers left the whole area full of ridges and valleys. I bet you could have a ball skiing in those woods."

Annie opened and closed her mouth several times before finally getting a sentence out. "You ski?"

"My grandkids do. Out in the fields behind our house. Always pushing me to try it."

Nick nodded. "You know, I had the same idea. I was thinking you could chop some trails through the woods. Hike in summer, ski in winter. Bring people into the B & B. What d'you think?"

Annie frowned. "It's a lot of work."

Neither man so much as glanced her way. What? Had she gone invisible?

Bill traced a finger along a ridge. "You could go into the woods here, follow along the river for a ways, then up this esker. It'd be awful pretty. Yeah, probably draw folks all year round if they got something like that to do right on site."

"That's just what I was telling Annie."

What was it with these guys? It was *her* property— not theirs. Nick was her nine-day husband and he was acting as if he would be around for the next ninety years. Who cared if Bill thought it was a great idea? Who cared if the whole town thought it was a great idea? In the end, she'd have to be the one to make it go. And the truth was, it was more than she cared to tackle. Nick didn't seem to have a clue about how different her life would be six months from now once the baby was born.

There—his lack of insight into her situation—that was another of Nick's flaws...one her brain would no doubt do its best to overlook. Good thing Nick was marrying someone else.

"Excuse me, boys, think we can speed up this nickel tour? I've got some phone calls I have to make this afternoon."

"Okay, okay." Bill turned away from the map and proceeded to lead the way through the museum.

Forty-five minutes later they finally stepped outside.

Bill put a hand on Nick's shoulder. "Listen, if you want some help cutting trails, I'd be happy to give you a hand. Being retired, I've got time to spare. Bet a bunch of the other fellas would help out, too. Map it out and we'll get it done."

A look akin to awe crossed Nick's face. "You sure? Wow, that'd be great."

"We help one another out around here."

Annie cleared her throat in warning to Nick and sent a message with her eyes: *Nice dream—not gonna happen.* Nick frowned.

"Annie and I have to talk this over some more," he said. "Tell you what, though, stop over sometime and I'll show you the property. You're not gonna believe it."

"I grew up here. I'll believe it."

Annie watched Nick and Bill shake hands. A feeling of melancholy washed over her. After hearing Bill echo Nick's enthusiasm, she had the feeling Nick was probably right—it was a great idea. But she was a single woman running a bed-and-breakfast. She couldn't also maintain trails and run canoeing and skiing expeditions. No way, no how.

She and Nick walked in silence almost all the way home. Finally, Nick said, "You know, I'm not trying to force you into something you don't want to do."

"You're not?"

"How could I? I'm not even going to be around. I just get carried away at the potential."

Yeah, and I get carried away just looking at you.

"It's just, Annie—"

Oh, no, here it came again.

"You've got the best piece of property around here. Right on the edge of town. Wilderness out your back door, civilization out your front—"

"Nick, I appreciate your interest in trying to help my business, I really do. But it just isn't feasible for a single woman…*especially a single woman with a baby on the way.*"

If that didn't drill it home for the guy, nothing would. He turned to look at her, his eyes boring into hers for a moment before he looked away. He shoved a hand through his hair and finally nodded, clearly not pleased with the conversation.

"Okay."

HOURS LATER, WITH DINNER long over and the sky beginning to darken over a perfect summer day, Nick stood in the doorway leading to the wide back porch and took in the scene before him. The sweet scent of roses hovered in the air.

Annie was kicked back in the porch swing spooning a hot fudge sundae into her mouth, bare feet and legs swinging beneath her like a kid. Luella sat in a nearby rocking chair, attention concentrated on her own bowl of unadorned vanilla ice cream.

Nick marveled at the tranquility of the scene, so opposite to the life he and Melissa led in Los Angeles. If he was there, they'd only now be making plans for dinner—or rather, choosing what restaurant to go to. They sure wouldn't be having dessert, barefoot, on a porch in the falling darkness.

His mind wandered over the extremes of his lifestyle. Most of his adventure trips involved roughing it in the wild—often for months at a time. He'd stayed away from L.A. for years, moving from one assignment to another. The lifestyle had suited him well—the only certain thing about it was the uncertainty. It kept him on his toes, fed his adventurous soul, left him wanting for nothing.

Life had been great until he'd come back to the States for a friend's wedding and discovered a nagging sense that something was missing in his life. Maybe it was because of his age; turning thirty-five kind of moved you into a new stage. Maybe it was knowing that this was the year he would have inherited his trust fund if Annie hadn't helped him out six years ago. Maybe it was his mother's death last year.

Whatever the reason, he'd gone back to L.A. looking for stability and a home base. And he'd found Melissa. And slid right back into the nonstop lifestyle he'd tried to leave behind.

Interesting. He'd never thought of it that way before.

Annie looked up at him, her smile radiating peacefulness. There had always been something so appealing about her, even when she'd been a down-on-her-luck waitress. He pushed through the door and joined her on the porch swing. "How's the scream?"

"Mmm. You sure you don't want some?"

He shook his head. "I couldn't eat another bite. Luella, I think that was the best roast beef I've ever had."

The old woman smiled and nodded.

"*Everybody* loves Luella's cooking," Annie said around a mouthful of ice cream.

"Then I'd better be careful not to overeat. Don't want to go back to the military overweight—won't be able to fit in my uniforms."

Luella scooped the last bit from her bowl. "Sure has been nice to have you around. Wish you could stay longer."

"Yeah, I know. But I've got a commitment...."

Luella put a hand on the armrest of the rocker and pushed herself to her feet. "I'm going on inside. Leave you young people alone. See you in the morning."

When she was gone, Nick turned to Annie. "She's not moving real fast tonight."

"Arthritis. Some days it's worse than others."

"And she still keeps working here?"

"Says she likes it. And, I think, she feels sorry for me because my husband is gone so much of the time."

"Oh, great. And I'm leaving in a week."

"She'll get over it." Annie smiled.

"Yeah, only I'm divorcing you after I get back to the military. Then she's really going to hate me."

Annie laughed. "At least you won't be here to face her wrath."

"That's comforting." His gut twisted a bit. He didn't want Luella not to like him.

He pushed his feet hard against the porch floor and sent them swinging. The gentle coolness of the night air brushed over his bare arms, filling him with a wistfulness that seemed to exacerbate the gnawing sense that his life was missing something. Impulsively he put an arm around Annie's shoulders.

She tensed and slanted a sideways look at him.

He grinned. "Don't panic—it's just me."

After a moment of what appeared to be serious consideration, Annie relaxed and settled into the crook of his arm.

"Tell me about the places you've been," she said. "What you've been doing the last six years."

Nick hesitated; for the first time since he'd become an adventure writer he didn't feel like telling his stories. Somehow it didn't feel right to spell out all the excitement he'd experienced, all the places he'd been, as though pointing out how dull this place was in contrast. Somehow, all the things he'd done didn't feel all that important anymore.

When he didn't say anything, Annie looked up at him in question. Finally he shrugged and proceeded to give her an abbreviated version of the past six years, a quick listing of locations and adventures, starting with that first trip to Nepal and finishing with the cross-country road trip that led him to her.

Annie twisted beneath his arm and ran a finger down the scar on his left cheek. "And how did you get this?"

"Mount McKinley in Alaska. Stupid of me. A misstep that could have cost me my life. Instead I received a warning, a permanent reminder to exercise some caution when I'm challenging nature." He rubbed her shoulder. "You get any scars since we last saw each other?"

She chuckled. "Only on my heart."

"Love still hasn't been kind, huh? I thought you learned your lesson with that idiot you followed to L.A. Maybe I should beat some sense into those jerks for not knowing a good thing when they have it."

"Yeah, well, it's probably good none of them stuck

around. I seem to have the perfect ability to choose the wrong type of guys."

"As in?"

"You know, the ones who aren't going to stick around for the long haul. The 'you're a great girl, but...' kind of guys. Problem is, when you're in the middle of infatuation you think, oh, this is the guy, he'll be here through thick and thin, through rich and poor, through labor and delivery." She laughed. "Haven't found him yet."

Nick wondered whether or not she would consider him the wrong type. Sitting as they were, with her in his arms, he sure didn't feel like the wrong type. Then again, he *was* engaged to another woman, so that probably made him the wrong type in spades. The thought didn't sit well.

They rocked in the still night air and he searched for something to say, some other subject that wouldn't be a painful reminder to Annie that she'd failed at love. Hell, even with marriage to Melissa in his future, sometimes he wasn't so sure he'd succeeded at it himself.

Chester trotted up the steps and dropped a yellow tennis ball at their feet.

Perfect. They could talk about the dog. The mutt clearly adored Annie.

"Doesn't he ever get tired?" Nick bent forward to scoop the ball off the porch floor and toss it into the yard. "We must have run ten miles this morning and now he's back for more."

Chester took off after the ball at warp speed.

"One nap and he's as good as new."

"That's what I was afraid of."

Nick stood and watched the dog tear back toward the porch with the now-retrieved ball. As soon as Chester neared, Nick reached down to snatch the ball from the dog's mouth and fire it back into the yard. With a bark of joy, Chester was after it again.

"Careful, he's going to take a liking to you."

Nick dropped down onto the porch swing.

"Enough of that," he said. "This morning's run wore me out."

Seconds later, Chester dropped the ball at Nick's feet and danced excitedly, waiting for the next round of fetch. Nick groaned. "I'm done, dog."

Chester barked at him.

Annie laughed. "I warned you. You're trapped now."

The dog jumped up to put his front paws on Nick's knees. He barked again.

With a sigh, Nick picked up the ball and let it fly as hard as he could. It landed in the lake with a plop. "That should take care of that."

Chester raced off again and Annie groaned. "Bad move."

"Why?"

In the moonlight he could see Chester come to a skidding halt on the beach, right at the water's edge.

"He won't go into the water."

"Great. The game's over."

"Not hardly."

As if in response to her words, Chester began to bark at the ball floating in the lake. And bark. And bark. And bark.

"How long does he keep this up?"

"Until someone gets the ball." Annie stood.

"I threw it, I'll get it." Nick took off for the beach, stopping at the water's edge to search the dark water. He dug his toes into the soft sand and let it massage his feet.

The dog kept barking.

"Shut up, you numbskull," he muttered.

Chester ignored him. Nick spotted the ball bobbing in a shaft of moonlight some fifteen feet off shore, and moving farther out every second. He stepped into the lake and began to wade through the water, still warm from the afternoon sun.

"Chester, hush!" Annie said from behind him. The dog quieted instantly.

Nick looked back over his shoulder and pulled his shorts up higher as he waded into thigh-deep water. "This stay pretty shallow going out here?"

"Yeah…but be careful, there's a—"

Her words came just as his forward foot slid over the edge of a slope and carried him into water up to his chest.

Laughter bubbled out of Annie. "Oh, Nick—"

"Drop-off. Thanks for the warning," he said. He reached for the ball and secured it in his hand, then looked back at Annie, laughing her head off, and decided it was payback time. He tossed the ball onto the grass and jumped to one side in the water, as though trying to get out of the way of something beneath the surface.

"Hey, what was that?" He looked down.

"What?"

"Something big. Brushed past me." He swung his arm as though fending something off. "What d'you have in this lake, anyway?"

"Nick?" She took a step toward him.

He jumped to the side. "There it is again! Hey!" He jerked the other direction. "Help! Annie!" He dropped under the water and shot back up through the surface. "It's got me!"

She screamed and dashed into the chest-deep water swinging her arms. Nick dropped below the surface again and came up next to her. "Loch Ness monster!" he shouted before grabbing her by the waist and lifting her up. She screeched and he burst out laughing.

She smacked him on the arm and smacked him again before beginning to laugh along with him. Like village idiots, they stood there in the lake, clutching each other, laughing in the moonlight. Her wet tank top clung to her breasts and droplets of water sparkled across her face like diamonds. He brushed them off one cheek.

And then he kissed her. He didn't mean to, the impulse just came over him. Later, he knew he was going to ask himself just what the heck he thought he was doing at that moment. But right then, all he wanted was Annie's lips beneath his.

It was no gentle kiss, either. Not a first-date kind of kiss at all. It was wet and sloppy and passionate and romantic, and he pulled her tight against him, could feel her body against his with only their T-shirts between them. And when they finally drew apart he was shocked at the sensations a simple kiss had invoked in him. This was Annie, after all, his friend Annie, pregnant Annie.

His wife, Annie.

His heart started to pound.

"Hey," he said, looking down at her. He brushed the long, loose hair back from her cheeks. She had a look of abject terror on her face. Probably wondering herself what he was doing.

"Sorry, I got carried away." He let go of her.

"You scared me half to death." She shivered and wrapped her arms across her stomach as she started toward shore. "Water's kind of cold."

He followed her out, mentally kicking himself for what he'd just done. *What had he just done?*

Maybe this kiss was just one of those passionate things people do in the midst of extreme emotions—like when they think they're going to die. Everyone had heard those stories about people making love with a stranger in the middle of a war. Yeah, that explained it. Annie thought he was about to be eaten by a sea monster, and when he wasn't, her emotions all came out in that kiss.

So what was his excuse?

The sensual nature of water, the moonlight, the warm temperature, the fact that she was here. *Love the one you're with?* God, was that what he was doing?

Guilt nagged at him. This was Annie—the woman who'd helped him out six years ago. The woman who'd been hurt too many times by the wrong guys.

And he, Nick, was engaged. He sure fit the mold for "wrong guy." How could he have forgotten Melissa so easily? Lingering doubts about his upcoming marriage crowded his mind, and he quickly shoved them back into the dark corner from which they'd escaped.

Nothing about this sounded like it would work out well for Annie. Kissing her had been about the worst thing he could have done. For her sake, he had to keep his distance from her. Starting tomorrow, he'd go back to Annie and Nick, good friends. And he'd forget all about the kiss. Because the last thing he wanted to do was to lead his friend Annie on.

CHAPTER SIX

ANNIE OVERSLEPT THE NEXT morning. She leapt out of bed in semipanic, a complete list of things she needed to accomplish running through her head, and half a smile on her lips over the kiss she'd relived in her dreams all last night. As she showered, her mental clock ticked off how far behind she already was. No time for makeup this morning. She pulled on her shorts and noted how snug the waist had gotten. These were her largest shorts—she'd have to buy some maternity clothes soon.

She wiped off the vanity mirror with a towel so she could see to put her hair up in her usual ponytail. Jeez, having a roommate—especially when he was still in bed—sure made it difficult to get dressed in the morning. Thank goodness she no longer had bouts of morning sickness.

She nudged the bathroom door open and spotted Nick in a chair by the window, the shade half drawn to allow the gray light of early morning to enter. She watched him for a moment as he alternately inspected his ankles and then scratched them.

"Fleas?" She reached down to switch on a table

lamp, then strapped her watch around her wrist and glanced at the face. Good—she'd made up some time already.

"Hummph. Looks like poison ivy," he said.

"How'd you get that?"

He glared at the dog stretched out diagonally on the bed. "Chasing your mutt through the woods yesterday."

Chester thumped his tail.

Annie swallowed a smile. "Should have kept him leashed."

"He pulled the leash out of my hand—remember?"

He bent to scratch his ankles again.

"Let me have a look." She stepped across the room and knelt on the floor beside his chair. An angry red, bumpy rash poked out from between the dark hair on his legs. *A runner's legs—muscled and lean.* Her face begin to warm and she stood abruptly.

"Yep, that's poison ivy." She reached out to pat Chester on the head. The dog rolled onto his back and thumped his tail all the more. Annie rubbed his belly.

"I've got to get downstairs." And then because she couldn't resist, she grinned and added, "I see the dog basket is working out nicely."

Nick snorted. "Must have been four times I shoved him off the bed last night. He just jumps back up when I fall asleep."

Annie glanced at her watch. "What do you expect? He's been sleeping on the bed ever since— Oh, my gosh!"

She stared at her hands, turning them palm up and

down. "He's probably covered in poison ivy resin!" She raced into the bathroom, shouting over her shoulder, "Strip the bed!"

She began to scrub her hands with soap and hot water. "This is just what I need. I'm already running late and now the dog needs a bath."

She stuck her head out of the bathroom. "The guests! Did any of them pet him yesterday? If he had poison ivy resin on his fur we could have an epidemic in the house—"

"Annie—take it easy! He got wet in a sprinkler yesterday—probably rinsed most of the stuff off him."

She dried her hands and stepped back into the bedroom holding an oversize bath towel. "Plain water won't do it. I'm not taking any chances." She threw the towel over the dog, who jumped to his feet and began to bark from beneath it.

"What are you doing?"

"He's got to go out and I don't want to touch him."

Nick threw back his head and laughed out loud.

"You may find this funny, but I have a business to run, and if anyone gets poison ivy from Chester—"

"I'll take the dog out."

Relief slid through her. "Thanks. Afterward, just lock him in here and I'll give him a bath later." She started for the door. "By the way, breakfast will be served in an hour."

"Crepes again?"

"Would you prefer the hungry man's breakfast? Eggs over easy, hash browns, bacon, sausage—"

He gave her a boyish grin. "My mouth is watering already."

She smiled back at him. "That would be at the diner. It's $1.99 every morning until nine o'clock. Here at Bailey House Bed & Breakfast, we'll be having spinach-and-mushroom omelets, seven-grain nut bread and fresh squeezed orange juice."

She slipped out into the hall before he could reply, but his groan was audible through the shut door.

HE WATCHED THE DOOR CLOSE behind Annie, then reached down to run a hand over the red bumps on his shins. "Chester, now I know why I never got a dog. You are just one big pain in the butt."

The dog jumped to the floor and pranced over to Nick's chair, wagging his tail as though he'd just been offered a treat.

"How would you like to go live at the pound?" Nick asked.

The dog's tail whipped back and forth in gleeful anticipation.

Nick shook his head. "Dumb as a stone. Come on, let's take a run."

Fifty minutes and seven miles later they were back upstairs.

Nick reached behind the shower curtain and turned on the faucet. Hot water sputtered and then burst out of the showerhead above the old claw-footed bathtub. The plastic curtain shivered under the spray.

He stripped off his sweaty running clothes and let them drop to the floor. Chester padded over from the doorway and turned a couple of circles before settling himself on top of them.

"Hey! Get off." Nick gave Chester a shove with his foot. "I don't want poison ivy all over the rest of my body."

He stepped into the shower and let the hot water cascade over his head and shoulders. "This is what it's all about," he said with a groan of contentment. He stuck his head out from behind the shower curtain to grab his shampoo from the vanity countertop and spotted Chester lying contentedly on top of his clothes again.

"For crying out loud! By the time Annie gets around to giving you a bath, everything in this room will be contaminated. Get over here."

The dog lifted his head but didn't move.

Nick exhaled irritably. He shoved the shower curtain aside and climbed out of the tub, water running in rivulets from his body to the floor as he stepped across the small bathroom. Chester jumped to his feet and began to dance in excitement.

Nick picked up the wiggling dog and held him as far away from his body as possible. "You're getting your bath right now."

Stepping back into the tub, he held Chester in the warm spray until his fur was thoroughly soaked, then set the dog down in the tub. Instantly, Chester tried to scramble over the side.

"No, you don't." Nick grabbed hold of the dog's collar and began to lather his hair with Annie's shampoo. The sweet smell of berries filled the air. He added more shampoo, scrubbing hard until the dog was nearly a mass of solid white suds. "If that doesn't get rid of poison ivy, nothing will."

"Nick?" Luella's voice carried through the open bathroom door. The dog's ears perked up and he turned his head.

"In here," Nick called, suddenly grateful Annie didn't have a see-through shower curtain. He stuck his head out. "What d'you need?"

"Annie sent up this calamine lotion for your poison ivy."

"Oh, thanks. Just put—"

The shower curtain jerked, and without even seeing what was happening, Nick knew Chester was escaping. He lunged for the dog and caught him by the scruff of the neck with one hand. The movement threw him off balance. His feet began to slip out from under him. Teetering, he grasped the shower curtain with his other hand and felt it tear under his weight.

He let go of the dog and threw his other hand back grabbing at air until his fingers connected with the shower hose. As if in a pirouette gone awry, he fell head-first over the side of the tub, plastic curtain clutched in one hand, shower hose in the other, the entire movement accompanied by the creaking of the metal shower curtain rod as it bent and collapsed, the crack of the showerhead breaking, and the sound of Luella screeching.

Clearly Luella was getting an eyeful. And Chester had escaped, soapsuds and all.

ANNIE HAD JUST SET breakfast before her guests when she heard Luella's scream followed by a loud crash. "Excuse me," she said to her guests as she backed toward the doorway. *Bon appétit.*

She took the stairs two at a time and arrived at the bedroom to find Luella sitting on the edge of the bed, with one hand over her heart. Beside her, Chester wiggled and shook, sending water and suds in every direction.

"Luella! What happened?"

Nick stepped out of the bathroom, a towel wrapped around his hips. "I fell out of the bathtub giving Chester a bath," he said, water dripping from his hair onto his shoulders. He held up an arm to show her his scraped elbow. It was all she could do to drag her eyes off his bare chest and look at the wound.

Luella nodded, her blue eyes wide. "I thought he'd killed himself for certain."

"The bathroom's kind of a mess." Nick winced.

Annie looked past him through the door. Her mouth dropped open. The floor was underwater. The shower curtain was ripped in two. The metal rod that used to circle the tub was bent into an unrecognizable shape. Even the showerhead was dangling, torn from the hose like a flower from its stem.

"You're certainly thorough," she said.

"It'll be good as new by tonight."

"A handyman, are you?"

"One of the best." His grin shot straight to her heart. "You'll come to wish you could keep me around here forever."

That's the problem, she thought to herself. I already do.

She looked at the dog rolling suds all over the bedspread. "I'll rinse Chester off in the basement laundry tub. Luella, can you take over breakfast?"

Without awaiting an answer, she wrapped the dog in

a towel and headed downstairs. Day three. They were just on day three and already too much had gone wrong. Besides the stress of lying about Nick, now she had to contend with that kiss last night and an almost constant attraction to him. What a hopeless case she was turning out to be.

HALF AN HOUR LATER, Nick stood alone in the bathroom, pad of paper in hand, making a list of the parts he was pretty sure he would need to fix the shower. If he was fixing a sailboat, this would be a no-brainer. But a shower? Still, how hard could it be?

Hard enough for someone who'd never done it before. What kind of idiot lied about his home-repair abilities to impress a woman? Annie couldn't care less that he climbed mountains—but fix her shower and her eyes practically gleamed with affection.

He stood on one foot and used his toes to scratch his ankle—this poison ivy was driving him crazy. He wrote *cortisone cream* on the sheet. Luella's calamine lotion wasn't doing the job.

He squinted at the destroyed rod and the showerhead dangling from the hose. Maybe he could swing by the library and get one of those fix-it books, the ones that gave step-by-step instructions for everything from appliances to home repairs. All he'd have to do was get it upstairs without Annie spotting it.

He shoved the list in his pocket and bounded down the stairs. Seeing no one in the hall, he sprinted out the door, shouting, "I'm off to the hardware store," before Annie had a chance to say she was coming along.

Once at the library, he flipped through several home-repair books until he found one that described exactly what he needed to do. He unfolded his sheet of paper and modified his list of needed materials. This would be a pretty easy job to complete.

He considered photocopying the necessary pages instead of checking out the book, but decided against it. Who knew what other projects he might undertake at Annie's in the next week? With this book close at hand, she never had to know he wasn't a handyman extraordinaire.

He checked the book out under Annie's name and headed up the street toward the hardware store. In the distance he spotted a familiar figure striding toward him—Father Thespesius out on one of his exercise walks.

"'Morning, Father," he called as the man neared.

"Nick! Good to see you! I trust all is going well?"

"Good, good. Just getting ready to do a few repairs." He gestured at the book.

"I imagine you're enjoying Luella's cooking?" The priest closed his eyes. "Be sure to ask her to make her oven-fried chicken while you're here. No offense to anyone above, but you'll think you've died and gone to heaven."

"I'll do that. Maybe tomorrow—I know tonight we're having pork chops."

The priest's eyes flew open and then narrowed. He swallowed and began to walk a circle around Nick, who turned with him.

"Luella's pork chops, you say? I don't suppose you'd have room for one more at the table?"

"I don't know—"

"Not that I would presume to invite myself—"

"No, I wasn't thinking that, it's just—"

"It so happens my housekeeper is gone this week and I've been cooking for myself, alone as I am…"

Nick nodded. Annie was going to kill him. "Father, we'd love to have you join us." He tightened his grip on the book.

The priest walked another circle around him, arms swinging. "You're sure you'll have enough food?"

"Absolutely. Why don't you come over about six?"

Father Thespesius bobbed his head up and down. "Thank you so much, Nick. I'll bring the wine." He strode off in perfect power-walk precision.

"Great," Nick muttered. "I'm gonna need it."

An hour later, he was back at home, new parts from the hardware store and old tools from the basement laid out in a row on the bathroom counter. Back behind the clothes hamper, where it couldn't be seen from the doorway, the fix-it book lay open on the floor.

He eyed the job at hand, then looked at the diagram in the book again. This was pretty easy stuff. First he'd take down the shower curtain rod. Then he'd deal with the showerhead. He climbed into the tub to get a better angle from which to work.

"I hope you don't fall out of there again." Annie stepped through the open doorway.

"Very funny." He glanced at the book behind the hamper and hoped Annie didn't come too far into the room.

She laughed, a sweet lilt that made him remember

the first time he kissed her—six years ago. The judge had declared them married and told him to kiss the bride. So he had. And afterward she'd laughed just as she had right now—with a kind of joyful abandon. It had touched him then, shot a jolt of happiness right into his heart, but he hadn't realized just how much, until later, after she was gone.

"Need any help?"

"Nah, I should be able to do it." He unscrewed part of the rod and she reached out to take it from him.

"How hard is it going to be?"

"Not too bad." *Even for a nonhandyman like me.* He cleared his throat. "Ah, by the way, I ran into Father Thespesius in town."

She looked at him expectantly.

"Nice guy. He was raving about Luella's cooking. Her chicken...and her pork chops."

"You didn't tell him, did you?"

Nick pursed his lips and put the wrench to the pipe again. "I think I did."

She frowned. "Think?"

"I'm pretty sure I did."

"Oh, no, Nick! He'll be calling, looking for a dinner invitation any minute now."

"I don't think so." Nick handed her another piece of the shower curtain rod.

"You don't know him well enough yet."

Nick shook his head. "He doesn't need a dinner invitation—he's got one already."

"Oh, Nick!" Annie wailed. "Father Thespesius has always been overly curious about my marriage. How are we supposed to keep this charade going when you invite him to dinner?"

"It was like I didn't have a choice—"

Annie glared at him.

The ring of his cell phone out in the bedroom broke the silence. Nick exhaled. It didn't matter who it was, he was happy to hear from them right now.

He climbed out of the tub, nudged the hamper over the book and bolted to the nightstand where his cell phone was charging. An unfamiliar number showed on his caller ID.

He dropped into the wing chair and put the phone to his ear. "Talk to me." He glanced at Annie and grinned.

A low voice whispered, "Ohhh Baby!"

"Hello?" He sat up and threw a questioning look at Annie.

She followed him into the bedroom.

"Oh Baby!" The voice took on an insistent edge. There was something oddly familiar about it.

A laugh welled up inside him and he held it back. "Minnow?"

"You're not supposed to identify me," she said, irritated. "I'm giving you the code word."

Annie leaned up close to him and he caught the scent of berry shampoo. He inhaled. It sure smelled better on her than on Chester. *Oh, baby was right.*

"What's going on?" Annie reached for the phone and he caught her hand with his to prevent her from succeeding. Their fingers interlocked. Their eyes met. His male anatomy started to react. Good God, all because of berry shampoo?

This was Annie. And he was engaged. He dropped her hand as if it was covered with poison ivy resin.

Minnow's voice blasted out of the phone. "Hel-lo? What's going on over there? I've got *big* news. Meet me at the fountain."

"Minnow," he said, fighting to keep his patience. "The two of us are right here—there's no reason to go to the fountain. Just tell us what's happening—"

"You're on a cell phone. There's no privacy—anyone can intercept it."

"Oh, for crying out loud. Just tell us what's going on."

"No. I'll call you back on the corded phone."

The line went dead.

Nick let out a sharp laugh as he let his head fall against the back of the chair. "Your friend is certifiable. She's calling back on the land line so we don't risk the chance that someone might intercept the cell phone signal and overhear us."

The phone on the other nightstand rang and Annie raced around the foot of the bed to snatch it up. She plopped down on the edge of the bed.

"Hello?"

Nick sat beside her and she held the phone between them so they could both hear. The scent of berries washed over him again and he forced himself to concentrate on Minnow's voice.

"Are you both there?" she asked.

"Yes," they replied in unison, and grinned at each other.

"Okay. Some guy just came in for a trim *and he was asking questions about you two.*"

"Who was it?" Annie asked.

"Nobody from around here. He talked kind of formal."

Nick looked at Annie. "What did he want to know?"

"Well, first I thought he was just a tourist 'cause he was blabbing about how quaint the town is, the old buildings and stuff. And then he started talking about your B & B, and next thing I knew he was asking how long you two have been married. And what do you do in your spare time. And how busy are you with reservations. And whether I thought Annie would ever move out of town to be closer to her husband."

She snorted. "Like I was too dumb to get suspicious. I knew right away he was up to no good. Maybe we ought to meet tonight to work up a plan of action—you know, strategize. Bet you a million bucks, he's going to hang around awhile."

Annie sighed. "We can't. Father Thespesius is coming to dinner."

"Of all the people you should be avoiding... Why did you invite him over?"

"Nick invited him."

"I didn't invite him. He invited himself."

"Be prepared," Minnow said. "He's the nosiest person in town. Jeez, Louise, you two! You won't have a secret left after tonight."

Annie flashed an I-told-you-so smile at Nick. "There's no getting around it. He'll be here at six."

"Well, then, so will I," Minnow declared. "You're going to need me to keep things sane."

"Oh, is that what you do?" Nick muttered under his breath.

Annie swatted him. "We're having pork chops."

"What's more important? Vegetarianism or helping the two of you. I'll bring along a soy chop. Just tell Luella so she doesn't give it to Father."

Annie looked at Nick and raised a questioning eyebrow.

Oh, hell. He shrugged. "The more the merrier."

"Okay, then be here at six," Annie said into the phone. "Your assignment is to keep the conversation off me and Nick."

"Righto. Once Father goes home we'll have our strategy meeting."

Annie hung up the phone and turned to stare at Nick. "What if someone's on to us?"

"How could they be? I've only been here a couple of days. This guy probably has some other reason for asking questions."

"Like?"

"Your land? Eighty acres right on the lake. The guy asked if you might move away to be near me. Maybe he's a developer."

She nodded. "Maybe…"

Nick held out a hand, palm up. "Or, maybe he's a reviewer. He asked how busy the B & B is. Those guys always go incognito so you can't try to influence their opinion."

She nodded again. "What if he's a private detective sent by your fiancée to find out the real reason you're staying in Wisconsin? What do you think? Is it possible?"

Nick stared at her a moment, a pit forming in his

stomach. Melissa? All he needed was for Melissa to find out he was in Wisconsin sharing a bedroom with…his wife. She'd be devastated; she thought he'd been divorced for years.

"No. I'm sure it's not Melissa. Now, don't panic, Annie. There's gotta be a reasonable explanation. Whatever it is, we'll deal with it. We'll find out who the guy is and what he's up to—and we'll deal with it…together."

CHAPTER SEVEN

FATHER THESPESIUS ARRIVED promptly at six.

"We're so glad you could come." Annie hoped he didn't detect any insincerity in her voice.

Nick squeezed her shoulder and a shiver raced through her. Grateful for his show of support, she looked up and met his gaze, felt herself start to sink into his dark eyes and jerked herself back. What a sorry case she was. All the guy had to do was touch her and all her thoughts turned to lust.

"Didn't want to be a minute late for Luella's pork chops," the priest said with a jovial grin. He handed Annie a bottle of red wine. "I know we should be having white. But in my business, red is always the top choice."

Minnow came up the front steps and followed him through the door.

"I hope you don't mind, we've invited Minnow to join us as well," Annie said.

"Not at all. Not at all." He turned to pump Minnow's hand. "Thought you were a vegetarian."

"I give it up for Luella's pork chops." She dashed past them into the kitchen holding a brown lunch bag.

Annie handed the bottle of wine to Nick, who eyed the label and whispered something under his breath like "Bet this is the same stuff they use in church on Sunday morning."

She stepped on his toes.

Fifteen minutes later, they were seated at the dining table, their plates full, the conversation light and flowing easily. Luella beamed under Father Thespesius's praise of her cooking and Minnow chatted on about the hair salon. Annie took another swallow of her lemonade, wished she could have some wine and forced herself to relax. Maybe this wouldn't be so bad after all.

Father Thespesius leaned forward. "Nick, have you given any thought to leaving the military and coming home to settle down now that you have a baby on the way?"

Minnow choked on her salad and Annie leapt to her feet to slap her on the back.

"Don't forget to chew before you swallow, dear," Luella said.

"Well, I...yes...not really...hadn't...too soon, anyway," Nick said. He tried to cut a bite of meat and dropped his knife with a clatter onto the plate.

Minnow stopped coughing. Annie stared at Nick. Apparently Nick wasn't a natural at lying. *Not like her.* A sick feeling settled in her stomach. She certainly had gotten adept at it the last couple of years.

"Annie's going to need you around here," the priest said. "Hard for a woman to run this place all by herself, especially with a young child."

Annie returned to her chair and smoothed her napkin across her lap. "Nick's income from the military really helps us stay afloat. I don't know if we could make ends meet here without it." Not bad; that should put an end to the questioning. She reached for her fork.

Father Thespesius took a bite of pork and talked around it. "All the money in the world won't do you a bit of good if you've lost sight of what's really important—love and family."

"My thoughts exactly," Luella chimed in.

Annie's stomach tightened.

Nick covered her hand with his. "We're not worried about that." His eyes bored into hers with a deep, albeit faked, affection. And though she knew this was an act, she couldn't prevent the warmth that flowed through her.

Eyes locked with Nick's, she nodded.

"Food's getting cold," Minnow said, shattering the moment.

Nick dropped her hand and everyone dug back into dinner.

"Luella, I know I said this already, but you have truly outdone yourself," Father Thespesius said after several minutes. He cleared his throat and Annie intuitively knew he was about to return to his previous topic—their marriage. "But tell me—"

Minnow leaned forward suddenly. "Did you hear the Carow boy was caught spraying shaving cream all over the mirrors in the teachers' bathrooms at the high school?"

Their heads swiveled in unison to look at her.

"No," Annie said, grateful for Minnow's effort.

"Doesn't that just sound like him?" Luella said.

The priest shook his head. "I'm going to have to talk with him again. Seems that boy is always getting into one scrape or another. Grew up without a man in the house." He settled his gaze on Nick again.

Oh, jeez, here it comes, whatever it is. Annie searched her mind for a topic, something—anything—to say that might prevent the priest from asking whatever the heck he was about to ask.

"Tolerably fine weather we're having, isn't it?" she said in what she sensed, too late, was an overly bright voice.

This time, all heads swiveled to look at her, forks half lifted to mouths.

"Tolerably fine?" Nick asked.

"Cinderella," Minnow interjected. "The prince says it when he meets Cinderella—in the television movie."

Nick snorted. "Well, now we know the *real* reason Cinderella took off at midnight."

"Actually, one of the stepsisters says it to the prince," Annie said. What an inane conversation. Still, anything was better than talking about her marriage to Nick.

"You know the lines to Cinderella?" Father Thespesius looked impressed.

"Well, why wouldn't she?" Luella answered. "It's one of her favorite movies, right up there with…" She turned to Nick and waited for him to finish the sentence.

He blanched and Annie prayed he would get it right.

"Ah… *It's a Wonderful Life?*"

"A round of applause for Nick Fleming, Husband of the Year." Minnow let out a strained laugh.

Annie stuck a spoonful of applesauce in her mouth even though she was now so stressed she would just as soon quit eating altogether. The sooner this dinner was over, the sooner Father Thespesius would go home.

"Speaking of husbands…" the priest said.

"Oh, oh!" Minnow waved her fork. "You know how Bill Butter left his wife and all those kids and took up with some woman he met on a business trip? Well, his wife was in today for a cut and color. And she told me that now, just a month after he left, he wants to come back. The best part is, she told him she needs some time to think about it."

"Which leads right into what I was about to say," Father Thespesius said.

Annie's heart sank. He was bound and determined to speak his mind. Of course, he'd had plenty to say about their long-distance marriage over the two years she'd already lived here. Whatever made her think Nick's arrival would make him stop?

She finished off her lemonade and refilled her glass.

"I wonder, have you really given any thought to what happens once the baby is born? What it will mean with Nick halfway around the world? A separation like this is just not a good situation under any circumstances. A child needs its father."

Annie stared at Nick, pleaded for help with her eyes. He lifted one eyebrow ever so slightly.

"You make a good point, Father," Nick said. "But there are married people in the military the world over. Somehow families survive. It takes a little more work to stay connected, but when you're as committed to making this work as Annie and I are…" He smiled at

Annie. "God willing, my job won't stop us from having the family we want. Maybe two boys and a girl. Or two girls and a boy. Or three the same. Right, sweetie?"

Annie's heart constricted and she nodded, unable to speak. He made it sound so real. The whole lie was getting completely out of hand. They were getting in deeper and deeper with no end in sight.

The sound of the front door latch clicking open filled her with relief. Any interruption was better than the subject at hand. Chester jumped to his feet with a bark and Annie leaned back in her chair so she could see down the hall. One of her guests, a stately, middle-aged balding man, stepped into the foyer and was instantly greeting by Chester, wiggling with excitement.

"Oh, Mr. Lewis!" Annie motioned him into the dining room. "How was the supper club?"

He stopped in the doorway and reached down to pet Chester's head. "Delicious. Thanks for the recommendation."

Minnow leapt to her feet and pushed through the heavy swinging door that led into the kitchen. "I'll get dessert ready," she tossed over her shoulder.

Annie frowned. What was the rush? They weren't even done with dinner yet. She turned her attention back to her guest. "I made a fresh batch of cookies so be sure to help yourself whenever you're hungry."

"Thank you. If you'd care to share your recipe, I'm sure my wife would love to have it." With a nod, he strolled down the hallway toward the kitchen.

Seconds later, Minnow barged back into the room through the swinging door, a frantic expression on her face.

"Where's the dessert?" Annie asked.

"Oh! Dessert! I decided we probably weren't done with supper yet!" She opened her eyes wide and gestured toward the swinging door. "Oh Baby, Oh Baby, Oh Baby!"

The code word? Annie threw a questioning look at Minnow and was answered with an almost imperceptible nod. She stood and crossed the room. "Actually, I *am* done, so I think I'll get the dessert ready after all," she said.

"I'll help." Nick pushed back his chair.

Luella set her napkin on the table. "Now, you just stay there, Nick. Let us women pamper you while you're home. I'll help the girls."

"Oh, no, no, no!" Minnow cried. "You made dinner. We'll get dessert." She slid her arm through Annie's and turned her in a circle, preventing her from going into the kitchen.

Annie held in a laugh. For a spy buff, Minnow wasn't too smooth at acting normal when times were out of the ordinary. Then again, maybe that was because Minnow wasn't too smooth at acting normal even when times were normal.

Mr. Lewis passed the dining room doorway, munching on a cookie as he headed toward the stairs. At the sight of him, Minnow spun through the door to the kitchen with Annie in tow. "Let's get dessert," she sang out.

As soon as they were in the kitchen, Annie dragged Minnow into the walk-in pantry and closed the door.

"What's going on? What's the matter with you?"

"It's him! The guy from the salon. Mr. Lewis is the one who was asking all the questions about you."

Annie could feel her jaw drop. "He's staying here."

"No kidding. I didn't want him to see me—to know that we're friends."

Annie's heart thudded into her stomach. There was more going on here than they realized. She let her head drop back and stared up for a moment at the bare light-bulb hanging from the pantry ceiling.

"You think he really knows something? Maybe he's just a developer wanting my property." Her tone brightened. "Or he could be a reviewer and I'll get a four-star rating in the bed-and-breakfast review book."

"Yeah. And maybe he's a P.I. hired by Nick's girl-friend."

Annie slumped. "That's what *I* said."

They stared morosely at each other.

The pantry door opened and Annie jerked upright. Nick stood in the doorway. "What are you two doing in here? You left me out there with Father Nosy and Mother Curious."

Annie grabbed the apple pie off the counter and pushed past him into the kitchen. "Sorry. Get the ice cream," she said. "Mr. Lewis is the man Minnow called us about today."

"The one asking all the questions?"

"The same," Minnow said. She pulled a five-quart pail of vanilla ice cream from the freezer. "Maybe he's from the IRS."

"I never thought of that angle. When did he check in?" Nick began to pace.

"Couple of days ago. He's supposed to stay a week." Annie began to cut the pie and lift it onto dessert plates.

"By himself?"

"Uh-huh."

"He said he has a wife. Isn't it kind of odd the guy is taking a vacation by himself?"

Annie shrugged. "I don't interrogate guests as they check in, you know. Might be kind of bad for business. Besides, he seemed normal enough." She watched Nick a moment. It was nice to have someone else to worry with. "So what do you think we should do?"

"Nothing—"

"That's silly." Minnow scooped the ice cream and dropped it onto the cut pieces of pie. "The guy could be ready to take the two of you down and you're going to sit around and wait for him to do it?"

Nick lay an exasperated look on Minnow. "What I was going to say is we do nothing until we figure out what the guy's gig is. Maybe he really is just a guest here."

Minnow snorted. "Yeah, and maybe I'm a nun. When he leaves his room, Annie, you get in there and look around—"

"I'm not going to go digging through his stuff."

"Couldn't you be making the bed and, oops, just happen to flip through his briefcase?"

She raised her eyebrows at Minnow. "No."

"Yeah, okay. Then we need to set up surveillance on him, every minute of the day. We need to know where he goes, who he sees—the works."

Nick shook his head. "No way. There's only three of us and it's a small town. Unless he's blind, he'd have to notice one of us showing up wherever he goes."

"I have to agree," Annie said. "We'll just draw attention to ourselves following him around. His staying here gives us some good chances to find out what he's up to without being too obvious."

She picked up two plates of dessert. "Now, let's get back into the dining room before Father gets suspicious."

HOURS LATER, AFTER EVERYONE had gone home, Annie wandered into the yard. The house was quiet and dark; Nick had gone upstairs, and suddenly the alone time she used to cherish at night, the time during which she prepared breakfast for the next morning, seemed oppressive.

The light from the nearly full moon bathed the yard in a silver glow. The air still held some of the heat from the afternoon sun and a warm breeze touched her skin and blew wisps of hair around her face. Beneath her bare feet, the soft grass teased her with its contrasting coolness. Ever since she'd come to Bedford, nights like this had made her feel as if she was one with the universe, part of a greater plan.

But tonight, all she felt was lonely.

Pregnancy made her more tired than usual, but she couldn't face climbing into bed with Nick right now. Not when he'd brought up children and pretended that, someday, they'd have three of them. Years ago, she'd once told him she wanted three children. Had he remembered that? Or had he just plucked the number from the sky?

She bent to pick up two orange life vests that had been discarded in the sand by her guests. She gave them a shake, then hung them inside the storage shed. She took hold of the rake leaning against the shed and attacked the beach, gathering pine needles, branches, leaves and other of nature's debris into a pile near the woods.

Three days with Nick and already she was a wreck. How would she make it to nine? Did she even want to try? Maybe something urgent should come up, like the military needed him back pronto. That would work; the military did stuff like that. People would accept it. The more she thought on it, the more she realized that was probably the answer to her whole dilemma about Nick. Get him out of here—and soon.

She stood back and surveyed her work, then wandered across the beach to the water's edge, her feet sinking into the wet sand, cool water lapping at her ankles. Holding her shorts high so they didn't get wet, she waded over to the pier and hoisted herself up to sit on the end, feet dangling in the dark water.

A pebble splashed near her feet and she jerked her head up and around to find the source. Nick stood at the end of the dock, grinning.

"Hey," he said. "Whatcha doing?"

Thinking of you. She shrugged.

"Mind if I join you?" Without waiting for an answer, he dropped down beside her, his muscled thigh coming to rest against hers, which was quite enough, thank you, to set her heart pounding.

She shifted her leg slightly to break the contact. "I thought you went to bed."

"I'm too restless to sleep. You worried about Mr. Lewis?" he asked.

Not as worried as she was about her feelings for Nick, but she wasn't going to say that. "Yeah."

"We'll get him figured out. And if he's up to no good, I'll pound him for you." He flexed a biceps.

She laughed. "Thanks. I feel so much better."

Problem was, while that might make her feel better on the outside, inside she was turning to mush. Of all the dumb ideas she'd ever had, this charade had to be the dumbest. Now was the perfect opportunity to tell Nick he didn't have to stay the whole nine days, that she would fly to Las Vegas—or wherever—for a quickie divorce.

He swung his feet back and forth in the water and the movement made his thigh rub against hers. She shifted away again and drew a breath.

Right now. Get him out of here before you throw your arms around him. She stared out across the lake at the dark wall of pines and hardwoods that lined the distant shore. *Say it, you gutless chicken.*

She opened her mouth and the words came out all on their own. "Nick, I had a kind of epiphany at dinner, a realization—"

"I think we did pretty well, considering Father Thespesius's questioning," Nick said.

"Well, yeah, but my point is, I'm worried we won't be able to keep this up for another six days—"

"Sure we will."

"No, what I mean is, it's going to get harder. Look at the monkey wrench Mr. Lewis has already thrown into the works."

"Annie, when I've got a mountain to climb I don't keep my eyes on the summit the whole time—otherwise the thing is too overwhelming. I set goals for where I want to be at the end of each day." He patted her knee. "We'll attack this beast one day at a time."

She sighed. He sounded like he was beginning to enjoy the whole situation. He wasn't getting it and she sure wasn't going to tell him that the real reason for her concern was the effect he was having on her every time she came near him. It was now or never. She had to move this man out of her life.

"Nick, look, you've been here three days already." Her words picked up speed as they rolled out of her. "If you suddenly got an emergency call from the military and had to leave, no one would question it. Everyone's met you now, they know you're real. Heck, you and I could say we're leaving for a little getaway. Then you go back to California and I stay away a few more days and come back here without you. No one the wiser."

"Annie, I don't have a problem staying—not any-more."

She could feel his eyes on her and turned to meet his gaze. Obviously he didn't understand. "I'm trying to say I'll get the quickie divorce. Now—tomorrow—as soon as we can."

"What about the museum opening?" His voice held more than a touch of bemusement.

She waved a hand as if it was no big deal. "Don't worry about it. If the military wants you back, it'll be easy enough to explain. Besides, I'd already decided last week to start hinting that we were having marital problems. That way, when I finally announce our divorce, it won't come as a surprise. Your leaving now would feed right into that."

Nick slanted his head and looked at her through narrowed eyes. It took all her self-restraint not to run her hand across his cheek, to touch the rough day's growth on his jaw, to—

"Damn!" he said, his eyes on the yard behind her. "Here comes Mr. Lewis."

Before she could turn to look, Nick's arm came up around her shoulders and his mouth came down on hers. Hard. Sensations shot through her, pleasure that made her heart thud, her skin shiver. She grabbed hold of the edge of the dock to keep from succumbing to the moment, to keep the rational side of her brain in control. *This was, after all, just a ploy to keep Mr. Lewis from coming over and asking questions.*

He held her jaw and kept her from moving away from him. His tongue slid between her lips and she sank beneath its erotic assault, meeting it with her own, because, she rationalized, *of course, we have to make sure this looks believable, and this is how one would kiss one's husband after months apart. After all, it's sure as heck how I would kiss my husband.*

His mouth moved over hers, insistent, and she let herself follow him, let her hand move to grasp his shirt and pull him closer. His mouth was on her throat, her jaw, teasing her ear, and she leaned into him, feeling his warmth, wanting more of him. *Control, control,* her brain warned, and she swirled her foot in the water, as if the cold around her toes would douse the fire building inside her.

Nick's hand came up to cradle her breast, braless because of the heat. He caressed her through her knit shirt, *combed cotton for extra softness, the catalog had said.* Yes, they were right about that. She was going to lose her mind over all that softness. He slid his hand beneath her shirt and she pressed into his palm, his touch rough and arousing and almost more than she could bear. Reality started shouting at her. Maybe this was going a bit too far for Mr. Lewis. She shoved the thought away. No, it wasn't. *Wanna bet?* Yeah, okay, maybe a bit.

She wrenched her mouth from Nick's and pushed back to stare at him. "What about Mr. Lewis?"

"What about him?" Nick asked in a husky voice. He pulled her toward him, his eyes heavy-lidded and hot. Her stomach flopped.

"I think we're doing more than he needs to see." She glanced over her shoulder; Mr. Lewis had apparently fled the scene—probably mortified over their open display of affection. Disappointment coursed through her and then evil took over her mind. That's all she could attribute it to, evil caused a sudden lie to burst from her mouth.

"Oh!" she said on a gasp. "Kiss me again—here he comes!"

When finally they came up for air, Annie's lips throbbed, her chin felt rubbed raw and she knew she had to put an end to this right now or she'd never be able to forget Nick even if he did leave tomorrow.

Nick glanced back at the house at exactly the moment she did. "He's gone," Annie said on a breath.

"Yeah. Nice job." Nick sat up straight.

She could hardly breathe and he said *nice job?* If he only knew. This had reached the point of being awful.

Talk about desperate. Here Nick was doing this to help her and she was pretending Mr. Lewis was nearby just so Nick would kiss her. This was pitiful—no, *she* was pitiful.

Oh, but the man could kiss. What she wouldn't give to wake up to that kiss every morning for the rest of her life.

Melissa. Right, Melissa was going to get that kiss, Melissa was engaged to that kiss. She, Annie, had no right to even covet that kiss—it was, after all, only on loan for nine days. She had to stick to her latest idea—get Nick out of here. How dumb it had been to ask—beg—force— him to stay. Sure, she might be convincing the town that they were happily married, but she was also convincing herself that she'd never gotten over this guy. *He had to go.*

Annie forced herself back on track. "There are just too many close calls. What if Mr. Lewis had overhead any of our initial conversation? As Minnow would say, it would have blown our cover. Nick, I'm letting you out of our agreement. We find the first flight tomorrow to wherever we have to go, get the divorce, then you head back to California."

THE HELL HE WAS GOING to leave. Nick watched Annie as she logically laid out their next plan of action. Was the woman immune to him? Two minutes ago he'd have sworn she was as attracted to him as he was to her.

When she'd first said he was free to leave, all he'd wanted to do was find a way to shut her up. Mr. Lewis had been a handy excuse—even though it was a lie. Lewis hadn't been anywhere in sight. Lucky for him, though, the man had shown up eventually; Annie would never have to know Nick made the whole thing up just so he could kiss her.

And had it helped? Apparently not. She seemed as determined as ever to get rid of him. Well, he wasn't going anywhere. Not until—

His brain skidded to a halt. Wait a minute. Annie was offering him the very thing he'd come here seeking—her signature on the divorce papers—and he was about to turn her down. What was wrong with him? His lawyer had called that morning with the news that he and Annie could get a quick divorce in Nevada or Alaska. All the pieces were falling into place. So why wasn't he jumping at Annie's offer?

Realization slipped through him slowly, like a soft breeze on a summer night. He didn't love Melissa. Not if he was feeling this attraction to Annie. The thought cleared his mind, made him see the past year with fresh eyes. He'd never actually loved Melissa at all. For a moment, his brain was so focused on the revelation he could think of nothing else.

"So we'll fly out tomorrow?"

He jerked his head up to look at Annie. "Uh. There's nowhere to go," he said. "I haven't heard back from my lawyer about who does quickie divorces."

"It's been two days since you called him. How hard can this be to figure out?"

Nick shrugged. "Besides, I can't leave Bedford yet. I made a commitment to judge the Women's Club flower arrangements contest tomorrow night, and I'm a man of my word."

"For goodness sake. They can find another judge."

"They asked *me*."

"That's only because I told them you're a gardening whiz."

"And now you're going to tell them you exaggerated just a bit?"

"Nick, the flower-judging is only part of the problem. If we're having trouble fooling Mr. Lewis, how on earth will we pull off you faking expertise about flower arrangements?"

He shook his head. "I'm not going to bow out. Don't worry—I won't blow it."

She sighed in defeat. "Fine. Call your lawyer tomorrow and we'll leave the next day."

"What about the museum opening?"

"It's not that big a deal."

What was up with her? "That was the whole reason you insisted I stay nine days."

She waved a dismissive hand. "Look, I said I'd sign the divorce papers. What more do you want?"

I think I want you. He looked out at the moon reflected in the dark lake. He had to end his engagement. He couldn't marry one woman when all his thoughts were of another.

He looked at Annie. "You can agree to sign the papers tonight. But I'm not going anywhere for a while." *At least, not until I find out how much of that kiss was real and how much was playacting.*

ANNIE'S STOMACH HAD TURNED to jelly. That's what was the matter. He was going to stay, and, soon, her whole body would be jelly. She wouldn't be able to walk without collapsing into a shivering, quivering heap on the ground. She'd have to lie there and say to people, *Don't mind me, I'll be fine in another six days.*

For heaven's sake, didn't he realize the effect he had on her? "You really don't have to stay," she said weakly.

"A deal is a deal."

She sighed mentally. If she kept protesting, he was going to get really suspicious. How could she not have realized that her old feelings for Nick might resurface?

Fine, he could stay. But, she would do her best to avoid him, keep him out of her sight, remain focused on the goal of making it through the next six days without letting Nick know how much she cared about him.

If only they weren't sharing a room.

If only they weren't sharing a bed.

CHAPTER EIGHT

STAYING AWAY FROM NICK was proving to be next to impossible. This morning, she'd walked into the bathroom and there he was, soaking in an oatmeal bath for his poison ivy. He'd grinned and said, "Throw me a towel, will you?" She'd whipped one his way before backing out in mortification. After last night's kiss, he probably thought she'd come in there on purpose.

She sighed and shook her head.

Once Nick had finished his bath, he'd discovered she and Luella were going to flip all the mattresses—a job that had been scheduled for the day he arrived and gotten postponed in all the chaos. He insisted that he be allowed to help and that Luella do something less strenuous.

So they'd flipped all the mattresses, just the two of them. Mostly him, actually, because he kept saying she should take it easy because of the baby. So she pretty much stood around and watched him—and his muscles. And throughout the entire ordeal the most intelligent sentence that had come out of her mouth was "You can double the life of a mattress if you turn it regularly."

She could have asked if he was nervous about judging the flower arrangements at the festival tonight, could have questioned him about his writing, could have told him the history of Bedford, for goodness' sake. But no, she babbled ridiculous things about mattresses.

It didn't help she'd decorated the inn so romantically that every room they entered further weakened her resolve, didn't help that her brain couldn't seem to let go of their interlude on the pier last night. And yet, somehow, she had to stay focused on the fact that his life was going somewhere that didn't include her.

Finally, to her immense relief, he'd gone off for a run and she'd come into town to have Minnow trim the ends off her hair. She sat in the vinyl beautician's chair facing the mirror, her head like a trophy on top of the black plastic cape covering the rest of her body. Minnow stood behind her, frowning at her reflection.

"That's it?" Minnow held up the ends of Annie's long sandy-blond hair. "One inch off the length? Come on, Annie, live a little, take a risk."

Annie looked at Minnow's fuchsia locks and grimaced. "Maybe another time."

"You don't have time to wait for another time. The moment is now. How long you been wearing your hair straight and long?"

"Not that long."

"That would mean…since high school?"

Annie shrugged. "So?"

"I rest my case. You've gone out of style and don't even know it." She began to comb out Annie's wet hair.

"Long hair never goes out of style."

"For teenage girls, it doesn't. You left 'teenage' behind ten years ago. And now you've let yourself fall into that old familiar rut."

"You mean the rut where you never change how you look because you look absolutely fine as you are?"

"No. I mean the rut where you don't care whether you look attractive to your husband or not."

Annie rolled her eyes. Good thing she and Minnow were the only people in the shop right now. "For goodness' sake—"

"He's from California. He *loves* that West Coast look. Why don't you give it to him?"

Annie stared at Minnow's rapt expression in the mirror. "Are you talking about Nick? He grew up in Chicago."

"He's a California boy now."

Annie talked to the mirror. "For this month, maybe. Anyway, who cares what he likes?"

Minnow swung the chair around so Annie was facing her. "You should. He's your husband."

Annie opened her mouth and then shut it without saying a word. She tried again. "Minnow. It's not for real, remember? He's leaving in five days. We're getting divorced. Any of this sounding familiar?" She waved a hand between them. "Hello? Not to mention, you know as well as I do that Nick couldn't care less what I look like."

"You shouldn't make assumptions. I've seen the way he looks at you. Now, consider what you'd look like if we cut you to shoulder length." She used her hands to demonstrate where the hair would end. "What do you think?"

Annie had to admit it changed her look entirely, but it wasn't her hair that concerned her at the moment. "What do you mean *the way he looks at me?*"

Minnow smiled like Mona Lisa and picked up the professional shears from the counter. "You ready?"

"No! I've got to be able to get it in a ponytail. I need to be able to get my hair out of my face when I'm in the kitchen. But what did you mean—"

"Okay. We'll take three inches off and add layers. Long, sleek layers. And we'll do some highlighting. Strawberry-blond. Sun-kissed. You'll look great."

"Minnow! What does he look at me like?"

Minnow grinned. "Oh. Right. He looks at you like... like he can't quite believe you're real—"

"Oh, great, he's repulsed."

"No, no. In a good way. It's like he thinks you're really special and he only now just realized it and he can't believe he never figured it out before."

"Really?" Annie's stomach flipped and a slow, mellow joy rolled through her. Then reality pounced on her like a cat with its claws unsheathed. "Minnow, he's engaged to someone else."

Minnow waved her scissors cavalierly. "The only thing I know for certain is that, right now, at this very moment, you two are married. When he looks at you there's something there. And when you look at the guy, you go goo-goo-eyed. Seems to me that if the guy you want is the guy you already have, then you should do whatever it takes to keep him."

Annie stared at her dumbfounded. Finally she said, "Am I that obvious?"

"To me, you are."

"Oh, God. I probably am to him, too. Last night Nick and I were sitting on the dock when Mr. Lewis came outside. So Nick kissed me to keep the guy from coming over and talking to us."

She could feel a blush coloring her cheeks. "Then I lied that Mr. Lewis was still nearby so that Nick would have to kiss me again. And he did. Only...he kissed me because he was playing a role. And I kissed him *because I meant it*."

Minnow swung the chair round again. "Layers. I'm cutting in some very cool layers. We're doing some highlighting and you are going to go for it."

"I can't do this."

"Yes, you can."

"There's more to catching a guy than getting a new haircut."

"Yeah, well, we'll cover the rest while I'm cutting. Are you with me?" She held the scissors poised at Annie's head.

Annie waited a long moment, her brain churning frantically in an effort to make sense of what Minnow was proposing. Finally she drew a deep breath and said, "Just keep it long enough for a ponytail."

Seconds later, she saw the first pieces of her hair fall to the floor. She closed her eyes briefly and hoped this sudden change didn't come across to Nick as an obvious come-hither ploy. "The hair is just the first step." Minnow's voice interrupted her thoughts. "You have to show the man you're interested. You have to prove to him that *you're* the woman he wants—not that bimbo, Melissa."

"And you're going to teach me these little skills?"

"Me and my team of experts." Minnow picked up a stack of fashion and women's magazines that were piled on the counter. "Just in time for the festival tonight."

Annie groaned. "I knew there was a catch."

"Now, while I'm turning your hair into a thing of exquisite beauty, you can take a few little quizzes I've gathered." Minnow held the magazines up one at a time, setting them back on the counter as she moved through a list of self-improvement topics. "I thought we'd start out with a little self-analysis. For example, *Just How Sexy Are You?* Once we've got that nailed down, we'll move on to *Do You Have What it Takes to Catch the Man of Your Dreams?* And then, just to make sure he's worth all the effort you're about to put forward, our final quiz will be *Is He a Player or a Keeper?*"

Annie let loose a chortle. "So once we're finished here, when I get home I can expect Nick will drop to one knee and ask me to marry him—or should I say, stay married to him?"

Minnow picked up a magazine from the counter and flipped it open to a dog-eared page. "Cynicism will get you nowhere. Now, you ready?"

Annie sobered. Nick was the man she'd always wanted. What the heck. She nodded.

Minnow grinned. "Be sure to answer as honestly as possible or we won't know exactly what you need to work on." She set the open magazine on the counter and straightened her back like a prim schoolteacher. "Now, let's get started, shall we? Question one. Just how sexy are you? If you were a dessert, you'd probably be (a) apple pie—sweet and all-American, (b) chocolate soufflé—decadent and irresistible, (c) cream puff—firm on the outside, but soft inside, (d) lemon torte—smooth and a little tarty."

Annie choked back a laugh.

"So, which will it be?"

"This is ridiculous."

"You want the guy or not? That's the real question. Are you willing to give it a try?"

Annie sighed. "I've always wanted him. Thing is, he's never wanted me. And I hate to sound like a broken record, but he is engaged to someone else."

"Annie, humor me here. Pick a dessert."

"As long as you agree my participation doesn't mean I'm going to do anything with the information. If Nick, on his own, decides to end his relationship—"

"Because he's fallen madly, passionately in love with you—"

"For whatever reason, then maybe, just maybe I might stick a toe into the water. But otherwise, jeez, Minnow, think how you would feel if some woman started coming on to the guy you were engaged to. I have to respect the choice he's made."

"Fine. Respect it. You just don't have to like it. And if you happen, along the way, to become what he's looking for, well, it's what's-her-name's loss. Now, pick a letter."

An hour later, her hair wrapped in tin foil, Annie was deep into an article titled "Unleashing the Real Woman

Inside You." So far, after three quizzes and two articles, she'd yet to discover any brilliant revelation that would make Nick suddenly decide he preferred her over Melissa. In fact, thus far, the only conclusion she'd been able to come to was that she was a combination apple pie and dry martini, and she appealed to guys who liked to play chess and dance the meringue.

Oh, boy.

The door to the salon creaked open and Vivian waltzed into the room and glanced around as if she was expecting a reception. "Oh, dear, where is everyone? I was hoping to sneak in and get my nails done before the festival tonight."

"At lunch." Minnow strolled to the front desk and checked the appointment book. "Jenny could squeeze you in at one."

"Thank goodness. Look at these cuticles." Vivian held up her hands before stopping to pat Annie on the shoulder. "I hope your stomach isn't aflutter in nervous anticipation, dear. We'll be announcing the festival's Pansy royalty winners before three o'clock."

Annie gave Vivian a wan smile.

"I'll be back in half an hour. Now, girls, I do have you both down to help pass out hors d'oeuvres tonight. So don't be late. Oh, and Annie! I met a guest of yours, Mr. Lewis, at the village hall. We had the nicest conversation. He was so interested in our little town that I invited him to the festival." She swept out the door with a flourish.

Annie turned a stricken face to Minnow.

"Let's not overreact," Minnow said.

"Not overreact? These are the words of wisdom from the woman who used the code word yesterday?"

"Yeah, but he was asking about *you* yesterday, not the town. Think about this a minute—maybe he's just a curious sort of guy, you know?"

"No." Annie pulled a hand out from beneath the black cape and began to gesture. "Maybe it's a front. Maybe he's trying to throw people off his tail by asking other kinds of questions."

"You're starting to sound like me."

"Well?"

Minnow frowned. "Okay, so I was thinking the same thing—I just didn't want to freak you out. This guy is up to no good, I'm sure of it."

"So what do we do?"

"Look at it this way—if he's at the festival, we'll be able to keep an eye on him without too much trouble. We can see who he's talking to—and then all we have to do is find out what he's talking about. There's three of us—only one of him. We just need to make sure one of us always has him in our sights tonight."

Annie nodded. "I'll talk to Nick."

"Which brings me to the subject of Pansy royalty." Minnow started to chortle. "You didn't tell me you and Nick were nominated—"

"I didn't tell Nick, either."

"Oh, God, you'd better hope you lose."

"I can't believe this even happened. Nominations have been closed for ages. Then suddenly they decided since Nick was back, we should be part of *the court?*"

"Not to mention, prince and princess."

"Please. The Women's Club wouldn't do that to me."

Minnow shook her head, still laughing. "Don't hold your breath. I just wish I could be there when Nick finds out."

AN HOUR LATER, ANNIE arrived home, swinging her hair across the back of her neck like one of those girls in the television commercials. She caught her reflection in the hall mirror and stopped to marvel at the way her hair shimmered in beautiful golden strawberry-blond-streaked layers. Minnow had been right. It was amazing what a difference a change in her hairstyle made. If only the quizzes and articles had been as helpful.

She lifted the back of her hair with her fingers and let it slip and slide back into place. Who would have guessed she could have hair like this? Though she hadn't done it for Nick—well, not really—she wondered what he would think of her new look. Or whether he would even notice at all.

Hoping to casually run into him, she checked the parlor and dining room to see if he was there, then swung into the kitchen. No luck. Hummph. Probably upstairs. Well, she wasn't going to go charging up there; she didn't want to be totally obvious. She had plenty to do to keep herself busy until he came down, including baking more chocolate chip cookies and finishing the cleaning.

But…if she made cookies right now, she'd have to pull her hair back and then she'd look the same as she always did. And with her luck, that would be when Nick would see her. Jeez, just what was she up to, anyway? Was she really buying into Minnow's makeover plan? Did she really want Nick if the only way he liked her was because of her hair? Her mind wavered on the reply. Whatever happened to "beauty begins inside"? Was it all just rot?

With a sigh, she pulled out a dust cloth and began to dust her way through the house. She really had to quit obsessing about this and get back to keeping herself so busy she didn't think about Nick. The time she'd just spent with Minnow had only made things worse.

She methodically worked her way through the parlor, adjusting a picture frame here, moving a knick-knack there, doing a more thorough job than usual, just to keep herself occupied.

The lawn mower engine roared past the parlor windows. *Hmm, he was doing yard work.* She forced herself to keep dusting. *All on his own without even being asked.* She wiped off the antique, marble-topped end table and its intricately carved wooden legs and claw feet.

The sound of the mower rose and fell as it moved back and forth across the lawn in front of the house. She dusted the top edge of a row of pictures hanging on the wall, and then the bottom edges and the sides. *What could be the harm in one little peek?*

The smell of fresh-mown grass drifted in through the open windows. She wiped off the window ledge with great precision, poking her dust cloth into every little nook and cranny. And then, as though her hand were possessed of a mind of its own, it reached over the sofa and used one finger to pull the lace curtain to the side just a bit.

Shirtless. The man was shirtless.

Sweat glistened across his tanned shoulders and on the black hair curling on his broad chest. She drew a shaky breath. What a picture.

He glanced up at the window. And waved.

She jumped back, letting the curtain fall shut, heart pounding, cheeks burning with embarrassment.

Shaking her head, she dropped into the big wingback chair facing the hearth. Just what did she want, anyway? She knew better than to go after Nick, yet she'd just spent two hours trying to figure out how to get him to like her.

She was trying to get an engaged man to fall for her.

Jeez, the more she changed, the more she stayed the same. This was reminiscent of the way she used to be. Wanting the wrong guy and refusing to accept that he was all wrong for her. Suddenly she felt like crying. He'd come to Bedford to get a divorce. He'd stayed to help her out. There was nothing more to it. And she was, once again, ready to play the fool for love—or lust or infatuation—or whatever it was she was feeling right now.

She squeezed the bridge of her nose with two fingers to hold back her tears. Time to put her hair up into a ponytail. Time to get back to the original plan. Four days down, five to go.

How on earth would she make it the next five days?

The front door opened and footsteps sounded in the nearby hall. Darn it all, she didn't want to see Nick right now—didn't want to face him like a beet-faced teenager caught stalking her latest crush. A teenager who'd gone out and had her hair cut and streaked to get his attention.

She jerked her legs up underneath herself and pulled her elbows in tight so she couldn't be seen from the hall. Thank goodness this chair had such a high back.

The footsteps paused at the entrance to the parlor, and she pressed herself into the chair as if it would help make her invisible. *Go away, go away, go away.*

"Yes, yes, I realize that," said Mr. Lewis from somewhere behind her.

She relaxed and let out the breath she'd been holding. It wasn't Nick at all, just Mr. Lewis on his cell phone.

"I don't dare appear unduly interested in their affairs," he said after a pause. "I haven't had a chance to talk with the housekeeper yet, but it's been my experience, you learn more from people when they are unaware of your motives."

Annie straightened a bit and turned her head so she could hear better. A soft breeze slid in the window and raised goose pimples on her arms.

"I'm still attempting to pull all the pieces together, but to the best of my knowledge—"

When he broke off, Annie had to keep herself from standing up and demanding he finish his sentence.

"It appears there's more to it than we thought," he said finally. "But I could be wrong. Just want to be sure I've got everything right before I leave. I should have a report ready within another day or so, with sufficient information to determine what course of action to take."

She couldn't make out his next sentence because he had begun to walk toward the kitchen. Why had she ever told the man he could have as many cookies as he wanted?

What the heck was he up to? Was he on to them or not?

She waited until she heard him head upstairs, then jumped to her feet and dashed out the door to find Nick. Glancing frantically from side to side, she finally spotted him pushing the mower at the far end of the yard along the edge of the woods. Chester pranced along behind him, obviously devoted to Nick.

In classic race-walker form, she hurried across the lawn, afraid to run in case Mr. Lewis looked out a window and spotted her. The breeze blew her newly shorn locks in her face and she shoved the hair out of her eyes, thankful she'd made Minnow leave it long enough to put into a ponytail even if she hadn't done it yet.

Nick shut off the mower once he spotted her and waited, one hand casually resting on the mower handle. Correction. Make that one strong hand, connected to a muscled bare arm connected to a broad bare chest. Annie steeled her resistance at this closeup sight of him. Chester bounded out to greet her and she reached down to pat his head and take a moment to reorganize her thoughts.

Straightening, she had every intention of telling Nick what she'd overheard. But her subconscious, that part of her mind that was completely aware of how little Nick was wearing, rammed itself forward again. Look at those abs, it whispered. *Washboard.*

Against her better judgment, she looked. *Legs... check out the definition in those calves. This guy has better legs than pro soccer players.*

And with him wearing those form-fitting, tiny running shorts, how could she not notice his muscled thighs and that small rear end and that— She gulped.

"What's the matter?" he asked.

She whipped her eyes up to his face and felt the blush race up her cheeks. "Uh, how's the poison ivy?"

"You came out here to ask me that?"

No, but she wasn't about to admit the real reason she was staring at his lower extremities. A silly grin crossed her face. She knew it was silly because she couldn't control the quivering of her lips.

"Are you all right?"

"Actually, no."

"Nice hair."

He noticed? The temperature of her cheeks rose. "Oh. Minnow convinced me to try something new."

He nodded. "Looks nice."

She nodded back.

He nodded again and his lips slid into a grin. "So you came out here because…?"

She let out a sharp breath. "Yeah. I just overheard Lewis on his cell phone. He is definitely up to something and I'm sure it involves you and me." She quickly related what she'd heard. "Not only that, but Vivian said he was down at the village hall asking questions about Bedford. She invited him to the festival tonight. Minnow and I thought we should do some surveillance on him there."

Nick nodded. "I really wonder what his gig is. He can't be a B & B reviewer—not with what you overheard."

"So cross that one off the list. What do you think he's up to?"

"Developer, maybe. Or, Minnow's theory, the IRS."

"Or something else. What if he's up to something we haven't even thought of. What then, Nick?"

He nodded. "I know. The bigger problem is that every possibility we've come up with could wreak havoc on your life if it comes out we're not what we say we are."

He wiped the sweat off his brow with the palm of his hand and she tried to stay focused on the conversation and not on how the muscles flexed in his tanned arm.

"It goes back to what I said before. Our best hope is that he makes a mistake. Lucky for us he's staying here. And even luckier, Vivian invited him to the festival. He'll never suspect we're keeping an eye on him. But when the guy finally trips up, we'll be there to catch him."

"I don't think I can take this kind of stress. I feel like I'm living in one of Minnow's spy thrillers. Except everything won't be tied up nice and neat on the last page."

"Annie, the more I think about it, the more I bet he's a developer. It fits that he'd be asking questions at village hall. And it would tie in with you because you have such a great piece of property."

"I don't know. What I heard of his phone call didn't sound as if he was after land."

Nick glanced at the thick forest behind him. "I'd be surprised if you didn't have developers after your land. Come on, I want to show you something."

"What about Mr. Lewis?"

"Nothing we can do about him right now. Come on."

He untied his T-shirt from the handle of the lawn mower and pulled it over his head, then started toward an overgrown footpath leading into the woods. Chester raced ahead and Nick stopped.

"Will he run away if we take him with us?"

"No. Just yell 'Chester McLester' and he'll come back."

"Chester McLester? Why doesn't this surprise me?"

Hearing his words, the dog bounded to Nick's side and sat down, tail whipping from side to side as he awaited his next command.

Nick lifted one foot and eyed the poison ivy bumps on his lower calf. "This little piece of information would have been helpful a couple of mornings ago."

Annie held in a grin. "Didn't Luella tell you? His previous owner taught him to answer to that name. Kind of a weird guy."

"No kidding. Come on, let's go."

"Wait a second, Nick. I'm serious about Mr. Lewis. Shouldn't we stick around to see what he's up to?"

"How? Sit outside his door? Follow him on his walks? Steal his cell phone?"

"Maybe."

He laughed, low and resonant, and she felt herself begin to melt. "Come on, this won't take long."

CHAPTER NINE

NICK RETRACED HIS STEPS and grabbed Annie by the hand, interlacing his fingers with hers. She let herself be pulled along into the woods, savoring the feel of his callused palm against her smooth one, and wishing he would slip those rough fingers through her new silky-smooth hair, and over her lips.

When the path narrowed, he let go of her hand and led the way, talking over his shoulder. "I hiked out here this morning, and I'm even more convinced. You're sitting on a gold mine."

Annie swatted at the mosquitoes that were feasting on her face and arms. "Seems more like a mosquito mine to me," she muttered. "What are you talking about?"

"You'll see."

Ten minutes later, they came to a halt at the river.

Nick looked at her, enthusiasm all over his face. "What do you see?"

"Ah, a dead end?"

He laughed. "Nope. A beginning." He pointed at the shallow sandy bank that sloped into the gently flowing water. "What do you see there?"

"This is a trick question, isn't it? A riverbank."

"Annie! It's a launching spot—"

"That was my next guess. And we would be launching…?" He'd better not say canoes and inner tubes.

"Canoes and tubes. I talked to the old guy who owns all that property where the river runs along his pasture. You put the canoes in here. And he's agreed to let you pull them out on his land."

Nick turned and gestured at the woods. "All you need to do is cut a narrow road in here to bring the boats in. Well, and build a storage shed. With a little grooming, that path we took would be a perfect route for guests to follow as they start their wilderness adventure."

She tried not to gape at him. Had he completely forgotten their conversation the other day? Just when did he think she would fit all this extra work in? She didn't have time to build sheds and roads—let alone give canoe trips down the river. And she sure as heck didn't have money to pay someone else to do it.

"I—"

"Don't say *no* so fast."

"So fast? I already said *no* yesterday. And you promised to quit bugging me about it."

He winced. "I know. But then I realized you weren't making an informed decision… In order to do that you have to fully understand what you're turning down."

"I do."

"No. You don't. I've been trekking through the woods, following the river, thinking this thing over. Here's the beauty of it. This part of the river—it's pretty calm. *You* won't have to go along on the adventures. Maybe you'd give some basic instructions before they set off. But that's it. A couple of hours later, depending on how long they want to be out, you pick them up at the end point."

He opened his arms wide as if to embrace the wilderness. "Bailey House Bed & Breakfast. Not just a place to sleep, but a place to awaken your adventurous spirit. Annie, it'll fill your rooms, summer, winter, spring and fall." He grinned. "What do you think?"

She had to admit, it did sound a bit intriguing, especially with his energy driving it, his passion for the plan. But ideas like this had to stand up in the cold light of reality. And the truth was, there was no way she could do it, not unless she hired help, and the thought of having any more to manage on her own was enough to kill any enthusiasm she might have. She shook her head in discouragement and started back toward the house.

"No?" Nick caught up with her. "Annie, it's perfect."

"There're all sorts of reasons it won't work."

"Name one."

One? She could name several.

"I don't own any canoes."

"An easy fix."

"There's no road in—and no storage shed."

"Another easy fix."

"It'll cost money—a decent amount of it, too."

"You gotta spend money to make money."

"I can't lift canoes by myself."

"The customers lift the canoes."

"I'm having a baby."

"You mean to tell me that once you have that kid you're never leaving the house again?"

"Ohh!" She threw her hands in the air.

"You have some of the weakest excuses I've ever heard."

She drew in a long, slow breath. *Fine. Just fine.* She stopped and turned to face him. He drew up short and narrowed his eyes as if trying to figure out what she was going to say next.

"Okay, Mr. Answer Man. I can't run a canoe business…" She winced. "I can't do it because…because… I've never been in a canoe before."

A grin slid across his face and his eyes sparkled. And then he threw back his head and laughed. She watched him for about five seconds, then spun on her heel and began to march through the woods. Well, march as well as one could when the path was overgrown with branches.

"Annie!" She could hear the laughter in his voice. He caught up to her. "There's nothing to it. Especially on a river like this one."

"Oh, please. This, the input from the adventure writer, the man who strives for ever-increasing adrenaline rushes. You probably consider roller coasters tame."

"Ah, some of 'em. But, Annie, you gotta admit, this idea has potential."

He was right about that. Potential for someone who had experience in the outdoors. But no potential for a woman who spent a childhood on military bases and an adulthood in cities. These woods were as close to nature as she'd gotten in all her life. She swatted at a fat mosquito on her arm.

"Let me show you—I'll take you canoeing," he said. "Humor me. Give me one little canoe trip before I drop out of your life forever."

Drop out of your life forever. Well, didn't that about say it all? "I don't think so."

That's all she needed—to be alone with Nick in a little boat for hours, herself overcome with lust and him merely trying to teach her the finer points of boating.

"Why not? Come on, a little canoe trip. We'll put in right here on your property and the minute you say *stop,* we'll stop."

She glanced over her shoulder. "Where's the canoe coming from?"

"There has to be somewhere to rent one in town."

"Nope." Good. His idea was dead in the water. Forgive the pun.

They broke out of the woods into her yard again. Nick dropped into step beside her. "Then I'll buy one."

She stopped. "Don't be silly. What'll I do with it when you leave?"

"It'll be the first of your fleet."

"I'm not going."

He gave her an assessing look. "Don't tell me you're afraid."

"I'm not afraid."

"Yes, you are. Then we're going for sure. You need a little excitement in your life."

Frankly, between Nick and Mr. Lewis, she could do with a little less excitement.

"Come on, Annie. How about tomorrow morning—ten o'clock?"

"Nick—"

"Enough excuses. We're going."

She sighed. "Better make it ten-thirty. I'll have all my morning chores done by then."

Nick patted her on the arm. "Don't worry, it'll be fun. Once I finish cutting the grass, I'll find a canoe."

She nodded and walked away as he started the mower again.

She was a failure, an utter failure, at sticking to her convictions. All she had to do was say *no* and mean it. And she couldn't even do that. Why did he have to get so involved in everything here? Couldn't he just play his role for nine days and move on? He was going beyond messing up her life and moving well into messing up her head.

She bent to pull some weeds from one of the flower beds. Well, all right, so he wasn't messing up her head so much as she was. It was *her* brain that turned last night's kiss into something it wasn't, *her* brain that was going to make the next five days a living hell. She ripped a particularly stubborn weed out by its long, tenacious roots.

And seeing how it was *her* brain, she could control it. She could be near Nick and not be overcome by want, by need…by insatiable attraction.

It might help if she concentrated on those flaws of his. It might help even more if he were ugly…or flabby. *Or not such a nice guy.* No, none of that mattered.

All she had to do was set her mind to controlling her brain—and not lose sight of the fact that he had a fiancée. Mind over matter. Forget the goal of staying away from Nick. That was next to impossible. She just had to remember: Fiancée, Melissa, engaged to be married.

That made everything so simple—and freeing. Now she could go canoeing without a worry.

She tried it again: Fiancée. Melissa. Engaged to be married. Yup, this would work wonders.

NICK WATCHED ANNIE WALK away and wondered about the sag in her shoulders. Could she really be that afraid of a canoe trip? She'd led too sheltered a life. She'd taken steps in the right direction by going to school and buying this place. But she'd gotten complacent just when she should have found a new challenge. He nodded to himself as he pushed the mower across the lawn. She probably didn't know how to take the next step. Well, he could take care of that—finding challenges was his specialty. He grinned. That's what he would leave her to remember him by—a splash of excitement in her dull, small-town life.

His thoughts turned to Melissa, and for the umpteenth time, he mentally reexamined his revelation of last night. Even in the light of day, away from the romantic influence of the soft summer night, the truth was undeniable. He didn't love her; he couldn't marry her.

He owed it to Melissa to tell her soon. She deserved someone who truly loved her, *someone who knew what love really was,* not someone who just thought he did. The longer he let this go, the greater her pain would be.

He glanced at his watch. Paris was seven hours ahead. It was always impossible to reach Melissa in the evening when she was on location. His best bet would be to catch her first thing in the morning. Which meant he would have to call at 1:00 or 2:00 a.m. His gut twisted at the thought of breaking Melissa's heart. He may not love her, but that didn't make it easy to hurt her.

A silver Lincoln pulled into the driveway and he watched Annie wave at the driver. Moments later, the door popped open and out stepped Vivian, dressed in a wild floral-print dress and big straw hat covered with matching flowers. No mistake about it—Flower Festival day had arrived.

Vivian stopped for a brief exchange with Annie before the two turned to stare across the wide expanse of grass at him. He hoped Vivian didn't decide to come out and say hello.

No such luck.

Vivian marched toward him, one hand on top of her hat to keep it from blowing off in the steady breeze, the other holding a rolled sheet of paper. Annie almost had to run to keep up with her.

He shut off the mower and waited for them to arrive, taking the time to admire Annie's long legs as she strode across the lawn in Vivian's wake.

"Nick! I have the most wonderful news for you," Vivian said in a breathless voice when she stopped beside him.

She reached out to rub his forearm, then lifted her hand to look at her palm, wet with his sweat. An expression of revulsion whipped across her face and disappeared beneath a weak grin. She patted her hand gently on the side of her dress.

"At any rate," she said, as though she had been interrupted midsentence. "I've come to announce that you and Annie have been elected Pansy Prince and Princess for this year's Flower Festival. Congratulations! Isn't it wonderful?"

Pansy Prince and Princess? Nick cleared his throat and raised an eyebrow at Annie.

"This is a real honor," Annie said hurriedly.

"I'm sure it is. Just what does being Pansy royalty mean?"

"You ride in a convertible in the parade," Vivian said.

Nick nodded. *Oh, joy.*

Vivian gave a gleeful laugh. "And of course, the two of you dance the first dance at this evening's celebration."

"Of course."

"All the past Pansy royalty come out on the floor for that dance—it's a lovely show of support for our fund-raiser."

"I'm sure it is." He drew the back of his hand across his brow. "This is quite an honor, I'm sure—and a surprise. To tell you the truth, Vivian, I didn't even know we were nominated." Maybe he should write his next article about the strange culture in small towns.

Vivian looked at Annie in surprise. "Didn't Annie tell you?"

"I didn't want to get his hopes up." Annie tried to smile. "You know, in case we lost."

"That wife of mine, what a sweetheart," Nick said to Vivian. "Always looking out for my best interests."

Vivian touched Annie on the arm and reached out with her other hand to do the same to Nick, then appeared to think better of it and patted the air near his sweaty biceps. "That's what love is all about. Your robes are being pressed as we speak. I polished the crowns myself just yesterday. You need to be at the Women's Club at six-fifteen to dress. The parade starts promptly at six-forty-five."

Crowns and robes? Nick slanted a look at Annie.

"Oh, and Nick, the prince always makes a toast. Just a few words. Nothing too spectacular. Something about the fund-raiser and the flowers. Don't forget to mention that the museum will be the recipient of the money raised tonight."

"No problem. Thanks for delivering the news, Vi."

"Vivian." She frowned at him before setting off for her car, one hand on top of her hat again.

Nick waited until she was backing out of the driveway before turning to Annie. She looked stricken.

"Nick, I'm sorry—I—never thought we'd win."

He let her sentence hang in the air so she would squirm a little. Her eyes widened. "Do you hate me?"

"Oh, no," he said. "Here I was, thinking you didn't have any excitement in your life—"

"I have plenty, thank you."

He smiled. *No, sweetheart, you don't.* But if he had anything to say about it, she would soon.

NICK ADJUSTED THE GOLD crown on his head and held up the purple velvet cape with its large yellow collar. How perfect—pansy colors. He hooked it around his neck and climbed into the convertible to sit beside Annie on the seat back. With the fall of early evening, the temperature had dropped down into the mid-seventies. Not low enough to make a heavy velvet cape comfortable, but a welcome improvement over the heat of the afternoon. He looked at Annie, regal in her own purple cape. He might look like a fool, but she looked magnificent.

The only saving grace for him was that he got to ride in a white 1972 Cadillac El Dorado—a big boat of a car, but what a beauty. He could almost overlook all the pansies decorating the car, just for the fact that he was riding in it.

The police car leading the parade set off its siren. The scream was promptly joined by other sirens from other police cars and the honking of the town fire engines—a noise combination that almost knocked him over.

Annie grinned at him and he grinned back, amazed to find he was looking forward to the night ahead. With a slight jerk, the car began to move. Nick attempted the royal hand wave that Vivian had tried to teach them: elbow, elbow, wrist, wrist, wipe a tear, blow a kiss. Now he really did feel like a fool.

From the corner of his eye he could see Annie watching him. He blew her a kiss and she burst out laughing.

"I don't think the man is supposed to wipe a tear and blow a kiss," she said. "That's my job."

They turned onto Main Street, both sides of which were lined with people who had come out to watch a parade that consisted of three police cars, three fire trucks, six tractors, one marching band, one float covered with pansies, two convertibles—one for the mayor—and a bunch of kids throwing candy. This was one easy group to please.

He waved and smiled and waved some more. "Do you think real royalty does arm-strengthening exercises so they don't get tennis elbow?"

Annie smiled regally at him but didn't answer, just went right into the method: elbow, elbow, wrist, wrist, wipe a tear, blow a kiss.

"Superb, my lady," he said in a British-accented voice. "Surely you are of royal blood."

"You may kiss my hand."

Nick brought the back of her hand to his lips and nearby parade-goers clapped and whistled. He grinned and began to kiss his way up her bare arm.

"Stop it!" With a laugh, she pulled her hand away from him. "Get back to work!"

"I rather liked the coffee break," he said. He began to wave again, his gaze sweeping absently over the spectators, not really focusing on anyone until he spotted Vivian, deep in conversation with—oh, no—Mr. Lewis.

Nick elbowed Annie. "Check it out. Ten o'clock."

As if she could hear him, Vivian turned slightly and, still talking, gestured directly at Nick and Annie.

"Oh, my gosh, they're talking about us," Annie said between clenched teeth and smiling lips.

Nick broadened his smile and waved directly at Vivian and Mr. Lewis. "Maybe he's just making small talk."

"He's getting a bit too cozy around town for me."

"Uh-huh. Let's hope he shows up at the festival and we can find out what this guy's all about."

THE PARADE ENDED HALF an hour later and everyone went into the community center for the festival. Nick headed off to judge flower arrangements and Annie reported to the kitchen for appetizer duty. A short while later, a tray of mini quiches in hand, she made her way through the large crowded hall, stopping to offer hors d'oeuvres to nearly everyone she passed. She spotted Mr. Lewis wandering among the flower arrangements. At least he wasn't talking to anyone...yet.

Where the heck was Minnow? She needed reinforcements. With this crowd, and Nick tied up judging flowers, there was no way she'd be able to keep an eye on Lewis by herself. Maybe she should offer him an appetizer. Maybe he'd choke on it and have to leave the party. Hmm, now there was a promising thought.

She scanned the gathering again and spied Minnow slipping in the front door. Relief washed through her. She pushed her way across the room, apologizing profusely to each person she bumped, but determined not to waste a moment. Grabbing Minnow by the elbow, she dragged her off to a corner for a strategy meeting.

"Where have you been?" Annie shifted the tray of appetizers to her other hand.

"Emergency. Some kid tried to dye her own hair and it turned orange. Why? What's going on?" Minnow grabbed one of the mini quiches off the tray and popped it into her mouth. She nodded at Annie. "Nice hair."

"That's what Nick said—"

"He noticed? Aha! He's hooked. All we need to do is reel him in."

Annie rolled her eyes. "It's hard not to notice when someone's hair is substantially shorter and blonder than it was two hours earlier. Especially when it's no longer in a ponytail."

"Hummph. Maybe. Still, you look really hip. You must have a great hairdresser."

"I do. Thanks. Now, listen, we saw—"

"Nice dress, too. Ooh-la-la. I didn't even know you owned a black sheath. What did Nick have to say about that?"

Annie huffed. "He said, Baby, I want to tear that thing off you and make passionate love to you all night long. Now, Minnow, be quiet a minute so I can tell—"

Minnow choked on her appetizer. "Oh, my God! He did?"

"Get real. He said, as he was putting on the sport coat Luella borrowed from her grandson, 'I can't believe people get this dressed up to buy flower arrangements.'"

"Oh." Minnow took a second hors d'oeuvre. "Well, if you ask me—if he noticed your hair, he noticed your dress. He's just trying to play it cool, that's all."

"Whatever! Can we drop that subject for one minute? I think we've got a real problem with Mr. Lewis. And if we don't take care of it, we won't have to worry about whether Nick thinks I look hot or not."

Minnow shopped chewing and swallowed. "What's he done now?"

"He was chatting up a storm with Vivian during the

parade. Like old friends. He's up to something and tonight we'd better get a clue about what it is."

"Is he here yet?"

Annie tilted her head to the right. Her crown started
to slip and she reached up to push it back into place.
"Near the bar. See him?"

"Yup. You know, just looking at him, he's suspicious. Think how weird it is that he's at this party.
Would you go to a party at some town you were just
visiting? I don't think so."

"He's obviously trying to get information about
something."

"Yeah." Minnow narrowed her eyes. "I'm gonna talk
to him."

"Be careful. If he figures out we're onto him he
might split town."

"You don't have to worry about *this* undercover
agent. Small talk is my secret weapon. I'll start out
with the weather and end up with what he does for a
living."

Annie gave a thought to Minnow's undercover act
at dinner the night they'd discovered Mr. Lewis was a
guest at the B & B. "If you think you can pull it off,"
she said dubiously. "But—" She spotted Vivian heading toward them. "Oh-oh. The slave driver's seen us. Vivian's been going crazy waiting for you so she can give
out the last work assignment. I'm getting out of here.
If you need me, I'll be mingling near our prey."

Holding the tray in front of her, she moved back into
the party, passing out hors d'oeuvres and greeting people as she worked her way toward Mr. Lewis. The man

was not going to have free rein here tonight—not if she could help it. She watched him stroll between the tables of flower arrangements, hands clasped behind his back, pausing every now and then as if taken by the aesthetic beauty of a specific arrangement.

Clearly a ploy. Well, he wasn't fooling her. Time to take matters into her own hands.

She stepped to his side, stomach slightly queasy with nerves. "Appetizer?"

"Thank you." He accepted the napkin she offered, then took one of the tiny quiches from her tray.

"Are you enjoying your stay in Bedford?" She hoped her voice didn't betray her by quivering.

"Very much. I love small towns."

"I take it you must be from a big town?" She grinned and held her breath.

"Milwaukee."

Aha. "Biggest town in the state. How'd you find your way to our little B & B?"

He frowned and she cringed inside, panicked that she was being too obvious. "I'm asking because we want to be sure to continue advertising wherever it works," she said in a rush.

"You're on the Wisconsin Bed-and-Breakfast Association Web site." He smiled.

"Of course. Well, we're glad to have you. And it's nice you've come to the festival. We don't get many out-of-towners."

"Vivian invited me this morning. She's been a fount of information about your town history. I understand she's on the board for your new museum."

Annie laughed lightly, as though the two were sharing a private joke. "Yes, she is. She's served on just about every board in town at one time or another. Lived here her whole life." She swallowed and pushed herself forward. "I take it you're doing some sort of research?"

"In a sense. Yes, I suppose you could say I am."

Annie's heart hammered so loudly in her ears she was afraid she wouldn't be able to hear his answer. She tightened her grip on the tray and forced her expression to remain calm. "I love research. What are you looking into?"

He smiled apologetically. "I really am not at liberty to discuss it. I'm sorry."

A wave of disappointment rolled through her. "I understand. My husband has the same situation…with his job."

She glanced at Nick, deep in thought as he contemplated the beauty of the particular flower arrangement he was judging. Wistfulness stabbed at her, a longing for him to love her, for their marriage to be real.

"I understand he's with the military."

Her heart seemed to slow. "Yes. Yes, he is."

"It must be hard for the two of you, with him gone so much of the time."

She nodded. My gosh, the tables had turned. Mr. Lewis was quizzing *her* now. If she wasn't careful, she'd end up helping him destroy her life.

"It is, but we manage. Love is a powerful cement." She took a step back and smiled brightly. "I'd better get back to work. Gotta get a fresh tray of appetizers before Vivian catches me loitering!"

She set off for the kitchen nursing her disappointment. Hopefully, Minnow and Nick would have better luck uncovering Mr. Lewis's motives.

CHAPTER TEN

CLIPBOARD IN HAND, Nick paused in front of a large flower arrangement and pondered its lines. He glanced at question three on the score sheet again. *Is there a pleasing ratio of large to small flowers?*

Hardly.

Some were big, some were medium, some were small. There didn't seem to be any rhyme or reason to the arrangement. But then, what did he know?

It was easy, they'd told him. All he had to do was give it a score—one through five, with five being the best. He scowled. This arrangement didn't really seem like a five or four…maybe not even a three. But a two? That seemed harsh; he didn't want to hurt someone's feelings.

What was wrong with him?

He scratched a two in the space and glanced wistfully back at question one. That question hadn't been so hard. *Are the flowers fresh, with no signs of dried edges?*

And then there had been question two: *Do the colors complement one another?* That had been pretty easy, too.

But there were six questions total and he was finding each more difficult than the last.

Not to mention it didn't help that the women who just "happened" to pass by were singing the praises of one or another centerpiece—generally their own. He looked at question four. *How well does the grouping of flowers draw the eye into the arrangement?*

How did he know?

He glanced around, hoping to find one of the other judges just as puzzled as he, but they were all intently scribbling on their score sheets, or staring, rapt, at whatever arrangement they happened to be judging.

A couple of attendees passed by, sipping glasses of wine while they discussed bidding in the silent auction on one of the flower arrangements. He nodded and moved out of their way. The *hideous* arrangement he was judging had already been bid up to forty-three dollars. Maybe the bidders knew something he didn't. He erased the two and wrote in a three.

Now where was he? Oh, yeah. *How well does the grouping of flowers draw the eye into the arrangement?*

About the only thing that would draw his eye into this arrangement was a bottle of beer stuck in the middle of it. He held in a laugh. Speaking of liquor, maybe that would help his judging skills.

And speaking of judging skills, where was Annie, his princess? Maybe she could lend him a hand with judging. He searched the crowd, finally spotting her near the bar, crown sparkling, a tray of hors d'oeuvres in one hand and a glass of soda in the other.

He turned the score sheet facedown on his clipboard and headed toward her. Vivian slid into his path.

"Oh, Nick, what a surprise," she said with a slow

smile. "How is the judging going? There are so many lovely arrangements, aren't there?"

He nodded.

Vivian touched his arm. "My own entry is a tasteful arrangement of yellows, golds and oranges, with some purple-blues thrown in for heightened contrast. Have you had a chance to see it yet?"

"No, but I'll be sure to look for it." He gave her his most charming smile. Vivian had just presented him with the perfect opportunity for information gathering. "Was that Mr. Lewis I saw you talking to at the parade? He's a guest at the B & B."

"Oh, yes, a very nice man. I combined mums with daffodils and daisies—all varying shades of yellow."

"Hmm." Nick nodded as though interested. "I imagine he's enjoying his stay?"

"Who?"

"Mr. Lewis, the man you were talking to at the parade."

"Oh...yes, I imagine he is. I invited him to the festival and it's so nice to see he was able to make it. He's very impressed with Bedford, you know. At any rate, my entry has a gold vase—"

"Did he say anything about Annie?"

"Just what an attractive couple the two of you make. It's on table four—"

"What is?"

"*My arrangement.* Nick, are we going to talk about Mr. Lewis or my entry?"

"Your entry, of course. I've just been wondering whether or not Mr. Lewis is happy with the accommodations. Our goal is to please, you know."

She waved a dismissive hand at him. "You needn't worry that he is unhappy with the B & B—he didn't so much as say a word about it. He was actually asking about Bedford—tourist things. The only thing he asked about you and Annie was how long you'd lived here, how long you'd had the B & B."

He wanted to know how long they'd lived here? Why did the guy care? Something was definitely fishy under the dock.

"That's it?"

Vivian nodded.

"Thanks." He tried to move past her.

She stepped to counter his escape. "It's a low gold vase. Number thirty-two."

He nodded.

"Bidding's already up to sixty-seven dollars, so it's doing quite well."

"You must be proud." He stepped to the left and she countered again. She slid her hand into the crook of his arm and began to pull him toward table four.

"Ah, I was just going, ah—"

"The thing of it is what with all your expertise in horticulture, I'm wondering if you might be able to stop by my house some afternoon and…give me some advice about my…hydrangeas. They just aren't blooming well this year."

They stopped in front of the table where her arrangement was displayed. She rubbed a hand along his forearm. "And I don't know exactly what to do to help them."

"Have you tried fertilizer?" he asked.

"Yes. But I've begun to think they need your magic touch. Annie seems to have blossomed since you arrived—I mean the flowers in her beds have. And, well, speaking of beds..." She smiled coyly.

No way. Was Vivian coming on to him? This woman wanted to win the contest—and nothing was going to stand in her way.

Looking for help, he glanced over at Annie. Her back was turned to him and she was engaged in an animated conversation with a small group of people he didn't know. He willed her to turn around and was disappointed when his desperate attempt at telepathy failed. Discouraged, he brought his attention back to Vivian.

"Ah, have you tried beer?" he asked.

"But—I don't have slugs."

Oh, was that what it was for? "I use it as a multipurpose cure-all with my plants," he lied. "Just sprinkle a bit over the leaves. You'd be amazed at the difference it makes. Kind of like with people—it relaxes them, helps them overcome their daily stressors."

Vivian had a look of awed horror on her face.

"In fact," he continued, "that's exactly what I was planning to do when I ran into you—get a beer." He squeezed past her, talking the whole time so she couldn't get another word in.

"As for your arrangement, I'm sure it will do well, as there are so many lovely arrangements. Why, I haven't seen so many stunning warts of ark...ah, works of art...since the last— Oh, there's Annie. I'm sure you won't mind—if you will excuse me, please."

Annie had finally turned in his direction—better late than never—and the grin that lit up her face seemed like a beacon calling him home. She raised her glass in a gentle toast and he was half tempted to take her in his arms and kiss her the moment he reached her side.

Instead, he whispered into her ear, "Saw you talking to our boy."

She set the tray on the bar and her smile faded. "He's doing some sort of research but won't say what it is. It's up to you—I don't think I should try to talk with him again. He'll get suspicious."

"I got some info from Vivian—what he was talking to her about at the parade. He was mostly asking about Bedford."

"Mostly?"

"He also asked how long we've lived here and owned the B & B."

Annie closed her eyes for a long moment.

Nick reached a hand up to gently massage the back of her neck. "Now don't panic. It's just small talk. I'll bet he's researching property to develop."

"Just as long as he's not researching people...and marriages." Annie took a swallow of soda.

"Yeah. This feels like a never-ending game of twenty questions. God, I hope we're all wrong about this. Because if any one of our theories is right, pulling this off will be a miracle."

"What'll be a miracle?"

Nick jerked at the sound of Father Thespesius's voice from behind them. *The miracle would be if Nick survived tonight.*

Annie's eyes widened and she exchanged a panicked look with Nick before he turned to shake hands with the priest.

"What's this about a miracle? You know we priests are always on the lookout for such things."

Nick's brain raced for an answer. "I, ah, Annie was just wishing I could stay in Bedford a little longer, and I said that if the military gave me any more leave right now it would be a miracle."

He put his arm around her shoulders. She rubbed his back affectionately and he pressed a kiss to her forehead. With any luck, the priest would fall for the whole thing.

Father Thespesius shook his head. "I'd sure like to see you stick around, too."

Nick nodded. "Wish I could. But duty calls. Join us for a glass of wine, Father?"

"Don't mind if I do."

Nick held up two fingers to the bartender. "Then I'd better get back to judging. Annie, sweetie, would you like to follow along as I judge? I think I could use another opinion."

She reached up to pat him on the chest. "Vivian would kill me. I'm assigned to pass out appetizers, and pass out appetizers I must. If you get too desperate, come and find me."

Nick took the two glasses of wine from the bartender and handed one to the priest.

"I'll walk with you," Father Thespesius said. "I may not have your floral expertise, but I know a little something about flowers."

"Thanks." Any input was better than none at all. He

just hoped the priest kept his comments confined to floral arrangements and stayed off marriage.

By the time an hour had passed, the two of them had consumed nearly three glasses of wine each and the judging was getting easier by the minute. What had he been so worried about when he started this job? There was nothing to this judging thing.

Nick squinted at the next arrangement. "Check out this one. What the heck do you think this is about?"

Father Thespesius read the title. "Lady in Lavender. Hmm." He tapped a finger on his lips. "Perhaps *Elephant in Lavender* would be more appropriate."

Nick snorted, then started to laugh. "Or Whale in Lavender."

"How about Dinosaur in Lavender?" Father Thespesius said between guffaws.

"Dinosaur with Twins in Lavender," Nick choked out as he pointed to some pink flowers on one side of the arrangement.

By then, the two of them were laughing so hard, tears streamed from their eyes and Nick had to hold on to the table for support.

"I hope the woman who did this one isn't watching us," he said between gasps.

"She's not. This one's mine."

Nick sobered instantly. "You did this? Seriously?"

The priest nodded, blue eyes twinkling.

Nick tried to hold in his laughter, really tried, but it burst out of him like the air from a balloon at the same moment a great guffaw of laughter exploded from Father Thespesius.

"Father, at least you'll get a five for effort." Nick marked a row of scores on the sheet. "We're done, let's go turn these pages in—"

"And have a glass of wine to celebrate."

Nick clapped him on the back as they walked toward the bar. "A man after my own heart. You know, for a priest, you're an all-right guy."

"I take that as a compliment."

"Yeah. I didn't think I'd like it in Bedford. Thought I'd hate it, in fact. Even Minnow isn't really that bad once you get to know her." As he said the words he realized he was actually beginning to like Minnow. "And Annie—she's changed, too—"

"You like her this way?"

Nick nodded. "This little town's been good for her."

He looked across the room and his eyes settled on Annie as she flitted her way along the far side of the community center. "What a change in six years. I should have known she'd turn out special."

"Six years?"

Nick looked up. Shit. What was that old phrase? Loose lips sink ships? "Months. I mean months. I know she's been happy here—especially the past six months." *Not a bad save.* "It's a great town. Good people. The kind of place you want to stay—" He broke off and gave his head a shake to clear his thoughts.

"The kind of place you can settle down in?" The priest smiled.

Nick looked at him and felt the room sway just a bit. *Right.* "No. I—I can't."

An expression of dismay settled on Father Thespesius's face. Nick could see genuine sadness in his eyes.

"My job is pretty important…to our country." He felt a flush of guilt for lying to a priest. "Father, I—all I can say is, everything isn't exactly as it seems."

The priest sighed. "I was afraid of that. Try to remember that every marriage has its ups and downs. Is there anything I can do to help?"

Nick shook his head. This was getting even worse. Now Father Thespesius thought they had marital problems. He looked at Annie again. She was deep in conversation, her lips curved up in a soft smile.

He supposed it would be all right for people to think they were having marital problems. It sort of fit with Annie's plans. At least it would make it easer for Annie when she finally announced their divorce.

Father Thespesius cleared his throat. "I think I'll take a pass on the wine and walk through to look at the bids." He took Nick by the elbow for moment and said, "Remember, those things hardest won are often the most appreciated."

Nick watched him walk away. He had a sneaking suspicion Father Thespesius had already figured out that there was more to his and Annie's marriage than met the eye. Even so, he felt certain the priest wouldn't speak of it unless Nick or Annie raised the issue. He brought his gaze to rest on Annie again as she laughed and smiled with friends.

Five more days and he wouldn't be looking at her again—probably not for the rest of his life. Something stirred within him, a memory of what it felt like when

Annie left town a week after their wedding. A hollow feeling. *Loss.*

He wasn't leaving for five days and he was missing Annie already.

A shrink would have a field day with this. Nick had money, the job he'd always dreamed of and a gorgeous fiancée—whom he was about to dump. And yet, in the midst of all that, here he was, attracted to, and missing, a woman he hadn't left yet.

Maybe this was human nature.

Maybe.

And maybe it was fate.

MINNOW SIDLED UP NEXT to Annie and nudged her in the side. "He's gone."

"Who?"

"Mr. Lewis. I tailed him all the way back to your house."

"You did? Did he see you?"

"Maybe. But he had no reason to think I was doing anything other than taking a walk."

"Probably went home to report in to mission control. He told me he's doing research—proprietary research."

Minnow's eyes widened. "Ooh. I'm dying to know what this guy's up to. We should search his room, Annie."

She rolled her eyes. "No way. That's all I'd need. An arrest for digging in the guy's luggage."

"Annie!"

She turned to find Vivian right at her elbow, holding the purple velvet capes across her arms.

"It's time for the toast. Where's Nick?"

Annie took her cape and swung it over her shoulders as Vivian pushed up on tiptoes and tried to see over everyone's heads.

"This is terrible. The band is ready to get started. Where is— Oh, there he is! Nick!"

She grabbed Annie by the arm and began to pull her through the crowd. Annie threw Minnow a look of long-suffering mock exasperation. "Duty calls. Talk to you later."

Minnow waved her away.

The moment they reached Nick, Vivian began firing statements at him in machine-gun staccato.

"We're ready to begin. Here's your cape. Get dressed. The band's waiting. Is your toast prepared?"

He looked at Annie. "I, ah, yeah. I memorized it." He hooked the cloak at his neck.

Annie swallowed a smile. This would be good. She knew he hadn't prepared so much as a sentence.

"Come along, then. We've got a schedule to keep."

Vivian lead the way across the wood dance floor to one of the standing microphones in front of the band. She tapped on the microphone and then blew into it, sending a *pfft-pfft* sound through the room.

"Hello, hello. Welcome, everyone, to our thirty-third annual Flower Festival. Once again, we've had a wonderful success and I'm sure we'll raise a great deal of money for our new museum. The flower-arrangement silent auction ends at ten, so be sure to bid high and bid often. And don't miss that particularly stunning arrangement, number thirty-two on table four. In a gold vase."

She smiled over the crowd. "Now, I'm proud to introduce our Pansy Prince and Princess, Nick and Annie Fleming. Nick, will you do us the honor of a toast?"

He stepped to the microphone. "Thank you, Vivian, and thank you to everyone who voted for us. I, ah, feel a little awkward up here. Well, awkward and honored. I've only been in town for four days and already I'm the Pansy Prince."

A chuckle ran through the audience. Nick looked at the floor a moment, then raised his gaze again.

"I have to tell you, all of you, you sure know how to make a guy feel welcome. I've been all over the world, and this is the first time in my life I really feel like I've come home."

He reached out and took Annie's hand in his. A knot formed in her throat. With his other hand, he lifted his wineglass high. "So let's do a little drinking and a little dancing, and raise some big money for the museum tonight."

A roar went up and the band swung into a rousing rendition of "Hail, Hail the Gang's All Here." Nick's thumb caressed the back of her hand, and Annie looked up into his dark eyes.

"I thought you didn't prepare."

"I didn't. That just came out."

She had to hold herself back from reaching up and taking his face between her hands and kissing him, from begging him to stay and give them a chance. From the corner of her eye she could see Vivian striding toward them, arms swinging, her mouth speaking words at them that were unintelligible until she was nearly upon them.

"No time for lingering. Royalty! Quickly. The line is already forming."

"What line?" Nick asked.

Annie grimaced. "You know how you and I are doing the first dance of the evening? Well, beforehand, there's a grand march."

Nick snapped to attention so fast his crown almost flew off. "A what?"

"Yes." Vivian nodded. "With all the past Pansy royalty."

Annie reached up to straighten his crown and brush her fingers through the black waves of his hair. "It'll all be over soon," she said in her most soothing voice.

"It better be. I feel like I'm in high school again. Aren't these people a little old for this kind of stuff?"

"Hurry, the music is about to begin." Vivian pushed them past a long row of previous royalty to the head of the line. "Twice around the dance floor, then stop in front of the band. Annie, put your arm through Nick's. Don't forget to smile."

The band struck up the music. Smiling, they paraded around the perimeter of the dance floor while the rest of the party-goers watched and clapped.

"Sweetheart, I think you're really gonna owe me when these nine days are over," Nick said through his smile.

"More than you bargained for, huh?"

"I pictured a week and a half of swimming and sunning. A vacation in Wisconsin's Northwoods."

Annie laughed. "Real life is so much more stimulating. Why vacation when you can be part of all this?"

"Yeah…this is right up there with climbing the Matterhorn."

She looked at him, ready to shoot back a witty retort, but the smoldering expression in his eyes stalled her response. Her breath caught.

"By the way, you look incredible tonight," he said. "Royalty becomes you."

Annie stared up at him, at a total loss for words; the only thought in her head was that she hoped her lack of response made her look mysterious and not idiotic. Could Minnow be right? Could Nick be interested, after all? And what if he was? Was it real or was it just a lust thing, an interlude before he went back to Melissa?

This was the man, after all, who had told her years ago he never wanted to get married. For him to have gotten engaged meant Melissa had to be something special. Would he really throw her over for Annie? The coffee shop waitress turned bed-and-breakfast owner-maid?

Or was she about to play the fool as she had so many other times in her life? As tempting as he was, she had to keep a grip on her emotions, on her responses to him. Unless he declared his undying love on bended knee, she had to guard her heart. This time, she wasn't getting caught short.

"Penny for your thoughts."

She started. No way was she sharing the truth. "Oh, just thinking about Mr. Lewis. Minnow said he went home. She followed him to make sure."

He nodded. "Quit worrying. There's only so much any of us can control. You've got a good life, Annie, and good friends. I really can't believe that whatever he's after will destroy that. Even if it is about you and me."

"I hope you're right."

"Know what you need? You need to leave this place and your worries behind for a few hours."

She laughed. "I'm not so sure a few hours would be long enough."

"It's a start."

"Any brilliant ideas?"

"Yeah. Tomorrow's canoe trip. Let's make it more than just a little trip. We'll pack a lunch and really get away."

"It sounds so tempting."

"All you have to do is say yes. I can take you places that'll change your life."

If he only knew.

"Trust me."

She looked at him. "Okay. You're on."

They halted at the stage and Vivian whispered, "You two dance now—alone."

Nick took Annie's hand and led her onto the floor. The band slid into the soft soothing melody of "Moon River," and Annie let herself sink into Nick's arms, up against his strong chest, her cheek to his. She closed her eyes and let the music fill her, the words seeming so much like both of their lives.

Nick nuzzled her neck and kissed her by the ear so softly it sent a tremor through her insides. She opened her eyes and raised her head to look up at him.

"You're something else, you know that?" His eyes seemed to darken and she felt her body respond. This wasn't what was supposed to happen. She was keeping her distance from him, remember?

"I am?"

"Uh-huh." His head dipped toward hers and he brushed her lips ever so gently with his own before pulling back to look at her again.

The music played.

"Wh-what are you doing?" she asked. This had to stop. She couldn't deal with it anymore.

"I'm kissing my wife."

"Why?"

"So everyone in town will know how much I'll miss her when I'm gone. We've got a job to do, Annie McCarthy," he said in a low voice.

His mouth came down on hers again and his lips lingered a moment before he brought one hand up to hold her head close to his chest, so close she could hear the beat of his heart.

She would remember this moment the rest of her life. And she would not forget again that *they had a job to do.*

Then the music changed and the moment was shattered and they pulled apart. And Nick grinned at her, a wide grin that indicated they had just pulled off the biggest scam in history. And she smiled back at him in just the same way because, after all, she had to keep him from ever knowing how hard she had fallen for him.

AT TWO-THIRTY IN THE MORNING Nick sat on the steps of the back porch and stared at his cell phone, stunned. As the night had drawn on, he'd found himself agonizing over how to call off his engagement to Melissa, what words to use that would cause the least amount of pain. He'd thought she might cry, might even get hysterical. What he hadn't been prepared for was the response he got.

Disappointment. *Melissa had sounded disappointed.* Resigned. Like she'd just gotten bad news that she'd already known was coming. Her voice had quivered just once, when she asked if he'd met someone else. He'd been quick to answer *no.* And then she said, "I really tried to like the outdoors, Nick. For you. But I think the only time I'll ever sleep in a tent again is if it's set up on a king-size bed in a hotel room. This is probably for the best." Then she'd wished him well and they'd ended the call.

Wow. He didn't love her. And she didn't love him.

He bent forward to rest his elbows on his knees. The moon, full and round, cast a silvery fairylike glow on the yard, and he felt as if he were in some surreal place. He should have known. Long fingernails and mountain climbing did not a pair make.

He supposed he should be happy he hadn't devastated her, supposed he should be devastated that she hadn't loved him after all, but all he could feel was relief that he hadn't married the wrong woman.

CHAPTER ELEVEN

ANNIE LOOKED IN TREPIDATION at the sleek silver canoe glinting in a ray of sunshine at the river's edge. "I still can't believe you actually bought a canoe. Isn't that a little extravagant for a one-day excursion?"

Nick set two paddles into the boat. He handed her a bright yellow life jacket and slipped into an identical one as he spoke. "The fact that you can't rent one around here bodes well for your business."

Why did he care so much? As if she was really going to start offering canoe trips. She glanced back down the narrow path that they had just followed to the river. "How'd you get it in here?"

"Paid two high school kids from the hardware store." He set their cooler in the canoe, then grabbed hold of one end and shoved the canoe partway into the water. "Okay. Get in from the center," he said, still holding on. "Take the seat in the middle. Keep your weight low."

Annie didn't move. "Do we have to paddle upstream to get home?" she asked, stalling.

Nick laughed. "Luella's going to meet us downriver at one-thirty. We'll just pop the canoe on top of my car and drive home. Come on, get in."

"I'm going." She tossed her sweatshirt into the bottom of the canoe, then hesitated a moment before climbing in after it. The canoe tilted a bit to one side and her heart skipped a beat. She tried to counter the slight lean and ended up dropping down onto the seat with an ungraceful plop.

Sacagawea she wasn't.

Sheepishly, she glanced back at Nick and was grateful to see he didn't seem to have taken notice of her clumsiness.

"We're off." Nick pushed the canoe into the water and deftly jumped aboard, taking several quick strokes of the paddle on one side to straighten them out and head them downstream. "Now for a quick lesson."

Twenty minutes later, Annie felt like a pro. Well, maybe not a pro, but certainly levels above novice. She had to hand it to Nick, he was a natural teacher, had a real knack for instilling confidence. Too bad he wouldn't be around longer—he would be the perfect person to run canoe trips for her B & B guests.

She gave herself a mental shake. Jeez, now she was buying into his idea. She forced her attention onto the scenery around her and marveled over how the canoe slid through the water, like a knife cutting soft butter, with hardly a sound or a ripple to mark its passing. A blue crane standing along the shore turned its head to watch them slip past. Overhead, high in the trees that lined both sides of the river, birds called and twittered to one another, unfazed by the boat gliding beneath them.

"I feel like I've gone back in time," Annie said in a hushed voice. "To the days of Lewis and Clark. What a country this must have been back then."

"Yeah. Gives you an appreciation for what we have."

They continued on for an hour, speaking a little but most of the time simply paddling. At times the water flowed faster and the ride became more exciting and Annie's adrenaline kicked in.

After a while, serenity eased its way through her and she marveled over it. Mr. Lewis, and what he was up to, no longer seemed so ominous. It was as if all the pieces of her life had suddenly fallen into the proper perspective—at least for the moment.

"I'm starting to see why you became an adventure writer. There's something really soothing about this, being out here, alone with nature." She glanced over her shoulder at him as she spoke.

"Now you're getting it. Way too many people try to escape their stress, soothe their spirits with booze and drugs. After living in L.A., I discovered this was a much better kick."

"And no hangover."

He laughed. "I'll warn you, though, it almost gets addictive. Fun, relaxing, exciting, all at once."

"Does it ever get old? When you're so far from home, in foreign jungles and on other country's mountains? Does it ever feel like *work* to you?"

Her questions hung in the air between them for a long moment.

"Does it ever get old? Or feel like work?" he repeated. "Sure. But it's my job—jobs are supposed to feel like work. I'm luckier than most people—my work is fun most of the time."

He didn't say anything more for a long while and

Annie began to think she'd irritated him, though she had no idea why. She struggled with how to bring the conversation back to the light-and-easy note where it had been.

"Hey, Nick…I didn't mean to pry. Forget I asked about it." She gazed up into the canopy of trees, the green leaves dappled with sunlight dancing in the breeze above them as they slid by.

"No, no—I didn't feel like you were prying. Just made me kind of think about things in a different way. When I left L.A., right after our wedding, I gave up my apartment. Went straight from one adventure to another all these years. Whenever I've had a few weeks between assignments, which wasn't too often, I stayed with friends—or my folks—or in hotels."

"Nothing wrong with that."

"But it wasn't home. And that was okay, actually. I liked the freedom I had. That's what I'd been striving for—complete freedom to go wherever I wanted to go, do whatever I wanted to do. And I found it."

Annie thought back over the past six years and smiled sadly to herself. He'd been looking for freedom and she'd been looking for a place to settle down. They couldn't be more opposite.

"Will Melissa travel with you once you're married?"

"Uh—"

"Haven't you talked about it?"

"Sure. Oh, yeah. It's just—well—she's got modeling to do…and, well… Annie, there's not going to be a marriage."

"Oh." *Oh?* She whipped her head around to look

back at him. "When did this happen?" she asked with feigned calmness.

"This morning. Two o'clock. I called it off."

Annie's heart pounded. She couldn't think of one single word to say other than *yippee!* and somehow she didn't think that was appropriate.

"Anyway, it's over. Guess I'm back to the life of a wandering adventurer."

She stared straight ahead and nodded, wanting to know more and afraid to ask. She had no right to push him for details. He'd tell her more when he was ready. She only wished he was ready right now. An awkward silence settled over them.

"You having a good time?" he finally asked.

"Yeah. This is really fun."

"Good. Now, think about all those people in Milwaukee and Chicago racing to work everyday. Parking downtown and walking busy city blocks to the office. Breathing in diesel fumes and smoggy air. Working late hours and getting home after dark. Got that pictured?"

"Uh-huh." What was he getting at?

"What do you think they would pay to get away to a place that soothes their stresses while they connect with Mother Nature? What would it be worth to them to go back to the simplicity of Lewis and Clark days if only for a weekend?"

"You should be in sales." This idea of his really did make sense for her business. Which was too bad. Because there was no way she could pull it off—not without any personal experience canoeing or hiking or

doing all those other things he had done. But maybe…
It might be worth looking into hiring someone, a part-
time person to be her adventure coordinator.

She glanced back at Nick to thank him for forcing
her to come along today, for giving her hands-on proof
that his ideas just might work. He was in the middle of
stripping off his T-shirt and the sight made her words
lodge in her throat.

Good Lord!

She whipped her head forward again. Focus. She
needed to focus. What was it she had told herself to
remember?

Fiancée. Melissa. Engaged to be married.

Well, that sure wasn't going to work anymore. She
wiped a hand across her brow. She was in real trouble
now.

"You wanna drive?" Nick's voice jolted her out of
her self-induced insanity.

"What? You mean like switch places with you?" She
didn't dare look back. "Isn't that kind of dangerous?"

"Not if you're careful."

"I don't think so."

"Put your paddle into the canoe and crouch down.
I'll just climb over you."

No way. She turned, determined to stop this non-
sense. "I don't think—"

He had already set his paddle on the floor of the
canoe. He looked at her and grinned.

"Get low. Here I come." He moved into a high
crouch, holding on to the gunwale on each side of the
canoe.

Annie hunched over. "Is this low enough?"

"Great." Seconds later, he'd finished his part of the maneuver and was squatting down in the canoe in front of her, his broad, bare shoulders a mere foot away. Thank goodness he'd at least put his life jacket back on.

"All you have to do is step backward over your seat," he said. "Hold on to the sides."

She made a face at his back. *Ten minutes ago she had found serenity and already she'd lost it.*

She took hold of the sides of the canoe and stepped back over her seat. This wasn't so hard. Another step or two and she'd be settled and ready to drive. A new-found confidence filled her. She slid her foot toward the rear and set it down, stepping awkwardly on the handle of the paddle. With a bit of a hop, she moved her foot. The canoe heeled sharply to the left.

Panic filled her and she threw her weight to the right to counterbalance the roll. The canoe rocked with her.

"Annie!"

Even before Nick's shout, she knew it was too late. The right side of the canoe slid under the surface, and she landed in the cool water with a splash, managing to grab a bite of air before her head went under. She had a feeling Nick wasn't going to be happy about this.

She popped to the surface and spotted him just a few feet away, treading water. "Sorry." She looked at the canoe, upside down in the river, and winced.

"You okay?" He swam to her.

She nodded, glad he'd made her wear a life jacket. "I'm really sorry."

"Don't worry about it. Happens to everyone. As

good a time as any for a lesson in what to do when the canoe tips."

He looked around. "You grab the paddles before we lose 'em. I'll get our lunch." He began to swim away from her toward the cooler, bobbing like a red-and-white buoy on the sea.

She took hold of one paddle and swam around the canoe looking for the other. Nick shoved the cooler toward her.

"I can't find the other paddle," she said. "Could it be under the boat?"

"Maybe." He rolled the canoe over so that it floated upright even though it was full of water. The gunwales were just a couple of inches above water level.

Stroking overhand, she worked her way around the boat again, meeting Nick on the other side. Still no paddle. "How could we lose a paddle?"

Nick looked downstream. "I didn't think the water was moving *that* fast. No big deal. We can still get home."

He grabbed hold of a line hanging from the front of the canoe and began to swim toward shore. "Let's get out of the water and regroup."

They pulled the canoe up on the riverbank and flipped it over to empty out the water. In the coolness of the shade, goose bumps rose on Annie's arms and she shivered. Nick pointed to a bright area through the trees. "Looks like some open space through there. You can warm up in the sun awhile before we get going again."

After a few minutes of picking their way through the

underbrush, they broke out into a sun-drenched meadow filled with tall grass and scattered wildflowers. Teal-blue dragonflies danced in the air.

"Wow. This still your land?" Nick gazed around him in appreciation.

"I don't think so. But, then, I don't know exactly where we are right now."

"You could cut a deal with the landowner. Have your canoe trips stop here so the people can take a break, hike around, have lunch. Annie—"

"I know, I know, I'm sitting on a gold mine."

He grinned. "At least you're getting into the right frame of mind."

He began walking in a circle, stomping down the tall grass. "Help me make a place for us to sit down, will you?"

Annie followed his lead, pushing down the grass with her feet until they had made an area large enough for the two of them and then some.

"Good thing I tied my shirt to the thwart or I might have lost it." Nick set the cooler down, then lay his wet T-shirt and their life jackets across the top of the grass to dry.

Good thing. Because if he was going to spend the rest of their trip naked from the waist up, she was going to have to hike back to town.

"My sweatshirt must have sunk. I'm glad I wore a tank suit." Annie stripped out of her shorts and lay them beside his shirt.

She sat on the cooler and shivered again, this time because of the sun's warmth instead of the cool water. Or was it from the nearness of Nick? *Oh, please. What*

was wrong with her that she had to dwell on the why?
Her mind had gone positively obsessive lately. She bent
to untie her wet sneakers.

"Hey, don't take off your shoes—let's go explore a
little. I promise we'll stay in the sun." He took her hand
and pulled her to her feet.

As they walked, Annie looked down into the long
grass. "Don't you worry about what's down there? Like
snakes or spiders or something ready to bite you?"

"Your feet are safe in shoes. Besides, to those little
guys in the grass, we're giant monsters coming after
them. Their first reaction is going to be flight."

Annie gave him a dubious look.

He led the way across the meadow, stopping to ex-
amine one plant or another, pointing out and naming
various types of butterflies that flitted about. Annie
marveled at the breadth of his knowledge.

"Take a look at all these milkweed plants. This is
probably a haven for monarchs." He stared down at the
patch of plants for a long moment before speaking
again.

"We lived in a subdivision outside Chicago, with lots
of woods and fields all around. When I was ten I
brought home a bunch of milkweed plants with
monarch caterpillars on them. Stuck 'em in the ground
by my front porch and watched them every day. Wasn't
long before each one had spun a chrysalis. You ever see
one?"

"Probably in a book."

"Pale green, almost iridescent. It's so incredible, it
makes you appreciate—respect—nature, what it has to

offer us. I watched those things and waited. You can't imagine what it's like to see a monarch butterfly work its way out of its chrysalis. From this tiny green case comes a beautiful, fragile butterfly that has the stamina to fly to Mexico in the fall." His eyes shone with the memory.

"How many did you have?"

"I don't know—ten, twelve, something like that. My grandma was visiting at one point and took one of my chrysalises home with her." His smile faded. "When she brought back the butterfly, it was dead, its wings permanently spread wide open, inside a big round paperweight. Some lady she knew made these things. I thought I was going to be sick."

In his story, Annie saw the boy who would become a man who reveled in nature. She reached out to touch his arm. "I'm sure she meant well."

"Oh, yeah, she did. Biggest heart in the world. She knew how much those butterflies meant to me and wanted me to be able to keep one forever. She died a couple years later. I'd take ten more of those stupid paperweights just to see her again." He shook his head. "Jeez, what am I doing? Getting maudlin when I'm supposed to be showing you how fun all this can be."

"I'm having fun." Her stomach grumbled as if to underscore her words. "Starving, but enjoying every minute of it."

"Luella's probably packed us a feast."

"Last one to the cooler is a rotten egg." She took off running across the field, laughing, no longer worried about critters deep in the grass.

They reached the clearing they had made and Annie dropped to her knees beside the cooler and opened the lid. "Look at this! Luella packed a picnic blanket."

She spread the large black-and-white-checkered cloth on the ground, then emptied the cooler of the rest of its contents—chicken sandwiches on homemade bread, a peach and a plum, a bag of cut carrots, string cheese, chocolate chip cookies and bottled water. "Dig in."

They didn't speak for several minutes while they wolfed down the sandwiches and carrots and string cheese.

Annie sighed. "I didn't know how hungry I was until I started to eat. You want the peach or the plum?"

"Peach."

She tossed it to him. "Ripe peaches to me have always been the taste of summer."

Nick took a bite and gave a groan of joy. "You pegged it." He swallowed. "Especially this one. Man, this baby is sweet." He held the peach out to her, juice running down the palm of his hand. "Try it."

Annie leaned forward and took a bite. The juice dribbled down her chin and he wiped it off with his thumb, rough against her skin—callused from hard work and adventure.

A tremor ripped through her insides. He licked his thumb and looked at her through darkened eyes. She could melt in those eyes. Uh-huh. She could melt in those eyes and slide all the way down that chest.

No fiancée. No Melissa. Not engaged to be married.

He leaned toward her again and she caught her breath. *I want this; I don't. I want this; I don't.* All she needed was a daisy with petals to pick and this idiocy would be complete. *I want this. I don't.*

All thoughts flew from her brain except the certain knowledge that he was going to kiss her and she was going to let him.

I want this.

She closed her eyes and waited. No kiss. She peeked through her lashes; his mouth was a mere inch from hers.

"Mr. Lewis is coming down the river," he said in a stage whisper.

She began to laugh and he captured her lips with his own, slid his mouth across hers with exquisite gentleness. She could taste the sweet peach juice that still remained on his lips, could smell the clean scent of soap on his skin. He pulled back and she reached for him, leaned into him, awash in the heady exhilaration of his kiss.

He took her face in his hands and kissed her harder, holding her head so she couldn't escape, and she wished it could go on forever. And she thought that maybe it might and she could die like this. Happy.

She could feel the heat of him, the heat of the sun on his back, and the fire beneath his skin. He pressed against her shoulder and rolled her down on the blanket underneath him, the hard length of him stretched out on top of her.

So this was Nick.

No one had ever felt like this before; *she* had never felt like this before. He trailed kisses over her eyes, her cheeks, her jaw, then took her mouth again while he slid a hand up her side, across the silky nylon of her tank suit, to cup her breast with only that very thin layer of material separating his hand from her skin. Fire shot through her and she thought she would explode.

She pressed up into him and raked her hands over his shoulders and down his bare back, trying to draw him closer, to feel all of him, as if she couldn't quite believe this was Nick and they were doing this.

She knew she should be thinking about the fact that he'd be leaving in a few days, that there was no way he'd leap from one relationship into another. She knew she should put a stop to this whole thing right now. But she couldn't do it. Theirs may not have been a true marriage, but it was a marriage. This was her husband. She had loved him when she married him and she would love him after he was gone. And she would have this one time with him to remember in years to come.

"I was lying," he murmured. "Mr. Lewis wasn't anywhere in sight."

"I'm shocked," she said in mock horror. She slipped her hands into the long dark hair at the nape of his neck, thick and wavy, and drew his head down so that she could kiss him again, so that she could drown in the lean, hard warmth of him. He eased his hand across her breasts and down the silky, slippy nylon tank suit, arousing her, touching her, sliding along her soft curves, pressing lower, harder, caressing as though the suit wasn't even there. She gasped and he teased her until she was breathless with need. His hand slid beneath the back of her suit to press her tight against him.

And then he stopped and pushed up and off her onto his knees. Breath ragged, he stared down at her. "Maybe this isn't such a good idea."

She met his stare for a very long moment. Now? He was going to have second thoughts now? She'd already been down this path and this was not the time she was going to start second-guessing things.

"Sure it is." She tried to act cool, tried to keep from grabbing him by the shoulders and pulling him down.

"You're sure? What about the baby?"

"It's not a problem. Believe me. I've read all the pregnancy books."

"Okay." With tantalizing slowness, he slid the straps off her shoulders and kissed the line of her collarbone, hands continuing to pull the suit lower as his kisses covered her throat and breasts, his fingers arousing her to exquisite joy as the barrier of nylon was slipped off and tossed to the side. She let herself revel in the moment, in his touch, in touching him, in wanting him, in finally knowing the hard planes of his body and the feel of his weight pressing against her.

After six years, she finally had her wedding night.

He looked down at her and pulled at the tie of his waistband, lowering himself onto her again.

And then he loved her, beneath the heat of the afternoon sun, with the cicadas in the background buzzing like a choir. Afterward, he wrapped her in his arms and she drifted into that lovely state between sleep and awake, where she could pretend that all this was real, that this was a typical day in her life instead of just an afternoon fantasy.

When she finally opened her eyes, she saw him up on one elbow, watching her. He brushed the loose hair back from her face and kissed the tip of her nose. Need surged through her again, fierce and urgent.

"Wore you out, did I?" He grinned.

"I never knew canoeing could be so much fun." She ran a slow hand across the black hair on his chest, across his belly and over his hip, marveling at his body's instant response to her touch.

"If you liked that, wait till I take you white-water rafting."

"Hmm. How about a sneak preview? And after that, I'd love to see what it's like to climb a mountain, and if you're really feeling educational, I've never been cross-country skiing, either."

His hand stroked across her breasts, fingers toying with her, tracing her curves. "This might take more lessons than I can give in one day. Perhaps you'll need tutoring on a regular basis."

She was aching for him already. "Whatever it takes," she said on a gasp.

He bent to her, his mouth following the path of his fingers. She sank into his luscious darkness again, let herself begin to spiral out of control. She could spend the rest of the day doing this.

And then he froze and lifted his head.

She dragged her eyes open. "What?"

"I think I heard something. Shouting."

She pushed up on her elbows. "Who would be nuts enough to be out here?"

He raised an eyebrow.

"Besides us, I mean."

He cocked his head to listen for a moment and Annie closed her eyes as if not seeing would help her hear better. Suddenly Nick's mouth was on hers again and his body was pressing her down. She sank into that delicious place she had just visited and longed to go to again. Her wariness dissolved beneath the onslaught that was Nick.

Only when they came up for air did she hear the shout—this time loud, close and definitely understandable.

"Ann-ie! Ni-ick!" came rolling over the meadow accompanied by the sound of a small boat motor.

CHAPTER TWELVE

ANNIE JERKED UPRIGHT. "Omigosh! Someone's coming!"

They both scrambled for their clothes. She grabbed hold of her swimsuit and wiggled into it while reclining, still hidden she hoped, in the tall grass.

"There! The canoe!" a voice shouted.

"Nick! Annie!" The first voice was joined by another.

"It's the police chief! Hurry up!" She tried to pull the twisted straps of her suit over her shoulders.

The crackle of a walkie-talkie and the murmur of voices carried across the meadow on the breeze. She looked at Nick and shook her head. "What is this, Grand Central Station?"

He snaked a hand up to grab her shorts and his T-shirt still drying on top of the tall grass. If she wasn't so afraid of being caught, she might have laughed at the sight of the two of them frantically dressing like high school kids caught necking in the back seat of a car.

He pulled on his T-shirt. "Ready?"

"Hold on a second." She lay on her back and wriggled into her shorts. "What do you want to do? Just suddenly pop up out of the grass?"

"Got a better idea?"

She shook her head.

"We were just having a picnic. Tipped over. Came up here to dry off and have lunch."

"Right." She took a breath to calm the pounding of her heart. "Okay, I'm ready."

Nearby, a crash sounded in the underbrush, accompanied by loud, deep barking. Before either of them could move, a huge black-faced German shepherd leapt into their midst, wagging his tail and panting, big drops of water dripping from his tongue.

Annie recoiled, then quickly recovered as she recognized the police chief's dog. "Thor!"

He danced toward her.

"I think we've been discovered." Nick stood and reached a hand down to pull her up beside him, waving with his other hand at the two police officers who were running toward them through the long grass of the meadow.

"Somehow, something is just not right here," Annie said.

"And what was your first indication?"

She purposely stepped on Nick's toes.

"Annie! Thank goodness! Nick!" the chief shouted. "Well, don't that beat all! We were expecting the worst and here you are safe and sound."

He looked from one to the other. "You all right?"

Annie nodded, hoping her face didn't have telltale Catholic guilt written all over it.

"Just…having a picnic," Nick offered.

"Tipped over," Annie said.

"Came up here to dry off and have lunch."

The other officer spoke into his walkie-talkie, announcing they had found the missing persons alive and well and that they would be bringing them in soon.

"We weren't missing. We went for a canoe trip," Annie said. "Luella knew where we were."

The chief chuckled. "Luella's who called us. Said she was supposed to pick you up at one-thirty just past where the river runs by old man Henkel's pasture." He shifted his gaze from Annie to Nick, as though expecting a reply.

Nick glanced at his watch. "I guess we lost track of time."

"How late are we?" Anne asked.

"Hour and a half." The chief shook his head. "Luella waited about thirty minutes for you to show up. Then your sweatshirt came floating down the river wrapped around a canoe paddle and she went into a panic. Thought there'd been an accident."

"Oh, my gosh! We tipped over. Everything got wet and we came up here to dry off—and have lunch." Annie's words rolled out in a rush. "Poor Luella. She must have been in a real panic."

The chief chuckled. "*Hysterical* would be more the word. She's got half the town stomping through the woods looking for you two. I was thinking maybe you just got waylaid somewhere." He looked at Annie and nodded. "Figured you were probably all right and would make it back in time, but better safe than sorry."

Nick picked up the cooler. "Guess we'd better get back and start apologizing."

"I got a little trolling motor on a rowboat out here. We'll tow you down to Henkel's place since ya only got one paddle. Come on, Thor." The chief slapped his thigh and set off toward the river, wading through the tall grass with his dog and the other officer right behind him.

Nick let them get several steps ahead, then leaned toward Annie and whispered, "I think he knows we really did get *waylaid*."

"No way. Why would you think that?"

"Your swimsuit's inside out."

She glanced down and a blush crept up her cheeks. Maybe the chief hadn't noticed; tank suits were rather the same inside and out, anyway.

Nick put his arm around her shoulders as they cut across the field toward the canoe. "Don't worry, sweetie. No one's going to care. We're married, remember?"

"Still…"

"Nah. If anything, they're jealous. Wish they were making love with *their* wives in a meadow."

He pressed a kiss to her lips and pulled her head against his chest for a moment. She could feel the sun's warmth still in his shirt, could hear the beat of his heart. And all she wanted to do was raise her head and kiss him and ask him to take her here again in the grass.

He'd called her *his wife*.

The thought sent a wave of joy and a stab of panic through her. What had she just done? In her quest to have this moment to remember him by, she had now ensured that she would *never* get over him. This was a man who had just ended his engagement, who had just said he was going back to the life of wandering adventurer. This was not a man ready to jump into another relationship. And he sure as heck wasn't ready for a commitment.

She'd wanted one time and she'd gotten it. She had a memory of Nick to carry with her long after he left Bedford. But she'd gotten herself a memory when what she really wanted was the man. She wanted him to really be her husband, to father her children, to have root beers at the diner with her, and haircuts at Minnow's.

How much more of a fool could she be? She should have stuck to her guns when she told Nick to leave a few days ago. She should have been up front and told him she had feelings for him—and then waited to see what his response was. But she hadn't. And now, here she was, stuck in some bizarre "almost married" state, hanging on to the fact that he'd called her his wife, and hoping that maybe he actually was beginning to think of her that way.

AN HOUR LATER THEY arrived home. The instant the police car pulled up in front of the house, a crush of people streamed out the front door to envelop them with good wishes and hugs and slaps on the back and laughter. Chester was beside himself in all the excitement, leaping and barking, and running in silly circles around the big pine tree on the front lawn.

Luella pushed her way through the crowd and down the steps until she stood in front of them, hands on her hips, her expression a mixture of anger and relief. Her look reminded Nick of one he had seen many a time on his parents' faces when he was in high school.

"I tell you, this old heart won't survive if I have to go through that again."

"I'm really sorry," Nick said. "We tipped over and pulled up on shore to dry off. I—we—lost track of time."

Luella's eyes glistened. "You two have taken twenty years off my life. And at my age, I can't afford to lose a one."

Nick swept her into his arms and kissed her wrinkled cheek. She swatted him away and motioned toward the front porch. "What's everybody doing standing out here? Let's go in and break out the Chablis!"

To a roar of laughter and scattered clapping, they all headed inside. Nick hung back and watched them go, watched Annie in her element, surrounded by this family she had found in Bedford.

He still couldn't get over how different she was from six years ago. The same Annie, and yet not her at all. Her face flushed and lips still reddened, a reminder of how they had spent the afternoon. The memory of her filled his mind, hot beneath him, her soft body illuminated in the afternoon sun, her lips swollen from kissing him.

Damn.

He thought of making love to her in a bed, amid the down pillows and the cool cotton sheets and the night breeze stirring the lace curtains at the windows. And he thought about the new shower he'd put in and how it had different massage levels—pulses they called them—and wondered if taking her in the shower under the hard pulse would be better than under the one called Spring Rain.

He looked up at the house, at the people filtering in through the door to celebrate Annie's survival. These people had learned in two years what it had taken him six to find out—this was one special woman. And she was his.

Wait. Hold it. Stop it right there. Where had that come from?

He'd just ended one commitment—he didn't need another one right now. He'd come here to get a divorce and ended up staying nine days. Five down, four to go. That was it. Whatever this attraction, this lust, this need for Annie was about, the fact was she lived in a small town in Wisconsin.

She was happy here.

And life in a small town would drive him insane.

Wouldn't it?

Just because he'd ended his relationship with Melissa didn't mean he was going to stay with Annie. He couldn't. This was her life—not his. He didn't want it.

Running from his thoughts, he took the steps two at a time and went into the house. Father Thespesius handed him an empty wineglass stamped on the side with the name of some vineyard in California, then proceeded to fill it with Chablis from the bottle he held.

"What Father, not red?" Nick grinned.

"Not a bottle of the stuff in this house. Luella says it gives her the migraines." He raised his glass. "Now, my boy, let's toast to your safe return—"

"You know we never were in trouble, don't you?"

"Now I do. But by the time we learned that, I think all the votive candles had already been lit."

"Really?" An unfamiliar warmth slid through him. He hardly knew these people and they had been lighting candles in the church and praying for him.

"I wouldn't have let anything happen to Annie," he said.

"I know. Just wish you could stick around." The priest smiled sadly. "I think Annie's really going to be at a loss when you leave."

Minnow appeared in front of them, threw her arms wide and wrapped them around Nick's middle. He looked down at her fuchsia hair and grinned, grateful for the interruption.

"You scared the living daylights out of us." She pulled back to look up at him.

"Minnow, I can't believe I'm saying this, but thanks for caring." He gestured at the crowded room. "Sure doesn't take much for people around here to have a party."

"Any excuse pretty much does it," Father Thespesius said.

Minnow nodded. "Once the searchers heard you were found, everybody came over here. Just happy you're okay."

Another person stopped over to shake his hand and another and another. Over and again, he heard how happy they were to learn he and Annie were all right, how glad they were that nothing serious had happened to "their Annie," and, by the way, did I ever tell you what happened to me on the river when I was a kid? By the time he even had a moment to look for Annie, more than an hour had passed.

He spotted her in the hall, trapped in a corner with Vivian, whose mouth appeared to be moving at warp speed. Annie had pasted an interested expression on her face, but he could tell by the glazed look in her eyes that she'd been talked at long enough. He took a step toward her.

"Did you have to call on any of your survival training while you were out there?" a familiar voice asked.

Nick jerked his attention from Annie and set his gaze on Mr. Lewis, who had come up beside him. He forced a casual smile onto his face. "Not really. We weren't ever in any trouble. Just had to get the canoe emptied out. Had a little lunch."

"I have a nephew who's in one of those elite units of the army. Probably not in the same one as you are, but he's always gone on some sort of survival expedition. You have anything to do with those guys?"

Nosy son of a gun. What did this guy want? Nick grimaced, as though torn about answering. "You know, I'm just not free to talk about what I do. Sorry. I can't even tell Annie the details."

Lewis chuckled. "That's what my nephew always says. I'll bet you two know each other—Frank Jackson. Sound familiar at all?"

Nick had the sudden urge to deck the guy. If he wasn't investigating them, then he was just plain irritating. He forced himself to mentally calm down. Right. And just maybe he was some nice guy staying at the B & B who was trying to make small talk.

Who could tell? Keeping up this whole charade was getting old. He saw Annie lean against the wall for support and her eyes caught his, pleading for help as Vivian talked on and on and on.

"Excuse me, Mr. Lewis, but it looks like a rescue is in order."

The man followed the direction of Nick's gaze and laughed. "Ah, yes, Vivian. I know exactly what you mean."

Nick made his way to Annie's side. "Mind if I borrow my wife a minute?"

Without awaiting her answer, he put his arm around Annie's shoulder and pulled her with him down the hall. "Had enough?"

"Oh, she could talk a leg off a mule."

"There's way too many questions being asked. Let's get out of here and go grab a burger. A greasy one with the works—"

"Fried onions—not raw."

"You learn fast."

"Onion rings."

He grinned. "And a chocolate malt. Large. Anywhere around here we can get such a thing? Besides the diner?"

"High fat, high carbs—just the menu at an old drive-in outside town."

"You game?"

"You bet—I'm eating for two!"

Nick grabbed her by the hand and sidled out the back door. Like kids escaping from a too-long church service, they raced down the driveway and jumped into his car, laughing gleefully at their escape.

"I'm not sure we're acting very appreciative, running away from our own survival party." Annie leaned back against the headrest and looked at Nick.

Her heart seemed to stop. A day's growth of beard darkened his jaw. A touch of sunburn colored his cheekbones and forehead. God, he was handsome. Maybe not to some people, but to her; the very sight of him literally took her breath away. And now, with the afternoon's memory still fresh in her mind, the smell of him still on her skin, she had to stop herself from reaching out and touching him, had to shove her feelings away before they burst to the surface like a bubble in the sea and she bared her soul to this man.

He backed out of the driveway, grinning at her. "Okay, so where do I go?"

"I forget you don't live here. Take a right and head out of town." It dawned on her that this would be the same route he'd take when he finally left Bedford, and *her,* for good.

Right now, with Nick in the seat next to her as if he was her date, or her boyfriend...or her husband... suddenly she couldn't hold back her desire for more, couldn't hold back the hope that maybe today had been something more than just a playful diversion for him.

Her mind churned with all the questions she wanted to ask and knew she couldn't. Nick had thought they should stop this afternoon, had given her the opportunity to say *no,* and she'd been the one to insist they continue. She had no right to pressure him now, to question him about why he'd ended his engagement and whether or not he had feelings for her.

"Take a left at the next road and then it's just down at the next crossroads. Harbough's Drive-In," she said.

Nick followed her directions, and she watched his hands turn the wheel, strong hands that had held her, caressed her just hours ago. She sat up straighter and shoved the memory away, almost grateful when the drive-in came into view, the lot half full of patrons, trays hooked to their windows. The smell of burgers and fries wafted into the car.

"This is perfect." Nick pulled the car into a parking space and Annie focused her attention on the teenage carhop, perkily dressed in a red-and-white uniform, who hurried toward them holding a pad of paper and a pencil.

Nick rested an elbow on the open window and started speaking the moment she reached him. "Two cheeseburgers with the works. Fried onions. Two orders of onion rings. Two chocolate malts. Extra thick—with spoons. As quick as you can. We're starving."

When the girl left, he turned his attention back to Annie. "It's a good thing we got out of the house. I can't tell you how many people were asking questions about the military."

"At least they all think it's top secret so they can't expect you to say much."

"Yeah. Except I'm feeling guilty. These are friends now and it's not easy to keep lying like this."

"Welcome to my nightmare. I was just about to set the stage for our divorce by dropping hints that our marriage was in trouble. And then you showed up."

"We seem to be plagued by bad timing."

She nodded, wondering what he meant and too afraid to ask. It might be best if they stuck with safer topics. "You were right about canoeing," she said, changing the subject. "It's great. No motor needed, no electronics, just nature."

"Sort of gives you a sense of control over your life, doesn't it?"

"Something that's been missing for me these past few days."

He nodded. "Just four more to go and you can go back to your original plan. Give it a month and then start mentioning we're having marital problems. Maybe we should be fighting in public instead of getting along so well. It might help the cause."

His words made her stomach tighten. She held up a hand. "Faking marital bliss is hard enough. I don't think I can fake marital discord, too."

"Good point."

The carhop showed up with the food and hung the tray on their open window. Nick dug a twenty out of his pocket and handed it to her, then began pulling the food into the car and passing it to Annie.

Her hunger had disappeared with his comment that they only had to continue the charade for four more days. She didn't want to believe this afternoon had been just a quick roll in the hay to him, a meaningless romp. But she'd be a fool to assume otherwise. Guys were so much more capable of separating the act from their emotions.

What they probably should do was talk about it. But Annie didn't want to start that conversation. She shoved an onion ring in her mouth.

Too many times in the past she'd stuck her heart right out in front, on the butcher block, thinking that once she and her new love discussed how they felt about each other everything would be fine. And time and again, she'd gotten her heart back in pieces.

She was no good at this relationship thing. Was too quick to want to figure out where they were going instead of patiently seeing the sights along the way. Her therapist had been great in helping her identify this character flaw. Still, it was one thing to recognize her faults, another completely to be able to solve them.

But this thing with Nick didn't fit in a standard relationship box. It wasn't as though they had months and years to discover charming idiosyncrasies about each other, months and years to fall into like, and lust, and mellow into long-standing love before having to figure out whether or not they wanted to stay together.

They had four days.

And then Nick was going away to—anywhere in the world and nowhere he'd be easy to reach—and there'd be no hope whatsoever.

She chomped on her hamburger and mulled over her options, grateful for the food. It kept her from feeling as if they had to talk every minute, and it kept her mouth full so she couldn't speak even if she wanted to.

Either she could talk to him right now about what had happened between them. Or she could talk to him tomorrow, or the next day, or the one after that. And then she would be out of days.

Or, she could say nothing at all.

As a preventative measure, she shoved a huge onion

ring in her mouth on top of a bit of burger, forcing herself to think this through before blurting out words of
love, passion, adoration, *stupidity*.

"Annie, about this afternoon…"

"Hmphghaah." Nice touch. She knew her cheeks
were bulging. She could hardly close her lips to chew
all the food she'd jammed into her mouth.

Here it came, *the* conversation, the one she'd been
waiting for. The only way she'd be able to participate
right now was if she spit all the food out of her mouth.
And she sure wasn't going to be that crude.

"We've known each other a long time, you know, as
friends. And we've been through a lot together. This afternoon…I don't know what it means."

Oh, grand. She was about to get the guy version of
what this afternoon was all about. Here came the news that
he'd had fun, but he hoped she didn't think this meant they
were in love with each other or anything, that he'd just gotten out of one relationship, that sometimes people just get
carried away and if everyone is adult about it no one gets
hurt. She took a gulp of root beer to wash down her food
and felt the lump slide all the way to her stomach.

"Oh, yeah. No big deal," she said cavalierly, antici-
pating the pain. She hoped her old therapist had an
opening for the day after Nick left.

Nick sat back into his seat. Some emotion washed
over his face; she couldn't tell what it was. Probably relief. "Really?"

"I mean, these things happen," she blabbered on. "I
know you just ended your engagement. We just got
carried away—"

"Yeah, we did. I—we—probably shouldn't have done that."

"It was the moment. The canoeing, the sunshine, the—"

"Relief from stress over Mr. Lewis."

"Exactly. Don't think that I have any expectations or anything—"

"So you're okay with this?"

"Oh, yeah. Believe me, it was no big deal." Burgers and onion rings roiled in her stomach as if to protest the lie.

"It wasn't?"

"Oh, I mean, it was fun. Don't get me wrong. But we both know it didn't mean anything."

He narrowed his eyes and didn't say anything for a minute. "Right. As long as you're okay that we…gave in to the moment. Hell, Annie. I just got unengaged. What am I doing making love to another woman already?"

Another woman? Another woman? Is that what she was to him? Just another woman? Despair rushed through her.

"I can't answer for you."

He exhaled. "You used to be able to help me out in these dilemmas."

"Oh, no, no more late-night coffee-shop counseling. All I ever did was pour you more coffee and listen to your escapades…and your dreams."

"You did more than that."

"Okay, I told you to go home and sleep it off, too."

He laughed. "Besides that. You used to say something. You were always preaching the same damn thing, something about belonging. I heard it so many times you'd think it would be imprinted on my brain."

A small laugh escaped her as her old words returned, words that had ultimately led her to Bedford. "When you find the place where you belong, you'll want to stay."

"That was it?"

She nodded.

"I seem to remember it being more profound."

"It is. It's not just about a place, it's about people, and jobs, and friends, and life."

Sadness seeped through her. Not only was he still searching, he might spend his whole life searching. Not everyone settled, not everyone found what she'd found here.

The realization hit her hard. She could either wait and hope that he decided he wanted her…someday. Or she could move on and put him out of her mind. Making love did not necessarily make a future. She'd known that already—just needed a little reminder.

For the sake of sanity, she knew there was only one answer.

Nick had to go back to his adventure life. And she, Annie, had to go back to her little life in Bedford, have her baby and raise it the best she knew how. If she was lucky, someday after a while, maybe months, maybe years, she'd meet a guy to help her purge Nick Fleming from her mind.

CHAPTER THIRTEEN

ANNIE PROPPED THE PHONE between her chin and shoulder and flipped the pages in her reservation book until she reached October. Even without checking she knew she had an opening. "Yes, we have room for you," she said with a welcoming smile in her voice. "Would you like to make a reservation?"

She glanced up at the sound of footfalls coming down the stairs and exchanged a friendly nod with Mr. Lewis before he slipped out the front door.

Hmm, where could he be going off to this fine afternoon? And what was with that large yellow envelope tucked under his arm?

A thought exploded in her brain and her heart plummeted into her stomach. *The report.* He was on his way to a rendezvous. *He was on his way to tell all.* What should she do? Should she stop him? Could she?

Was she nuts?

The sound of the caller's voice over the phone line interrupted her frenzied thoughts. "Oh, yes, I'm sorry, a bit of a problem here. What was it you were saying?"

She stretched, trying to see out the front window, but the coiled cord wouldn't reach. In desperation, she swooped the phone base off the desk and set it on the chair, gaining several feet of length. She stretched farther…could almost see out the window…just a little farther…

The phone crashed to the floor. And the caller was still talking and Annie had no idea what he was saying. This was ridiculous.

"I'm terribly sorry, we have a little emergency here right now. Would you mind calling back in about an hour? I'll go ahead and pencil you in—Hudson was the name? Thank you so much."

She practically threw the receiver onto the base where it lay on the floor, then looked frantically in either direction as though the action would help her gain some sort of insight. Darn it all. Where had Nick said he was going this morning? Was he out for a run? Or running errands? Why hadn't she paid attention?

Stupid question. She hadn't paid attention purposely, because she didn't want to be paying attention to him anymore. All she'd wanted to do was get through the next few days.

Her mind raced. Nick was nowhere to be found. And Minnow was at work. Which meant it was up to her—and the only thing she could possibly do was follow Mr. Lewis to see who he was meeting. Maybe he'd set the envelope down somewhere and she could grab it and run. Maybe she could happen into him downtown and invite him for a cup of coffee. Maybe she could spill coffee on the envelope and he'd have to bring it home to repackage and she could get a look at what was inside. *Maybe she should calm down.*

She tore upstairs to grab a cell phone and shove it in her pocket, then raced downstairs and burst out the front door, only to skid to a halt on the porch. Lewis wasn't even a full block away yet. At least he wasn't into power-walking or he would be long gone by now. She drew several slow breaths, then paced the length of the porch and back, waiting for him to get far enough ahead so he wouldn't take notice of her.

After a few minutes, she scampered down the porch stairs and crossed the street. Adrenaline pumping, eyes locked on Mr. Lewis's back, she slid along the inside of a leafy hedge in front of one house and cut through a neighbor's flower bed. She skidded in the dirt and looked down in disgust, lifting her feet to glower at the mud now squished on the sides and bottoms of her just-washed sneakers. Who watered their flowers so early in the morning? This spy life wasn't all Minnow made it out to be.

She looked up again just as Mr. Lewis stopped and started to glance back over his shoulder. Annie spun and pressed herself against the side of a big maple tree. Then she rolled her head slowly to peer around the tree to make sure he had continued on his way.

Aha! Time for action again. She wiped her shoes on the grass—bottoms first, then sides—to remove some of the mud, and set off after Mr. Lewis again.

A wave of power rolled through her. She was the cat; he was the mouse. It was almost like a dance—only he didn't know he was dancing. One, two, three. Look, move, hide. One, two, three. Look, move, hide.

She grinned as she stalked him, moving from one

front yard to the next, stopping to hide behind bushes, trees, fences, whatever was available. She pressed her back into another tree and peered around the trunk. Clearly, she'd rushed to judgment about how hard this was—espionage was easy as a piece of lemon meringue pie.

"Annie, what on earth are you doing?"

She snapped her head around and smacked it into a low-hanging branch as she smiled weakly at the elderly woman who had stuck her head out the screen door of a nearby house. A white miniature poodle shot out of the house and charged at her, barking like mad.

Annie glanced up the street in alarm. She scooped up the squirming dog and hurried to hand it over to the woman.

"Good morning—afternoon—Ruth. Just going downtown."

"Heard your husband's back. You're not hiding from him, are you?"

For crying out loud, this was how rumors got started. Annie shook her head.

"'Cause I remember what my Carl was like, rest his soul, when he would come back after being gone just a couple of weeks on business. These men and their needs, you know. Don't blame you one bit for hiding." Ruth's smile was filled with sisterly understanding.

Annie struggled to speak. "Oh, no, nothing like that. Just got a little tired. Of walking, I mean, walking." She pointed at the tree. "Thought I'd take a rest. Really nice to see you again."

She took off at a run before the woman could ask any

more questions. Ruth's voice floated after her. "Come over any time you need to get away, dear...."

Jeez, by the time Nick finally left Bedford, this whole town was going to think she was nuts. She'd have to move even if they didn't know she was lying to them.

She raced to the corner and looked both ways. Now where'd Lewis go? What the heck? How could he have gotten away from her? She hadn't wasted that much time with Ruth.

Spotting him almost two blocks up, she slowed her pace to an amble, stopping now and then to stare at something on the ground or in a store window, as though she were just window-shopping. Mr. Lewis stopped at the new museum and tried the door. Ha! He should've asked her about that—the grand opening wasn't for a few more days.

The day before Nick was leaving.

The thought dampened her mood. She watched as Lewis cupped his hands around his eyes and leaned against the glass to look into the museum's front picture window.

Then he crossed the street and she followed at a block's distance, ducking into shop doorways so he didn't spot her if he happened to look back. He stopped at the blue mailbox on the street corner.

Her breath caught. She froze. His rendezvous wasn't with a person. It was with the U.S. Postal Service. She opened her mouth to shout, then stopped herself, watching in horror as he swung open the mail slot and dropped the yellow envelope inside.

She had failed.

He spun on his heel like a man quite pleased with himself and started back along the route he'd just come. Any closer and he would recognize her.

With a gasp, she threw herself into a thick arborvitae hedge, coming out with an "oomph" as she landed in someone's yard on the other side. Spiderwebs clung to her face and she wiped them off with the frantic motions of someone with severe arachnophobia, which she didn't have. At least she hadn't known she had it until this moment.

She spat flat pine needles out of her mouth. "Minnow, you're wrong," she muttered. "This spy business sucks."

She rubbed her grass-stained knees and peeked through the evergreen branches, waiting until Mr. Lewis passed by. He was whistling, for God's sake, acting like a man who had just won the lottery—or one who had just completed a difficult assignment.

Despair filled her. She couldn't deal with failure of this magnitude alone. Pulling the cell phone from her pocket, she dialed Minnow's salon.

Relief washed over her when Minnow answered the phone instead of the receptionist.

"Oh Baby," she whispered into the mouthpiece.

"It is? Oh, my gosh! What? What? When? Why—"

"You sound like the rules for proper newspaper reporting," Annie said.

"I'm dying here! What's going on?"

"I'm on a cell phone—"

"Don't talk! Come to the shop. I've got too many customers right now to leave. But give me a hint."

"Lewis."

"As in Mr.?"

"Uh-huh."

"Get over here!"

"On my way."

Annie pressed the button to auto-dial Nick's phone and left a message telling him to come to Minnow's salon as soon as possible. By the time she reached the salon, her mind was churning and one of her knees was bleeding from her dive through the arborvitae.

If Mr. Lewis had finished his report, whatever it was about, something was bound to change...and soon. They were out of time. She needed to know what he was up to. And she needed to know now. Her livelihood, her life, depended on it. If she needed to start some sort of damage control, she had to know.

She walked into the salon and nodded at the receptionist. "Just gonna talk to Minnow."

She spotted Minnow at the farthest station squirting liquid from a plastic bottle onto about a hundred tiny perm rods wrapped with gray hair—all on one head. Minnow looked up and waved.

One of the other stylists was sweeping up pieces of dark brown hair from the floor around her chair. "Hey, Annie. Met your husband at the Flower Festival. You get tired of him, you let me know," she said.

Annie gave her a wan smile. *In a pig's eye.* That woman came on to every guy in town. "Minnow, you got a minute?"

"Meet you in my office." She wrapped a plastic bag around her client's hair and secured it with a clothespin.

Annie opened a door along the back wall and

stepped into the laundry room. The washer vibrated as it spun, the dryer hummed and the room had the overall temperature of a sauna. She lifted a clean washcloth from a basket, wetted it in the laundry tub and dabbed at the blood on her knee.

The door opened and Minnow popped into the room. "Whew. Kind of warm in here."

"At least it's private."

She took in Annie's skinned knee and disheveled appearance. "What happened to you?"

"All in a day's work for a spy. I dove through a hedge."

A grin lit Minnow's face. "I'm impressed. What's going on?"

"I followed Mr. Lewis—"

"Tailed him."

"Whatever. He left the house carrying this suspicious yellow envelope. So I tailed him and got to watch him mail the thing off."

"The Report!"

"That's what I thought—"

"Did you try to get it?"

"How? He stuck it in the mailbox before I even realized what he was up to. I thought he was going to meet someone—not mail the dang thing. Now it's in the big blue box on the corner of Main and Washington, waiting to be picked up and sent on its way."

"To a destination that could bring about the destruction of your life in Bedford."

"A bit melodramatic, but probably true."

Minnow shook her head. "Desperate times call for desperate measures. Stick your hand down the slot.

Sometimes there's a big pile of mail in there and the envelope will be close to the top. All you have to do is grab it."

"Right. And sometimes there's a cop nearby who'll arrest you for mail tampering or postal theft or whatever they call it."

"Okay, okay. On the other hand, that envelope might be your undoing."

"On the *other* hand, so would committing a felony. And that undoing would happen first."

"But on the other hand—"

"Let's not waste any more hands on this. I'm not gonna do it. This whole mess started with a simple lie. Next, I'll be stealing. And who knows what would come after that. Assault and battery?"

Minnow rolled her eyes. "Did you tell Nick about it?"

"I can't reach him. Probably doesn't want to talk to me, anyway." She couldn't keep the dejection out of her voice.

She lifted the washcloth off her knee. "You got a bandage?"

Minnow pulled a first-aid kit out of an upper cupboard and handed it to her, then began to fold the white towels in the laundry basket and stack them on the dryer. "Yesterday, after the big rescue, I could have sworn you looked like a well-loved woman. And he looked like a man in love."

"It's all an act. At least on his part."

"Oh, come on. I saw the guy yesterday, how he was watching you at the party. You did it, didn't you?"

Annie pursed her lips and applied a flesh-colored bandage to her knee.

"Coy won't work. Where?"

"In some meadow after the canoe tipped. Oh, and did I mention he ended his engagement to Melissa?"

Minnow brought her hands together with a clap and let out a squeal. "I told you so! I knew you two belonged together."

"Don't get so excited. It was just a thing of the moment. A case of love the one you're with."

"You're not kidding me, Annie. It's me, remember? I know how long you've liked this guy." She shoved aside a pile of folded white towels and hoisted herself up to sit on the dryer.

"Yeah, well, I fell for him six years ago and now I've only made it worse. I wish I hadn't convinced him to stay because it's like I'm doing Chinese water torture to myself."

"No way he's not feeling anything. No way. I can see he's attracted to you."

Annie contemplated Minnow's words. "Yeah, but *attracted* doesn't necessarily equate to *wanting to stay here.* Last night we kind of came to an agreement that we shouldn't have done what we did."

"He needs a push. The new *Cosmo* has an article about—"

"You're reading too many magazines again." She sighed. "I don't have time to spend being lovesick—and I don't have time to try to fix it. Forget about Nick for a few minutes and concentrate on the bigger problem. What do I do about Mr. Lewis? Anything? Or do I just sit tight and wait?"

The door opened a crack and the woman with her

hair in perm rods stuck her head into the room. The odor of perm solution wafted in with her. "Minnow, the timer's going off," she said.

"Oh, right! Let's get those rods out." She jumped down off the dryer. "Annie, let me think about all this stuff awhile. Maybe I can come up with something—like an idea from one of the spy thrillers I've read."

Just what they needed, advice from fiction novelists. "All ideas are welcome," she said in desperation, and followed Minnow out into the salon.

"Say hi to that husband of yours," the other beautician called as she passed by. "Tell him to stop by for a complimentary 'welcome to Bedford' cut."

Annie eyed a bottle of green kiwi-melon shampoo on the rack and considered unscrewing the top and lobbing it at the woman like a grenade. Restraining herself, she shoved through the door and strode down the sidewalk in the direction of home, her emotions a jumbled mess of anger, fear and—damn it all to hell, life wasn't fair—*love*.

NICK SAT AT THE BAR in the Deer Fly Inn, a rustic tavern in the next town up the road, just east of Bedford. The place was cool and dark, with paneled walls and beer signs everywhere. He wrapped his hands around the nearly empty mug of Miller High Life in front of him on the bar.

He'd needed to think and there was nowhere in Bedford he could do it—not without someone coming up to talk about Annie or ask about the military or just shoot the breeze. And if he tried to think at Annie's place, he'd have to see Annie.

And that was no good, either.

So he'd gone out for a drive and ended up in this little hole-in-the-wall. Which, as far as he could tell, was just about perfect. He was anonymous here, just some guy passing through town.

Outside, the day practically glowed from the bright afternoon sunshine. But inside, the atmosphere was subdued, dark, quiet. The bar was empty of patrons except him and a couple of guys playing pool. He hadn't been in a tavern in the afternoon in a long time and the feeling was odd. Almost as if he'd gone back to college or something. He half expected a bunch of guys to tumble in the door and join him for a cold one.

He finished off his beer, wiped the foam from his upper lip and shoved his glass at the bartender for a refill.

The heavyset man pulled the tap back and filled Nick's glass. "You staying around here?"

Nick nodded. "Bedford."

"Nice little town."

"*Little* is the definitive word." He focused his attention on his glass and the bartender moved away to wipe down the other end of the bar.

When you find the place where you belong, you'll want to stay.

Nick tipped up his glass and took a swallow of beer. This stuff was going down way too easy. Thing was, Annie did feel like a place where he belonged. And if he was honest with himself, sometimes Bedford did, too.

But "sometimes" wasn't good enough.

What if he made a mistake? What if he stayed in Bedford because of Annie and then ended up hating it? No doubt he'd then end up resenting Annie.

"Wanna talk about it?"

Nick looked up at the bartender. "What?"

"Whatever it is you're drinking to solve. Woman?"

"Sort of."

The bartender chuckled. "Give me the condensed version."

Nick shook his head. "Too complicated."

"All right, then here's my best advice for decision-making. Free of charge. List your options. Do pros and cons for each. Make a decision and don't look back."

Nick nodded. "Thanks."

The bartender pulled a bag of beer nuts off the display behind the bar and tossed them at Nick. "On the house," he said, before ambling into the poolroom to chat with the boys back there.

Pros and cons. Okay. Plenty of pros for Annie. Fun and smart and pretty and caring and sexy in a down-to-earth sort of way. The only con, really, was the town she lived in. The closest thing to real excitement around here was the annual Flower Festival.

It really came down to two choices. Either go back to the life he'd led before, the constant stimulation of new people, new countries, new adventures. Or stay with Annie in Bedford, where he'd probably end up feeling trapped, like a dog tied to a post.

He was a man without a place where he belonged. *Exactly the same as he'd always been.*

Hell. He had a major proposal out for consideration

with the TV networks—a proposal that could make him a household name. And if that one didn't go through, he had plenty of other ideas, all with the potential to make him a real player in the adventure market.

Which gave him his answer. He knew where he belonged. For him there was only one choice—go back to the life he'd chosen six years ago.

The thought was so sobering, he reached for his beer.

And then his cell phone rang for the second time since he got here and he answered it, expecting Annie's voice. Instead, he heard Minnow whispering the code word and diving into a description of Annie's latest escapade with Mr. Lewis.

"She's headed home and I think she could use some support," Minnow said.

"All right. I'm on my way." He shoved the half full glass of beer to the side, picked up his change from the bar, leaving a few bucks for a tip, and stepped out into the stifling heat.

DEEP IN THOUGHT, SLOUCHED down on a bench outside the local coffee shop, Annie didn't even notice Nick's SUV until he hung out the window and shouted, "Hey lady, want a ride?"

Her heart flopped in spite of her best intentions to feel nothing for him. "You missed the debriefing."

"I got here as fast as I could. What's up?"

She crossed the street and climbed into the vehicle, recounting the afternoon's events as she directed him to the mailbox on the corner of Main and Washington. Nick pulled over to the curb and they got out and stared at it.

"That's the one, huh?"

"Minnow thinks I should stick my arm in the slot and try to get the envelope."

He snorted. "And go directly to jail."

"That's what I said."

Nick pulled down the handle and peered inside the dark opening.

"Nick!"

"I'm just looking."

"See anything?"

"Tonsils. Adenoids."

She slapped his arm. He dropped the handle and the slot clanged shut with a sense of finality.

"So what do we do now?"

Nick screwed up his face. "I guess we ask him."

"Ask him? As in…Mr. Lewis, we have a tendency to be incredibly nosy and we're wondering if the report you've been compiling has anything to do with either of us? And if it does, would you mind sharing your information?"

"I'm thinking something more along the lines of…Mr. Lewis, I'm a top-secret military man. And *ve have vays to make you talk.*"

"Works for me."

He took hold of her arm. "I'm not kidding, Annie. I really think it's time we asked the guy a few questions. Maybe not specifically about the report. But about what he does for a living."

"The not-knowing is killing me." She looked up into his eyes for support. Big mistake. Sex was in them—hot and steamy and long and lush. She could smell the faint odor of beer on his breath.

"Have you been drinking?"

A slow smile slid across his face. "Busted."

"What have you been up to today?"

"Thinking. Had some serious thinking to do." He slid his hand around hers. Her heart quickened and goose bumps prickled at the back of her neck. What was this? Romance? Could Minnow be right? Might he feel something for her after all?

He touched his lips to hers in a chaste kiss, then deepened it, pressing her up against the mailbox as his kiss made her heady with want.

"Vivian just came out of the diner," he murmured.

Disappointment surged through her. She should have known this was just an act. Scene ten, take one. When was she going to learn?

CHAPTER FOURTEEN

NICK SAT BACK IN HIS CHAIR and watched Annie on her hands and knees furiously scrubbing the kitchen floor. "By the time Lewis finally gets back here, this place is going to be spotless," he commented.

"I can't just sit around and wait. I'll go batty. If he doesn't hurry up, Luella will be back from her meeting. Now that we've decided to confront him, the least he could do is show up."

"'Confront' sounds a bit aggressive."

"How about 'interrogate'?"

"Oh, yeah, that's so much better. There's an old saying, you catch more flies with honey than with vinegar."

"All I can think is that, for the first time in my life, I have something worth keeping. And now I could lose it all. I'm getting obsessive and I hate it."

She sat back on her haunches and looked at Nick. "Where could he be? We've been waiting almost two hours already. Throw me that towel on the table, will you?"

Nick tossed the towel at her. "At the risk of sounding like Minnow, why don't we put together a plan?"

"Such as?"

"How we're going to ask him what he's up to. If we charge at him firing questions—"

"He'll get suspicious and clam up."

"Yup."

"Okay, spy boy, what do you propose?"

He grinned. "How about good cop, bad cop?"

"Doesn't he sort of need to be a prisoner for that to work?"

"No. I've seen it on TV and—"

"Minnow is really rubbing off on you."

"Watch it… Seriously, we work the guy. You go after him tough for the info and I'll be the nice guy, his friend."

"How come I can't be his friend?"

"Because it's your B & B."

Annie huffed and started to dry the floor with the towel. "Fine. So he comes in the house and I say, 'Beautiful day, isn't it? Want a chocolate chip cookie?'"

"That's too nice. You're supposed to be tough."

"I can't even be pleasant to the guy?"

"What you say is, 'Hi, Mr. Lewis. Do you have a few minutes?' Then you invite him to sit down. But you stay standing—a psychological advantage."

A laugh burst out of her. "Tell the truth. You *have* been talking to Minnow, haven't you?"

Nick put on his best hurt face. "I can come up with good ideas on my own."

Annie wiped her hands on the towel and pushed herself to her feet. "Okay, so he sits down—"

Nick stood. "As the good cop, I'll offer him the cookie—"

"How domestic."

He ignored her, ignored the sparkle in her eyes, the rosy flush of her cheeks, the upturned corners of her lips that were almost begging him to kiss them. "Then I say, 'Annie's a little concerned about something—'"

"Only I'm concerned? Aren't we both? We're married, remember? If the husband is concerned, too, it gives it more credibility. Men always pay more attention to what other men think."

"They do?"

Annie looked up at him and nodded. He could see the fear in her eyes, the worry in the set of her lips. He took a step toward her and reached out a hand to cup her cheek, to reassure her everything would be all right. Her eyes filled with questions. They stared at each other for a long, long moment, his brain shouting at him: *Keep away from her. If you stay here you'll be miserable for the rest of your life.*

He dipped his head—what did his brain know, anyway?—and put his mouth to hers. She kissed him back, deep and fiery and long. Her hands were grasping his shirt and pulling him close and he knew he was making a mistake—this was Annie and he was leaving in three days—but, oh man, she was hard to stay away from.

The front door slammed and they broke apart breathless and gasping and staring at each other as though shocked by what they'd just done.

"He's back!" Annie ran her hands over her face and drew a breath.

"Easy. There's no rush."

"Yes, there is." Annie started for the hall and Nick grabbed her arm.

"Wait a minute. Let him go to his room, get settled. We don't want to scare him by being too in-your-face." *Plus, you look flushed, and just kissed, and this isn't the best state for us to be seeing Mr. Lewis in.*

"Right. Right. You're right." She began to pace from the pantry to the stove and back again, nearly running into Minnow as she crept through the kitchen doorway, dressed in black clothes, wearing a black stocking cap and gloves, and carrying a black briefcase.

"Was that you in the foyer?" Annie asked, disappointment evident in her voice.

"Nice to see you, too."

Nick stifled his own discouragement and dropped into a kitchen chair. "New fashion, Minnow?"

"You'd never cut it in the espionage business. These are my undercover clothes."

"Yeah, but it's not dark yet."

"They help me get the job done and that's all that matters." She popped open the briefcase and pulled out a large yellow envelope. "May I present one yellow envelope retrieved from the mail—"

"Oh, my gosh!" Annie blurted out.

"Retrieved from the mailbox on the corner of Washington and Main. My first attempt at intelligence gathering is a resounding success." Minnow gazed at the envelope in her hands as if she were holding a newborn child.

"You stole the envelope?" Nick couldn't keep the accusation from his voice.

"You stole the envelope?" Annie's voice, on the other hand, was filled with relief.

"*Stole* is such a harsh word. I prefer *borrowed*." Minnow handed the envelope to Annie, who looked at it and grinned.

Nick couldn't believe what he was seeing. "Annie, you just took possession of stolen property—"

"Not quite," Minnow said. "I waited at the box until the mailman came to empty it, then I told him Mr. Lewis at the B & B had asked me to see if I might be able to get back an envelope he had accidentally mailed this afternoon."

"And he believed you?" Nick shook his head.

"Well. It helped that it was Bob Drenconin and he's been asking me out for the past six months. 'Course, now I have to go dancing with him on Friday night."

"Bob Drenconin? You're going out with *Shake-It-Baby Drenconin?*" Annie began to chortle.

Minnow sniffed. "It was the only way I could get the envelope. And I told him the minute he shouts *shake it, baby, shake it,* I'm outta there."

There was a time, Nick thought, he would have found this conversation strange. Now it didn't bother him at all. And the realization that it didn't bothered him even more.

Annie looked closely at the front of the envelope and set it on the table by Nick. "Do you know the person it's addressed to?"

He shook his head. "Never heard of him. The only thing I do know is, if we get caught with that envelope we're in deep trouble."

The three stared at the envelope.

Annie ran a finger under the address line. "What are those initials—WFRA? Isn't that a radio station?"

Minnow scrunched up her face. "I don't get it. He works in radio?"

"So what do we do now?" Annie looked at Nick.

"Open it," Minnow said. "We need to find out what he's up to."

"Put it back," Nick said.

Annie fixed an intent look on the envelope. Nick could almost see the struggle inside her, could feel her pain of trying to balance the need to know with doing the right thing.

Annie sighed. "Get it out of here, Minnow. Get it back in that mailbox before I'm tempted any more than I am right now. I may be a liar but I can't be a thief."

"Are you crazy? All that effort and we're not going to find out what's inside?"

Annie shook her head. "Sorry."

"You mean I'm going out with Shake-It-Baby Drenconin for nothing?" She looked from Annie to Nick and back to Annie again.

"I'll make it up to you." Annie stepped slowly across the kitchen and paused to gaze down the hall.

"Just get that thing out of here before— Mr. Lewis! How was your day?"

Nick jumped to his feet, snatched up the envelope and shoved it at Minnow. "Get rid of it—"

"Beautiful day, isn't it?" Annie was saying.

Mr. Lewis stepped into the room and smiled at Nick and Minnow.

A panicked expression flashed across Minnow's face and she nodded, all the while hugging the envelope to her chest. "I really need to get to the post office. I'm expecting a mailing. Hairdressing supplies. And I have to mail in these orders!"

She barked out a too-loud laugh. "Have to run or I'll miss the last pickup." She spun and raced out the back door before anyone could say another word.

The room hung silent in her absence. Annie did a little shrug and smiled apologetically at Mr. Lewis. Though she looked calm, Nick knew she was a wreck inside. His heart went out to her.

Mr. Lewis smiled. "I just wanted to let you know, I've finished my business in the area. Once I gather my things together, I'll be checking out."

"Now?" Annie squeaked out. "Wouldn't you like to sit down and talk a little?"

Mr. Lewis shook his head. "I'd like to be home before dark, so I really must get going."

"How about a cookie?" Nick mentally cringed at how ridiculous he sounded.

"Thanks. I'll grab one on my way out."

He exited the room before either of them could say another word.

Nick turned to Annie. "That went rather well, don't you think?"

"Oh, yeah. Good cop, bad cop. Just like the movies."

"I've got a better idea. As soon as he's gone we search his room for clues." Now he really was sounding like Minnow.

Annie's eyes widened and she nodded. "Okay.

Maybe there'll be papers in his garbage can—the first draft of whatever he sent out."

She squared her shoulders and went to the desk in the foyer.

"Don't keep us waiting, Louie," she muttered under her breath. "As Minnow would say, we have a clandestine operation to launch."

Forty-five minutes later, Mr. Lewis came downstairs carrying his suitcase and attaché case. Stomach a mass of jumbled nerves, Annie finished his paperwork and thanked him for staying with them. It took every ounce of her inner strength not to let the man see how anxious she was for him to be gone.

Nick handed Mr. Lewis two chocolate chip cookies and walked him to the door. "Here's that snack for the road."

As soon as Mr. Lewis had stepped onto the porch, Annie pushed the door shut. She hesitated, one foot on the stair. Nick spied through the lace curtains in the parlor to make sure the man drove away.

"Is he gone?"

"Just...pulling...out. Let's go!"

Like desperate children on an egg hunt, they took the stairs two at a time and raced down the hall to Mr. Lewis's room. Annie threw open the door and paused in the doorway with Nick at her shoulder. Late afternoon sun poured through the west-facing window and illuminated the cozy room.

"There'll be two garbage cans," Annie said. "I'll take the desk, you take the bathroom."

She turned the desk garbage can upside down on the

rug and looked with dismay at the assortment of mis-
cellaneous snack wrappers, crumpled papers, banana
peels, apple cores, tissues and other items that were now
strewn across the floor. Yeeck.

"Hey, hey! Annie, Nick!" Minnow's voice carried
into the room.

"Upstairs!" Annie sat on the floor and began to sift
through the garbage she had just dumped out.

Minnow charged into the room and drew up short,
a shocked expression on her face. "You're searching
Lewis's room? Isn't that against the law?"

"Nothing like the pot calling the kettle black," Nick
called from the bathroom.

"Hey, I remailed the envelope! No one's the wiser."

"Lewis checked out—it's not his room anymore."
Annie began to gingerly lift the trash off the floor and
return it to the waste can.

"You should have told me you were going to do
this—I could have come back sooner. This is my kind
of thing."

Nick stepped into the bedroom. "Bathroom's clean,
Annie. Nothing in the garbage but garbage."

"You're sure about that?" Minnow tossed her fuch-
sia-tinted hair and put her hands on her hips.

"Yeah. But feel free to double-check."

Minnow went into the bathroom and shut the door.
Moments later the shower started. Nick looked at Annie
and grinned.

"Don't even ask," Annie said.

Nick laughed and bent to pull aside the bed skirt and
look under the bed. "Nothing but dust balls under here."

Annie turned her attention to the dresser and desk, opening every drawer—and finding nothing. Her discouragement grew. She held the Bible spine side up and gave it a shake, hoping a note might be hidden in its pages. But all that fell out was a dried four-leaf clover someone had stuck in there to press.

So much for good luck.

While Nick stripped the blankets and sheets off the bed, Annie flipped through the pages of the local tourism directory, searching for anything that might help them uncover Mr. Lewis's motives. She spotted a scrap of notepaper wedged into the fold and gave a strangled shout just as Nick tossed the bedding on the floor and said, "This guy didn't leave so much as a business card behind."

She jumped to her feet, stomach flopping with excitement. "Look at this, look at this! A phone number!"

"With a name?"

"No—but it's local… Kinda familiar. Huh. You have your cell phone on you?"

Nick shook his head. "Maybe it's time to join the twenty-first century and put phones in the rooms."

"Kills the romance."

"Sure helps in an emergency."

Minnow opened the bathroom door just enough to stick her head out in a cloud of steam. She was fully dressed. "You guys find something?"

"A phone number. Minnow, what are you doing in there?" Nick asked.

"I'll be right out." She ducked back into the bathroom, leaving Annie and Nick to stare at each other.

A moment later, the shower shut off. Minnow opened the bathroom door and waved one hand to clear away the steam rolling into the bedroom. "Whew, it's like a steam room in there." She flipped on the exhaust fan. "You were right. The bathroom's clean."

"What were you doing?"

"Oh, well, I read a book once—"

"I should have known."

Minnow frowned. "The victim had written the killer's name in the steam on the bathroom mirror. But the mirror unfogged before anyone found the body, so the name disappeared. Once the CIA agent turned on the shower and the mirror steamed up again, the writing became visible. They solved the case!"

Annie held in a smile at the expression of restrained disbelief on Nick's face. "You thought Lewis might have written some key information on the mirror?"

"Never know. Leave No Stone Unturned, that's my motto."

Nick snorted.

"Enough, you two! Let's go call this number and see if it means anything or not." Annie waved the scrap of paper in the air like a flag and the three raced downstairs to the front desk.

"I'm too nervous—you call." She handed Nick the phone, then read the number off to him as he punched it in.

"It's ringing." He grinned and clenched a determined victory fist at shoulder level.

Annie held her breath and said a prayer that this was the break they were looking for.

"It's a recording—" Nick held up a hand for silence.

Annie and Minnow crowded closer. Suddenly his smile faded and his mouth dropped open. Annie's heart thudded against her chest wall in fear.

"It's the museum." Nick set the phone back in its cradle. "The phone number for the new museum. Lewis was probably looking for something to do—"

"When he wasn't investigating me." Tears stung at the back of her eyes and she reached up to squeeze them back with her fingers. "Heck, this morning when I followed him he even stopped there and looked in the window."

She wandered into the parlor and dropped down on the edge of the sofa. "I'm getting a worse and worse feeling about this. The guy wouldn't talk about what he was researching. And now it's like he went out of his way to make sure he didn't leave behind even a trace of what he was doing."

Minnow sat on the arm of the big wing chair and let herself fall sideways into the seat cushion. "You know, he's probably just a businessman who came to town for an entirely different reason. Building a new manufacturing plant or something."

"Minnow, you were the one who raised the suspicions in the first place. Are you telling me you're changing your mind now?"

"I don't know what to think."

Annie blew out a breath. "Then think about this. If he doesn't care about Nick and me, why was he asking questions about us?"

Nick sat beside her and put an arm around her shoulder. "Who knows? Small talk. Maybe he's just using us to start up conversation. We would be natural icebreakers for him because he was staying at our place."

"I suppose."

"Annie, this is getting nuts. There's nothing you can do about the guy. Give it a rest."

He was right. Minnow's spy mania had made them all a little crazy. Her attraction to Nick and her pregnancy had made her hormones run rampant. And the fact that they were faking a marriage and lying to everyone in town had just made them paranoid. They were probably seeing trouble where it didn't even exist.

Which meant she could either keep worrying about something she couldn't control and drive herself and Nick insane in the process. Or she could take a deep breath, relax and wait to see what happened.

The second choice seemed infinitely better for her psyche.

"Okay. Let's give it a rest."

Minnow raised her hand. "I move that Mr. Lewis was just a nice guy on a business trip."

"You're making a motion?" Nick shook his head.

"All in favor say 'aye.'"

"Aye," they chorused.

Annie forced herself to smile. She only wished she felt as confident about this as they were all pretending to be.

CHAPTER FIFTEEN

SO FAR SO GOOD. Almost twenty-four hours had gone by and not a word out of Mr. Lewis. The guy was probably a salesman or something equally nonthreatening. And he, Annie and Minnow were probably just three idiots with oversize imaginations who should be writing spy novels of their own.

Nick wiped the sweat off his face and bent over the storm window lying across two sawhorses in the garage. He pressed glazing compound into the groove along the glass, then drew a putty knife over the compound to form a neat triangular bead. Straightening, he stood back to survey his handiwork, immensely satisfied with himself. Five windows reglazed; all they needed was a coat of paint and they'd be ready for fall. Good thing he still had the fix-it book from the library so he could continue to pretend to be a master of home repair.

He thought again about Mr. Lewis. More and more he was convinced that Minnow's imagination had blown this whole thing out of proportion—and he and Annie had bought into it way too easily. Now with just two days to go until the museum opening, he could see the brass ring. Annie could go back to life as she knew it. And so could he—adventures all over the world, lots of new people and new places. *But no place to call home.*

He wiped his hands on his shorts and headed across the yard for the house, his mind already chasing down the idea of a cold beer and a refreshing dip in the lake. It was so hot he was half tempted to strip down naked and dive in right now. Wouldn't that be a hit with the guests?

He took the stairs two at a time and crossed the porch, entering the kitchen, where he spotted Annie emptying the dishwasher. "Hey, got the windows all glazed. Only thing is, they can't be painted for a week—not until the glazing cures."

"Thanks. I'll do it before the snow flies."

He smiled. She had at least three months to finish the job. "Want to go for a swim?"

"Ahh, tempting, but I've got too much to do."

"You're making me feel guilty."

She laughed and he headed upstairs to change into his swim trunks, all the while thinking about Annie, about swimming, about life again. Some night, when the B & B didn't have any guests, he might just take her skinny-dipping. The old Annie would never consider it, but the new Annie…

What was he thinking? He was leaving in two days. He wasn't staying in Bedford and would probably never return. He wouldn't ever be taking Annie skinny-dipping. He gave the door to their bedroom an irritated shove and stepped inside.

He crossed the room to the window and stared out

over the back lawn to the lake. And thought of Annie. And making love to her in the sand, rolling her beneath him in the shallow water. Jeez, he was obsessed. He felt like a teenage boy in the throes of uncontrollable hormones.

A beep sounded in the room and he turned, recognizing the sound from his cell phone, alerting him that a voice-mail message waited. He dialed into his message center and sank into the chair by the window to listen to his messages. Two, both from his agent, neither one saying anything except that Nick should call—quickly.

He punched in the number and waited through several rings until his agent answered.

"Jack, it's Nick. What's up?"

"Nick!" His agent's voice boomed, and Nick jerked the phone away from his ear and gave his head a shake.

"Right here."

"It's about time! I've got good news. What you've been waiting for."

Nick frowned.

"You there? Get ready—your proposal's been accepted! Not only do we have a television and book deal, but they'll fund half of it, too."

"They bought it?"

"Pack your bags—you're going to Outer Mongolia," his agent said in a glee-filled tone.

Nick couldn't believe it. *His proposal had gone through.* He, a team of scientists and a TV crew would spend the next year chasing down the elusive Almastis, a race of yeti-like creatures in Outer Mongolia. And afterward, he would have an exclusive contract to write a book about the experience. This was the big break he'd been working toward.

But what about Annie?

He glanced around the bedroom filled with everything that was her. The lotion she used that smelled like vanilla, the new dog bed in the corner that had never been used, the—

"Nick? This connection stinks. You still want this, don't you?"

Did he? "Absolutely."

"Good. Because you need to be in New York the day after tomorrow to sign the contract."

The museum opening was the day after tomorrow. "I can't be there that soon. Change the date."

"You don't have a choice. The head man is leaving for a month in Europe—he's got exactly one available day to meet and it's the day after tomorrow. You know how these guys are. Meeting's already set for first thing that morning."

"I've got a conflict."

"More important than this deal?"

Nick hesitated. "Why the rush? They've been sitting on this proposal for almost six months. Now suddenly we only have one day to get it done?"

"Nick, what's the matter? This is what you wanted. You gotta get when the gettin's good. You don't want them to change their minds or get someone more well known."

He couldn't bring himself to answer.

"Nick? Talk to me."

He drummed his fingers on the armrest of the chair.

What was the matter with him? This was exactly what he'd been working toward for almost six years now.

He drew a long, slow breath. His dreams were about to come true. He'd wanted to do this proposal before he came to Bedford. He'd probably be happy to do it again once he left. He had to stay focused on his goals, not let all this extraneous stuff confuse the issue. Annie would understand. It wasn't as though he and Annie were anything but an afternoon fling. She knew that. She'd understand.

Would she?

Sure. Hadn't she been the one to tell him he was free to leave a couple of days ago? Wasn't she the one who said she'd make up an excuse about the military needing him back right away?

Hadn't she told him after they'd made love that she didn't have any expectations? She'd accepted their relationship for what it was.

"Thing is, I've got my car out here," he said, stalling.

"So you fly back to Wisconsin when we're done and drive the rest of the way to L.A. Big deal. Come on, are you with me?"

Nick sighed. "Yeah. Yeah, I'm with you. I'll see you in two days."

He shut off the phone and stared at the wall. Ecstatic. He should be ecstatic. So why wasn't he? He'd wanted this to go through in the worst way. Would have sold his soul for it two months ago. He thought about Annie again.

When he'd put together the proposal, it hadn't bothered him that he wouldn't see Melissa for a year. But now, the thought of not seeing Annie for a year made his gut ache. A year? If he did this project, he would probably never see her again.

He closed his eyes and let his head drop back against the soft cushion of the chair. Mistake number one: making love to Annie. He thought of their afternoon in the meadow, of the connection they'd shared. No, that hadn't been a mistake. That had been the first right thing he'd done in a long time.

He rubbed his face with his hands and contemplated his future. He had to tell Annie. She'd had a way of cutting through the gray and getting to the black and white. Together they'd figure out what he should do.

ANNIE SHIFTED THE BASKET of clean towels onto her hip and tapped on the bedroom door, then entered without waiting for a reply. She dropped the basket onto the floor by the bathroom and grinned at Nick slouched in the wing chair.

"You forget where you put your swimming suit?"

He didn't return the smile. "I just got a call from my agent."

"Bad news?"

"Yeah. No! Great news. Remember that proposal I told you about the first day I was here?"

"The one about Big Foot?"

He nodded. "They're called Almasti. Anyway, my proposal's been accepted."

Her heart soared for him. "That's wonderful!"

"Some people think the Almasti are Neanderthals

that survived. I'll be part of an expedition trying to track them down. We hope to capture one, get some skin, hair and blood samples, fit it with a radio transmitter and turn it loose again." He grinned. "About ten years ago, a team of Russian and French scientists tried to do the same thing—and failed."

"I thought those sort of creatures were a myth."

He shook his head. "Too much evidence exists for them to be a myth."

"Where are they?"

"Mongolia. I'll be there a year."

"Mongolia." *Halfway around the world.*

Her soaring heart plummeted into her stomach and a massive lump of disappointment rose in her throat. She tried to swallow it down and smile at the same time. She'd known he had aspirations—what had she really thought he would do? Stay with her? In Bedford? Population 7,500? She knew better.

He clasped his hands together and leaned forward to rest his forearms on his knees. "Annie—about what's happened—between us…"

Her stomach lurched and the fake smile on her face collapsed. "We've covered all this, remember? Don't worry about it. I don't expect you to stay or anything. We're both adults, we know what this stuff is all about."

She began to move around the bed, straightening and smoothing the bedspread as the words rolled out of her like a river. "This sort of thing happens and no one should get too carried away about it. Of course, we'll still be friends—we'll always be friends, right? But you and I are so different—so very different that—"

"Annie. Shut up."

Bent over the bed, arms outstretched, she froze and looked up at him. This was it. Now he would tell her it had been fun and he was leaving forever and thanks for the memories.

"Annie, I care about you. A lot. But I'm not the kind of guy— You put it best yourself—I'm always off chasing the next adventure. And this is a once-in-a-lifetime opportunity."

He was leaving. She sat on the edge of the bed facing him and blinked hard to hold back the tears. She'd known when she started this thing that he was going to leave, so she had no right to be disappointed now.

Thing was, she was way beyond disappointed. *Devastated* might be a better choice of words.

"Opportunities like that don't come along every day," she said as chirpily as possible. No way was he going to know she was dying inside.

He shoved a hand through his hair. "The thing is, they want me in New York for a meeting—day after tomorrow."

"The museum opening."

"I tried to change the date, but it was no-go." He looked down at his hands. "I agreed to be there. I leave tomorrow."

"No problem. I'll just say the military suddenly called you back." Her voice cracked and she hated herself for showing weakness. "Listen, thanks for helping me out by staying as long as you did. I think we really pulled it off."

She started for the door, eager to get out of the room before Nick saw her break down in tears.

"Come with me." His words, spoken quietly, stopped her in her tracks. Holding her breath, she turned slowly.

To Mongolia?

He nodded.

"To traipse through the mountains?"

"Only for a year. After that, I'll show you the world, Annie. Places you've never seen, things you've never done."

"I tip canoes."

"We won't be in a canoe."

Leave Bedford? She looked around the room. "Leave this house? Leave what I've built here? Raise my baby on the road?"

"It'll be an adventure. Come with me and you won't have to worry about what's in Mr. Lewis's report."

A weariness rolled over her. He didn't get it. He would never get it.

"I'm not an adventure girl," she said flatly. "I'll *never* be an adventure girl. What I want is here, don't you see? And what I need is someone who wants the same thing to share it with me. I don't care what's in Mr. Lewis's report. Not really."

A tear rolled out of her eye and she wiped it away. "Oh, I do care, but there's nothing I can do about it, anyway. Adventure? Mongolia? Do you know how much of an adventure it was for me to actually buy this place? And then to be caught in a lie about being married? And then to have you show up? I already have more adventure than I can handle."

She threw her hands up in frustration. "All I've ever wanted was to find a place where I belonged, where people invited me to block parties and baby showers, where they stop to talk in the front yard. Where I bring them chicken soup when they're sick and they mow my lawn when I'm gone. I've found that here."

She shook her head sadly. "You go, Nick, because you have to. Because I want you to. Because that is who you are. But this—" she spread her arms wide "—is who I am. I'm fresh lemonade. And you're Jack Daniel's on the rocks. And there's no way one is ever going to become the other."

NICK RESTED HIS HANDS on the railing surrounding the back porch and looked out across the lake. Dusk had fallen, bringing a slight drop in temperature, but not enough to disperse the heat. He watched Annie down at the beach, raking the sand in preparation for another day. A couple of guests who had checked in this morning stopped to talk to her, and she gestured as she answered their questions. Even from this distance he could tell she was smiling. Even from this distance he could tell that Annie had found the place she belonged. He envied her that.

Maybe he could belong here.

No. This was her place, not his. People had to find their own way—not piggyback on someone else's happiness.

Annie bent to pick something from the sand, then let loose with a sidearm swing. A stone skipped across the water—one, two, three skips before it sank. He smiled when she bent again and sent another stone bouncing atop the water.

Annie claimed to be a city girl, but she'd taken to the country pretty easily. He loved the enthusiasm he'd seen in her eyes when he'd taken her canoeing. She'd shoved aside her fears and wasn't afraid to try.

If this week had done nothing else, it had made him realize that he hadn't, as Annie put it, found the place he belonged yet. He didn't think he'd done this much introspection since Annie left him the week after their wedding.

It was possible, he supposed, that he might be one of those people destined to always be searching. One of those guys who never married—or else married six times. One of those guys who had the greatest adventures all over the world, with lovers in every port, and an empty apartment back home. The thought made his shoulders sag. What had Father Thespesius told him? Things hardest won are often the most appreciated.

Maybe those things never won were the same.

Annie bent to grab another stone and send it bouncing over the water. Three skips—embarrassing. The girl needed a lesson.

And a little convincing.

He trotted down the steps and across the lawn to where she stood facing the lake, hands on her hips, an expression of frustration on her face.

"Need some help?" he asked, teasing.

She laughed and he felt himself slip into the joy of the sound. He couldn't imagine never hearing her laugh again.

"I've gotten as high as nine."

"Not bad. Once I got fourteen."

"Liar." Her eyes sparkled.

"Really. It was the perfect stone. Round, flat, smooth, like it was polished. And the water was mirror-flat. That baby just kept skipping and skipping and skipping."

He walked across the beach, head down, bending every now and then to pick up a stone, only to discard it. Finally he spotted just the one he needed. He dug his fingers into the sand and triumphantly pulled it out.

"Now, watch the master." He bent at the waist and let the stone sail out from a sidearm pitch. He straightened just as it hit the water, skipped twice and sank with a plop.

Annie laughed. "Two? The master got two?"

"It must have hit a wave." He looked out over the still lake and winced.

Annie laughed harder. "Yeah, a ghost wave."

"Let me try again." He let a stone fly, not really caring whether he got a long series of skips or not. Then he looked at her. "Annie, have you thought about what happens if Mr. Lewis does expose us? What will you do then?"

She turned and stared at the house, now a gray shape in the rapidly falling dusk. "I don't know. I've tried to think about it and honestly can't come to an answer."

"Would you come with me then? If he blows your cover?"

Her eyes saddened and she shook her head. "It's not so simple as all that, Nick. You know that."

Yeah, he did.

He looked up at the sky and noted a line of dark clouds that had appeared on the horizon. Storm coming in. Kind of felt like his life. Nothing was simple any-more. Frustration filled him at his inability to make this work.

He pointed at the sky and Annie looked up.

"The radio said we'd get thunderstorms tonight," she said.

They watched as the rapidly moving dark clouds de-voured the dusky gray blue sky. In the distance, light-ning flashed and muted thunder rumbled toward them.

"It's going to be a good one." Annie tilted her face upward and closed her eyes. "Here comes the wind!"

The temperature dropped so quickly Nick swore they lost ten degrees in a matter of minutes.

Annie squealed. "Here it comes. We've got to close the windows!" She ran for the house and he followed her, reaching the porch just as lightning cracked over-head and large, fat drops began to fall.

Luella met them at the door. "I've closed up the first floor already."

"You check the second floor; and I'll get the third." Annie ran for the stairs.

Racing through the second floor, Nick slammed down the open windows against the rain pelting the glass. Within minutes, he was back downstairs, bypass-ing the dining room where Luella sat chatting with the new guests. He was in no mood for small talk—or ques-tions about the military.

In fact, he was in the kind of mood you get when a vacation is just about to end—and you're ready to go home, but you don't really want to go. Man, was he be-coming a head case.

He took a wineglass from a kitchen cupboard and filled it from the box of white wine chilling in the refrigerator. Before he left town, he really had to buy Luella some decent wine.

Annie rounded the corner and he raised his glass. "Thought I'd watch the storm. Want to join me?"

"Sure." She poured herself a glass of lemonade, then flicked off the kitchen light. "We'll be able to see better."

"I haven't been in a Midwest storm in years. They're the best."

They stood in the doorway in the dark, not speaking, and watched the storm increase in ferocity. Lightning ripped open the sky, followed by blasts of thunder that shook the house. The few lights that glowed in the house flickered with every blast. Rain, blown almost sideways by the powerful wind, hammered against the windows and roof.

Nick shoved open the door and stepped out onto the porch, into the driving rain.

"Don't go out there. It's dangerous."

He walked down the steps to the yard and lifted his face to take the full brunt of the storm. The warm rain slashed his skin like needles.

"Nick! Get back in here! You'll get struck by lightning!"

He looked into the darkness. Lightning lit the sky and he caught a glimpse of Annie in the doorway. She motioned him in.

And he motioned her out.

Therein lay the problem. He was alive out here, not

just drifting through life, but feeling it, experiencing it. And for Annie, life was best when she was peeking out from behind the door. She'd come quite a ways since she was in L.A., but then, so had he. So instead of getting more alike, they had just stayed that much apart.

Here he was thinking, if only Annie could throw open the door and run into the rain. And there she was, probably thinking, if only Nick could learn to be happy watching instead of partaking.

He had to give her credit—she'd pegged it correctly. They were as different as Jack Daniel's and lemonade. Question was, why could she accept it and he couldn't?

He shoved the wet, dripping hair out of his eyes and motioned her out again. *Come on, Annie, take a chance, a little risk. Come out on the porch at least. Meet me halfway.*

He could see Annie's silhouette behind the screen door, watching him, but not moving.

Come on, Annie.

SHE WATCHED HIM DANCE in the rain, arms outstretched, feet kicking water up out of the puddles that had formed all over the lawn. Her lips turned upward. He was so unafraid. He went out and challenged life on his own terms. He was everything she wasn't. She leaned her head against the screen. Everyone knew you don't go out in thunderstorms.

He turned toward her and waved her out again.

"I suppose you talk on the telephone during storms, too," she shouted.

He threw back his head and laughed as the rain poured over him. "Sometimes I even take a shower."

She couldn't help but smile. What would it hurt to join him out there? Depending on your point of view, *safe* and *secure* could also be defined as *stifling* and *boring*.

Good Lord, where had that thought come from?

She wrapped her hand around the doorknob. Her heart started to beat a little faster. She hadn't gone out into a storm on purpose in her whole life.

She waited a moment more to gather her courage, then gripped the doorknob more tightly and turned it. In that instant, Nick began slogging through the grass toward the porch.

A sense of relief filled her that she didn't have to go out after all...a sense of relief and a sense of regret.

She let go of the handle and stepped back to get out of his way. He shook his head like a dog, and water flew out in every direction, spattering her with droplets.

She laughed and reached back to flip the light switch on again. "Better hang your clothes on the line in the basement before Luella catches you dripping all over the floor. I think there's some clean towels in the dryer."

He started for the basement door. "You missed it out there, Annie. It was something."

Was it? She'd been happy with her life until he'd shown up—still was happy with it. Just because his fulfillment included dancing in the rain and canoeing didn't mean hers did.

It had taken her a heck of a long time to just get to being who she was now. If therapy had taught her anything, it was that she couldn't make herself over for a guy. She'd tried to do that too many times and all it ever got her was heartache.

He was leaving tomorrow, for goodness' sakes. If she'd changed who she was just because he'd been here for nine days, who then, would she be when he was gone? In retrospect, it was a good thing she hadn't gone out into the rain.

And it would be an even better thing when he was gone.

CHAPTER SIXTEEN

NICK PICKED UP HIS EMPTY duffel from the floor, gave it a shake, and concentrated on packing his belongings, as if the very action could ease his discontent. He went into the bathroom and took his toothbrush from the holder, removed his deodorant, after-shave and razor from the medicine cabinet. He slipped his towel from the rack and threw it in the hamper, then stepped from the room, pausing in the doorway to look back for any last items he might have forgotten.

His gaze fell on the new showerhead he'd installed, the new shower curtain rod. Those would be the only reminders for Annie that he'd even been here.

He heard the hall door open and turned just as Luella entered, carrying a stack of his clothes.

"Here's the last of your things. Still warm from the dryer." She set them on the bed and looked at him for a moment before clucking her tongue and shaking her head.

"I'm old enough now to say whatever I want. No one gets too mad when I do, because they figure I'm just an old woman, and old women, well, what are you going to do about them?"

Nick swallowed a grin. "Something on your mind?"

"Sure is. Nick Fleming, it's not right you're going off again. This is no kind of a marriage, with one person always away. And the two of you seeing each other only a few times a year."

He nodded. Wouldn't be his first choice for marriage, either.

"Annie's happy now. Happier than I've ever seen her. I don't want her to go back to the way she was before."

"What do you mean?"

"I know you two were having some problems...."

"She told you about that?"

"No. But it wasn't hard to tell. You never came home to visit, didn't send letters or call her. She didn't talk about you like she used to when she first bought the place. I figured the rose garden might be getting a few thorns, if you know what I mean."

"No relationship is perfect."

"No. But they take work. Forgive me for speaking out so, but it doesn't seem to me you're working at this very hard."

Nick felt his eyes widen and his mouth drop open. If she only knew.

"It's my job, Luella. I can't just not go back."

"But you could apply for a discharge or whatever it is that you do to get out of the military."

He was half tempted to tell Luella the truth so she would understand. But then Annie would be left behind to pick up the pieces. And no way would he do that to Annie.

"I appreciate your concern, Luella. Annie and I have talked about my leaving the military, but I'm just not ready yet."

"Hummph. Haven't talked enough, then. You just think about what I've said." The old woman left the room, shaking her head.

Irritated, Nick lifted the stack of clean clothes, shoved them in his duffel and turned his thoughts to the meeting in New York. By tomorrow this time, he would be on the verge of signing a contract for one of the most visible projects he'd ever been involved in. He'd be guaranteed more money than he'd ever made before, virtually assured of instant fame. People would kill for the opportunity that had presented itself to him.

Just because Annie had turned down his offer to come with him, didn't mean he shouldn't be happy with where his life was headed.

ANNIE PULLED OPEN THE kitchen drawer and began to empty its contents onto the counter. What a mess. How did things get like this? Why did she save things thinking they might come in handy? What a packrat.

She felt a prickling of sweat on her skin. The air had gotten heavy with humidity as the morning heat met the remains of last night's storm. She sorted rubber bands, paper clips and twist-ties into piles. She needed to get better control over all this stuff she saved, over her life. She needed to restore order. Now.

She thought of Nick, upstairs packing, getting ready to walk out of her life as simply as he had walked in.

She gripped the edge of the drawer for support. How had she allowed herself to fall in love with him?

She began tossing things into the garbage can. It felt good to clean house, get rid of some of this junk, restore order, maintain some control. She worked quickly, finishing that drawer in several minutes and turning to the next.

Luella's voice startled her. "Ahh, it's a drawer-cleaning sort of day. Closets next?"

Annie turned. "Is there something wrong with putting things in proper order?"

Luella touched Annie's cheek. "No, dear. But he's upstairs packing and you're down here sorting. Shouldn't the cleaning wait until your husband is gone?"

Annie turned back to the drawer so Luella wouldn't see the tears in her eyes. The old woman was entirely too astute. Whoever said the mind dulls with age was wrong, wrong, wrong about Luella. If this was a dulled mind, Annie was almost glad she hadn't known the woman when she was younger.

"He's your husband, Annie, and you don't know when you'll see him again. Go upstairs. He's leaving today."

Annie stared down into the drawer and fought the temptation to tell Luella the truth. She wanted Luella to understand. Yet, what would it accomplish to tell Luella that he was never coming back, that she would never see him again, that he was going off to chase Neanderthal men in Mongolia?

"Avoiding him doesn't change the fact he's leaving," the old woman said softly. "Don't let yourself have any regrets once he's gone."

Luella took Annie's arms from behind and gently pushed her toward the hall.

NICK LOOKED UP AND SMILED as Annie came through the doorway. "One thing about traveling light—when it's time to leave, there's not a lot to do. You come to help me?"

She shook her head. "Luella thought I should spend some time with you because you're leaving today."

"She lectured me on the state of our marriage."

"Sorry. It's only because she likes you."

"I know. But I get the feeling she thinks I'm a jerk because I won't leave the military and stay home with my wife."

"When I go back down, I'll reinforce that it's a joint decision. You want breakfast before you take off?"

"Just coffee." He pulled the zipper shut on his duffel and hefted it off the bed. His eyes met hers and he saw regret there, and suddenly he wanted to kiss her and lay her down across the bed, to feel her with him again.

"Hey, Annie."

"Yeah?"

Stupid, stupid adolescent infatuation. Don't humiliate yourself by begging. "Thanks—for everything. I'm glad I stayed. Hope everything works out for you."

She nodded. "Thanks."

Half an hour later, they sat in the kitchen making small talk like strangers and sharing a cup of coffee before Nick left for the airport in Milwaukee. He watched

Annie pour cream into her decaf and stir it longer than was really necessary.

"So you're sure it'll be okay I miss the museum opening?"

"No problem. Minnow's spreading the word that you received an urgent call from the military and had to leave."

"She's a good friend."

"I never would have thought you'd ever say that— not after the first night you met her."

"I didn't say she isn't annoying sometimes."

Annie smiled knowingly.

Luella entered the room with the mail and set it on the table next to Annie. She waggled a finger at Nick. "You tell the general, or admiral, or whoever it is you report to, that you need time off to come home more often."

Home. He'd begun to think of it that way, too.

He thought of the divorce papers Annie had signed last night, now tucked away in his computer bag, ready for filing at the courthouse. He'd come to Bedford for Annie's signature so he could be free. And he'd ended up getting her signature so that he could set her free. What a switch.

Luella took a step toward him. "I'm leaving for the market, so best I give you a hug now."

Nick stood and embraced the old woman. "Thanks for everything, Luella."

She pulled his head down to kiss his cheek in exactly the same way she had the day he arrived. "You take care of yourself. I'll keep an eye on Annie, make sure she doesn't overdo it. And you give some thought to what I was telling you upstairs."

She pushed through the back screen door and it banged shut behind her. He really should fix that thing.

The pit in his stomach grew.

Annie topped off her coffee and began to riffle through the mail. "Bills, bills and junk mail." She held up an official-looking gray linen envelope. "Look at the trouble advertisers go to just to make it look like they're legitimate mail. No company name—just a return address. How much you want to bet this is a credit card application?"

"Platinum, preapproved with a $10,000 limit." Nick grinned, though he didn't feel very funny. He really should get going. Just stand up, say goodbye and get on his way. All he was doing right now was prolonging the agony.

Annie slid her thumb under the flap and ripped the envelope open. With great flourish, she removed the letter inside and shook it flat.

"Very nice," she said with a nod. "It's addressed directly to me. *Dear Ms. McCarthy. It is my pleasure to inform you—*"

She shrieked, the sound so shrill and loud he reacted with a jerk, splashing coffee across the table. He jumped to his feet and threw a dishtowel on the spill.

"Annie! What?"

"We got it! We got the grant!"

He snagged the letter from her hand and began to read aloud. "It is my pleasure to inform you that the Wisconsin Foundation for Renovation and Antiquities has approved your application for a grant in the amount of $10,000 for your General Store Museum. Checks are cut quarterly, and yours should arrive in approximately six weeks. Our investigating representative, Mr. Edward Lewis—" Nick's jaw dropped open.

"Mr. Lewis?" Annie said with a squeak. "Mr. Lewis was here for the museum?"

Nick felt as if a weight had been lifted off his shoulders. "Wisconsin Foundation for Renovation and Antiquities? WFRA?"

"It wasn't a radio station!" Annie let out a laugh.

Nick began to read again. "Our investigating representative, Mr. Edward Lewis, was extremely impressed with your endeavor and asked that we let you know immediately of this approval."

Annie jumped to her feet and danced across the room, arms in the air. Nick grinned at her. "Let me guess. He was checking out board members to make sure everything was on the up-and-up."

"I sat on the board, I wrote the grant proposal—of course they'd want to make sure I was legit. Boy, have we been blind."

Nick exhaled and contentment filled him. Annie was free, she could stay in Bedford as long as she liked. "We did it, Annie. We pulled it off."

He opened his arms and she did the same and they fell into each other's embrace, dear friends celebrating a shared victory. He spun her in a circle and kissed her one last time, so that he might never forget what she tasted like.

"Come with me." He searched her eyes for some sign of hope and saw only the faint shimmer of unshed tears.

"Stay," she whispered.

They pulled apart. She patted his chest and he reached up to intertwine his fingers with hers.

"Take care of yourself," she said. "Don't get any more poison ivy. I'm pretty sure they don't sell calamine lotion in the mountains of Mongolia."

He tried to smile. "I'll send you a postcard."

She smiled back at him, but her eyes were sad. "I'll hold you to it."

He kissed the knuckles of her hand.

"You'd better get going or you'll miss your plane."

He nodded. "Annie...I'm sorry."

"For what? I think we're even now."

Maybe so, but his heart felt pretty much like it was ripping in half. He knelt down to rub Chester's head with both hands. Unbelievable, but he was even going to miss this crazy dog. "See ya, mutt."

Standing, he walked out the screen door and out of Annie McCarthy's life. The door banged shut behind him like an exclamation point on the end of a sentence.

SHE REFUSED TO CRY. Annie emptied the dishwasher, baked a few sheets of cookies, took out the garbage. It was too quiet in the house to stay inside. She wandered down to the lake, to the pier, to dangle her feet in the water, with her one true-blue companion, Chester, at her side. She waited, hoping Nick would change his mind, would surprise her by sneaking across the yard to sit on the dock beside her. She waited, even though she knew in her heart he wasn't coming back.

At least she still had her life—*her wonderful life.*

A knot caught in her throat and grew until a sob broke loose, followed by another and another. The pain of loss ripped through her and she wrapped her arms around her middle and bent forward, great heaving sobs racking through her. She had let Nick go.

Suddenly, somehow, her wonderful life seemed like a consolation prize, hollow and meaningless. How wonderful a life could it be, really, when so much of it was built on a lie? When the person you loved most wasn't there to share it with you?

Sobbing, she viciously kicked at the water, breaking its smooth surface and sending ripples out in every direction. That's what her first lie had been like, ripples, spreading out and out, changing perceptions and breeding more lies just to keep the truth from being discovered.

She loved this town, loved the people—and she'd been lying to them since the day she got here. And lying to herself. She'd convinced herself it was okay to lie in order to get this house, to live in this town, to have these people as her friends. When in her heart she knew, she had used them by lying to them.

It didn't matter that she hadn't meant to harm anyone. It didn't matter that one lie led to another, that she already had another lie planned in order to finally get to the truth—some months down the road she planned to announce she and Nick had divorced. No matter that it was truth and a lie all in one. It was really just one colossal lie.

Here she was worried that she might lose the affection of the people of Bedford, when the truth was, the people of Bedford didn't even know her. Not the real her.

She wrapped an arm around her dog and buried her face in the back of his neck. "What's happened to me, Chester?"

He licked her face.

The odor of dead fish wafted into her nostrils and she straightened. "Ugh. Nick was right—your breath is awful."

He licked the tears on her cheeks.

"Yeah, I know. You love me no matter what. Problem is, that's your job."

She kicked the water again and watched the spray fly out onto the lake. She had really screwed up this time.

Realization dawned slowly, came over her like a sunrise, fingers of light seeping into her soul until, suddenly, everything was clear. She didn't want this life anymore—not like this. The people of Bedford had trusted her, had believed she was who she said she was. They deserved to know the truth.

And her baby deserved to be born into a life free of deceit.

Whatever the consequences, she had to clear this mess up, had to let people know the truth. She had taken charge of her life several years ago, changed herself from a wilting violet to a woman strong enough to own her own business.

She was strong enough to do this, too.

The only question was, how to tell people? Her mind flittered over her options… A newspaper ad? A door-to-door literature drop? Tell Vivian? She smiled. Vivian would have the word all over town in no time. Unfortunately, with Vivian's skills at embellishment, the story might become completely different in the retelling.

She dropped her chin to her chest, thinking. She supposed she could tell a few people at the museum opening tomorrow.

No. She could tell them all.

A shiver raced through her with the grand realization that before her lay the best opportunity of all to clear the air. Nearly everyone in town she would want to reach would be at the opening.

Once the speeches were done, the ribbon cut, and the applause finished, she would step up to the podium again, most likely for the last time ever in Bedford.

And she would tell the truth.

AN HOUR INTO THE MEETING with his agent, publisher and the studio head on the fifty-fifth floor of an ostentatious glass-walled New York skyscraper, Nick realized he hadn't been listening to the conversation for the last twenty minutes. Though he'd been nodding his head, his thoughts were all on Annie. And on the museum opening at seven o'clock. And on Minnow, and whether or not Annie had told her that Mr. Lewis was a spy after all—in a sense.

He warmed at the memory of his first day in Bedford. How Annie had flung herself into his arms and kissed him. And then Minnow had showed up, fuchsia hair and all, and started them thinking about espionage and undercover operations.

He started to chuckle.

The other men broke off their discussion to look at him.

"Sorry," he said, swallowing his laughter.

The men returned to their negotiations, discussing the details of the expedition, the documentary, and the book Nick would write when the search for the Al-masti was over.

Damn! He'd left that home improvement book in the garage, hidden behind a bag of birdseed. He'd planned to sneak it back to the library when Annie wasn't around and had forgotten all about it. He'd better call her later and tell her where it was—or she'd owe one big fine. Probably never let him live it down.

He really should call her, anyway. On the plane, he'd come up with a great idea for the B & B. She could offer two-day canoeing-camping trips on the river—a back-to-nature package that was included with a week's stay at the B & B. Instead of tents, they could stay in tepees. That would bring in a few guests. How many people had ever camped out in a tepee before? And once that was under way, maybe what they could do was offer—

His brain screeched to a halt. *They?*

He was going to Mongolia for the next year. There would be no canoe trips, no tepees, no hotel guests, no hiking, no camping...*no Annie.*

He looked at the three men who were intently discussing his future—a future full of fame and money and adrenaline rushes.

And no Annie to love.

He loved her.

The sudden revelation made the hair on his arms stand up. He loved her and he'd left her to do the museum opening alone, to face all those people and lie one more time by saying her husband's meager nine-day military leave had been cut even shorter.

He loved her. Suddenly his great Almasti search, with all its potential for fame and wealth, no longer seemed so significant. He'd been all over the world, thinking the next thrill, the next rush would be the thing that satisfied the odd, empty space in his spirit. But it never did. The only time he'd ever really felt at peace, completely at home, was during the last week in Bedford...with Annie.

When you find the place where you belong, you'll want to stay.

He wanted to stay with Annie. Wherever she was, was where he belonged.

He glanced at his wristwatch. Two-fifteen. It was just past noon in Wisconsin. Bedford was a three-hour drive from the Milwaukee airport. If he could catch an early afternoon flight, he'd be back in time for the ceremony tonight. Just in time to tell everyone in town how much he loved his *wife*.

He pushed his chair back from the big mahogany conference table and stood. The three men looked up at him in surprise.

He cleared his throat. "Gentlemen. The deal is off."

"Nick?" Jack jumped to his feet.

"I don't want it."

"Are you talking to someone else about this?" the publisher asked. "We'll match their offer."

Nick looked directly at him, a fifty-something guy, graying around the temples, probably more than a few pounds over his high-school-graduation weight. Comfortable-looking. "You got a wife and kids?"

The man's expression showed his surprise at the question. "One wife, three kids—seventeen, fifteen, eleven."

"Any regrets?"

Jack shook his head in warning. "Nick, we can talk about this stuff later."

The publisher held up one hand and gave Nick a wry smile. "No regrets. Although, life in my house is sometimes more adventure than I want after a day of work."

"Adventure. What an interesting choice of words."

The man leaned back in his chair, an understanding smile on his face. "You've gotten a better offer. And it's got nothing to do with this proposal, does it?"

Nick grinned. "Nope. Go ahead and find someone to take my place. I've got to get to the airport. I tipped a canoe in Wisconsin and I have to get back in time to right it."

He picked up his briefcase, pulled out his cell phone and strode from the room, already dialing his travel agent.

THE PLANE LANDED RIGHT on schedule. Nick pulled his bag from the overhead compartment and waited impatiently for the people ahead of him to clear the aisle. The museum opening was two and a half hours away and he had a solid three-hour drive ahead of him—if he stayed at the speed limit.

Before too much longer, he was heading out of the parking ramp, windows down, the soft, warm summer breeze slipping in one side and out the other.

He turned the radio on and let the music fill him with

its rock and roll rhythm. Across the airwaves came a song from his high school days, the words about the incredible joy of finding love. He threw back his head and laughed. He felt just like he had the summer after graduation. Totally free. Old enough to drive, old enough to make major decisions, old enough to fall in love, and waiting for it to come along and turn his world upside down. Except it hadn't happened. Until now. Until Annie.

They'd lost six years while he'd tried to chase down the place where he belonged. He didn't want to lose another day. He turned the radio up and began to sing along.

He pictured Annie's face when he arrived. Pictured her shock, her smile, her laugh, her throwing herself into his arms just like she had the day he arrived. Only this time the kisses would be real.

He set the cruise control for seventy-five miles per hour and kicked back. An hour passed and another, the miles flying away under the wheels of his car. Before too long he would be there.

He passed a sign that read Bedford, 5 Miles. It was closer than he'd realized. Anticipation made his stomach jump and he sped up. Minutes later, he passed the gas station at the edge of town and waved to the owner as she cleaned the windshield on a customer's car. He tried to stop smiling.

It took a moment for his brain to register the police car parked on the side street. He glanced at his speedometer and found himself going at least twenty miles over the limit. In the rearview mirror he watched the squad car pull out behind him, red lights flashing.

Nick hit the brakes and pulled over, muttering a curse under his breath. This was good for at least a fifteen-minute delay. And he was already late. He bent to dig his wallet out of the laptop case on the seat beside him.

"You know how fast you were going?" a voice asked from the driver's side window.

He turned. "Chief! What are you doing writing tickets?"

"Nick? Aw, some of the guys wanted to go to the museum opening so I said I'd take a shift. I thought you left town—military needed ya back."

Nick shook his head. "Not anymore. I'm staying home." *Home.* It felt good to be here. "I wanted to surprise Annie but I'm running a little late."

The chief pushed his sleeve back and looked at his watch. "More than a little. You better hurry up—it started twenty minutes ago." He grinned. "Hey, I got an idea."

ANNIE WATCHED AS THE MUSEUM director cut the blue ribbon that stretched across the sidewalk in front of the building. A flush of fear ran through her. While everyone else clapped and cheered, her heart pounded with anxiety. Her introductory speech was past; now she just had to contend with the truth.

She forced her feet to walk up the steps to the platform on which the podium was housed. She cleared her throat. The air seemed to buzz around her; her head grew light. No fainting allowed. Not now. Later would be okay, but not now. She grasped the microphone with one hand to stop from trembling.

"There are refreshments inside." Her voice sounded unnaturally loud and high. "Please come in, tour the new facility and join us as we celebrate our grand opening."

The crowd clapped and began to move together toward the museum doors.

What a dumb move on her part. She should have told the truth before inviting everyone in. This was terrible; no one would be left to hear her confession.

"Wait!" Her sudden pronouncement came out of the PA system like a shout.

All eyes swung to the podium.

"Before you go..." She swallowed hard. "There's one more announcement I need to make today. Actually, it's a confession."

The crowd quieted in anticipation and she struggled to ignore the churning of her stomach. By the time she finished this announcement, everyone would know that she had spent the last two years lying to them. Her reputation would be in tatters. She would probably have to move out of town.

Tears threatened at the back of her eyes. She reminded herself sternly that she had no one to blame for this mess but herself. She alone had told the lies that got her here today.

"I, ah...don't know quite where to begin. Nick and I— We— Nick didn't go back to the military. He actually isn't in the military at all. Never has been in the military. He's a writer. An outdoors writer. He travels around the world, goes on adventures and writes about them."

She could see confusion on the faces in the crowd.

"We don't much care what he does, Annie," someone shouted.

She smiled sadly and looked down. This was harder than she'd thought it would be. "The thing is, Nick and I—we're not married—well, we are married, but..."

Why on earth hadn't she written down what she was going to say before she got up here? Now she not only would be remembered as a liar, but also as a blabbering idiot. The crowd shifted restlessly, anxious to get into the party.

She had to get this out fast. "The truth is, until Nick showed up a week ago, I hadn't seen him since we got married six years ago. We didn't love each other then and I thought we were divorced years ago. Somehow the paperwork fell through the cracks. It didn't go through, so we were still married—"

"Spit it out, Annie," someone called in a friendly voice. "What are you trying to say?"

The bottom line. Tell them the bottom line. She inhaled.

"I've been lying since the day I came to Bedford. I lied about being married so I could buy the B & B. I lied about meeting my husband on trips. The baby is—artificially inseminated. It's all a lie. I didn't mean for it to go on, but I didn't stop it. Then Nick showed up to tell me our divorce never went through."

She drew a deep breath in preparation for the next statement. "And I convinced him to stay a week and pretend to be my husband so you wouldn't learn the truth. He's gone now—back to his real life. I'm sorry. You don't know how sorry I am."

A police car headed down the street toward them, siren blaring. A murmur ran through the crowd as they turned in unison to watch the car pull to a stop in front of the museum. Annie sighed. Leave it to Vivian to have some last-minute addition to the grand-opening celebration that she failed to mention.

The front passenger door opened and a man stepped out. Annie's eyes widened. Her stomach flopped. If she didn't know any better, she'd think it was— *Nick?*

The crowd burst out in a roar of cheering and laughter, of people calling out his name and welcoming him back. Like a wave rolling off the shore, they stepped back to let him through. Nick shook hands and exchanged greetings as he moved through the crowd toward her. Annie closed her gaping mouth and stared.

What on earth was going on?

He took the steps to the podium two at a time and grinned at her.

"What are you doing here?" she asked. Her eyes darted toward the crowd that had obviously pressed forward so they wouldn't miss a word of the exchange.

"I forgot some stuff."

She hadn't noticed anything left behind. "Like what?"

"My toothbrush."

The crowd tittered again and moved closer.

"What?"

He nodded. "And my favorite socks—they're probably under the bed."

Was he nuts?

"My dog—I also forgot my dog."

"He's *my* dog."

Nick shook his head. "I distinctly recall you telling me he was *my* dog." He scanned the faces of the crowd until he spotted Luella. "Luella, didn't Annie always say Chester was my dog?"

The old woman nodded vigorously.

"You're not taking Chester to hike through Mongolia! Luella, didn't you hear anything I just said three minutes ago?"

Luella beamed. Oh, good. Everyone had gone nuts. She had the distinct feeling she had been put in an asylum for the insane.

"I forgot something else, too," Nick said softly. He took a step toward her.

"I forgot that it took me a long time to forget you after you left six years ago. I forgot what it did to me to see you again after all these years." He paused. "I forgot how much I love you."

She gasped and tears sprang to her eyes. A lump formed in her throat so large she couldn't speak, couldn't swallow, couldn't breathe.

"I canceled out of the project," he said.

"You're not going?" she choked out.

He smiled and shook his head.

"But it's your dream—"

"My dream is bigger than that. I have a canoeing-adventure business to start…tubing, rafting…cross-country skiing in the winter…hiking… That is, if you'll have me."

If she would have him? She shoved the back of her hand across her eyes. Did everything between them always have to have a complication? Now she had to tell him his dream wouldn't happen in Bedford. Would he still want her then? She glanced down.

"I won't be staying here. They know. I've told them the truth about us…about my lies."

A murmur ran through the crowd.

"Then we'll go somewhere else," Nick said. "I don't care where I live—as long as it's with you."

She raised her eyes to his.

"Marry me, Annie. Or rather, stay married to me."

She pressed her lips together and fought back the tears stinging her eyes. "You've gone insane, haven't you?"

He thought about it a moment. He'd spent years searching for unusual experiences, things to make his adrenaline rush, to give his life a sense of meaning and excitement. And yet, the more of that he'd done, the less he felt like he was finding what he was searching for.

Until now. Here in this little town, with this woman and her bizarre friends and acquaintances, he felt more alive than he'd ever felt before. If this was going insane, then he would embrace it the rest of his life.

"Maybe I have," he said. "But they say there's only a very fine line separating insanity and genius."

"Come on, Annie. Say yes!" someone shouted.

Startled, she glanced at the crowd.

"The microphone's on." Nick looked at the podium, searching for the off button and not finding it. "Looks like everyone's in on this conversation."

"I'm having a baby, Nick. *A baby that's not yours.*"

He looked at her belly, ever so slightly rounded. "Luckily our child will have two parents who love it very much. Now, what do you say?"

"Yes! She says yes!" Father Thespesius worked his way forward through the crowd.

"We forgive you, Annie," someone shouted. A myriad of other voices echoed the words.

Father Thespesius stepped up to the podium. "I think what these folks are saying is, we don't want you to leave."

His final words were almost drowned out by a chorus of cheers and whistles and shouted agreements. In the midst of the commotion, Annie heard a familiar voice shouting her name.

"Hey, Annie! Annie! Annie!"

She spotted Minnow with her arms raised above her head in victory. "It's a wonderful lie!" she shouted.

Annie's eyes widened and her tears burst forth.

"So will you—" Nick began.

"Yes," she whispered. "Yes, yes, yes!"

She threw herself into his open arms and a huge cheer went up among the watching crowd.

"Everybody inside for the party!" Father Thespesius announced into the microphone. "We've got an opening and a marriage to celebrate!"

The group streamed into the museum. Nick slung an arm around Annie's shoulders and walked with her toward the entrance.

She cast a sly smile his way. "Whadya say we cut out of here and go canoeing?"

He raised an eyebrow in surprise. "I didn't realize you enjoyed it that much."

"Oh, but I did." She grinned.

"Annie McCarthy, I do believe you're a fellow thrill-seeker." He bent to kiss her lightly on the lips. "If you thought canoeing was fun, wait till I take you white-water rafting."

"I thought you'd never ask."

He laughed out loud and gathered her into his arms, knowing that from this day forward he would be embarking on the greatest adventure of his life.